Give my dear American
friend !

China , Zhang Aixia

Give my dear American

OUTLAWS
OF THE MARSH
水　浒　传

By
Shi Naian
and Luo Guanzhong
Translated by Sidney Shapiro
Adapted by Jin Shibo

Foreign Language Teaching and Research Press

（京）新登字 155 号

水 浒 传

SHUI HU ZHUAN

施耐庵、罗贯中著

Sidney Shapiro 译

金诗伯改写

* * *

外语教学与研究出版社出版发行

（北京市西三环北路十九号）

外语教学与研究出版社编辑部排版

华利国际合营印刷有限公司印刷

新华书店总店北京发行所经销

开本 736×965 1/32 12 印张 170 千字

1991 年 9 月第 1 版 1996 年 7 月第 4 次印刷

印数：35001—45000

* * *

ISBN 7-5600-0168-8

I·4

定价 12.80 元

s novel, the editor has put on the observed columns some of the battles where daring morality, he could not escape in adapting Store.

EDITOR'S NOTE

One of the best known and best loved of the ancient Chinese novels to have come down through the ages, Shi Nai'an's *Outlaws of the Marsh* is based on a peasant uprising which took place in the reign of Hui Zong, a Song Dynasty emperor who ruled from 1101 to 1125. The story tells how and why one hundred and eight men and women banded together on a marsh-girt mountain at the junction of present-day Shandong, Henan and Hebei provinces.

The little outlaw band gradually grew into a formidable army of thousands, gaining fame far beyond the borders of the region. It fought brave and resourceful battles against the oppression and cruelty of despots and tyrants. The troops sent against the forces of Liangshan Marsh suffered one defeat after another.

The present adapted version of *Outlaws of the Marsh* is based on the excellent English translation of the novel by Sidney Shapiro, published by Foreign Languages Press, Beijing, in 1980.

The adapted version set forth in three books, each high-lighting three chieftain of the Liangshan Marsh stronghold.

In order to retain the suspense of the original

1

novel, the editor has taken the liberty of cutting some of the details, where doing so would not resulted in factual inaccuracy.

Editor

December 1984

2

CONTENTS

CONTENTS

BOOK ONE

CHAPTER ONE — LU DA

1

Our narrative of the gallant deeds of the outlaws of Liangshan Marsh opens with the appearance on the scene of Lu Da, known later as Lu Zhishen.

Lu Da was a major in the border garrison of Weizhou. He was a stalwart fellow, six feet tall, with a girth of more than two meters. A full beard framed his face. He had an irascible temper, and easily flew into a rage.

One day, as he was strolling about the town, he made the acquaintance of a young man called Shi Jin along with Shi Jin's former arms instructor, Li Zhong.

Lu Da invited them to have a few drinks with him. They went to an inn down the street and took their places at a table. The waiter, who knew Lu Da, greeted them respectfully. He soon brought wine and covered the table with platters of meat and vegetables.

Each of the three downed several cups. They talked of this and that, and compared methods in feats of arms. But when their conversation was at its liveliest, they heard the sound of sobbing in the adjoining room. Lu Da immediately became incensed. He snatched plates and dishes off the table and smashed them on the floor.

"You have the brass to allow people to wail in the next room and disturb us while we are dining," he bawled at the waiter. Shi Jin and Li Zhong tried to pacify the fuming Lu Da. "Don't be angry, sir," said the waiter. "I would never permit anyone to disturb you. The people weeping are an old man and his daughter, who make their living by singing in taverns. They didn't know you and your friends were drinking here. They can't help lamenting their bitter fate."

"There's something peculiar going on here," said Lu Da. "Bring them here to me."

In a moment the waiter returned with a girl of about eighteen, followed by a man in his late fifties. Wiping her eyes, the girl made three curtsies. The old man also greeted Lu Da and his friends respectfully.

The girl told the diners their story. She and her father were from the Eastern Capital. Their family name was Jin, and the daughter was called Jade Lotus. They had come to Weizhou to visit a relative. On the way her mother fell ill and died. The old man and his daughter were having a hard time. Butcher Zheng, nicknamed Lord of the West, saw Jade Lotus and wanted her for a concubine. He sent his men to wheedle and threaten. Finally he signed a contract promising the old man three thousand strings of coppers for Jade Lotus.

However, in less than three months his wife drove Jade Lotus out of the house. On top of that, Butcher

Zheng demanded that they 'return' his money, although they had not in fact received a single coin from him. They didn't know what to do.

The old man had taught Jade Lotus many ballads when she was a child, and they then began to make rounds of the inns, singing. They gave Zheng most of what they earned each day, keeping back a little for travelling expenses so that they could go home.

"Ours is a hard lot, and we have no place to seek redress," said the girl. "That's why we were weeping just then. We didn't mean to offend you, sir. Please forgive us."

"Where does Zheng live?" asked Lu Da.

"He has a butchery at the foot of Zhuangyuan Bridge."

"Bah!" said Lu Da contemptuously. "So he is only Zheng the pig–sticker, the dirty rogue who runs a butcher shop under the patronage of our garrison commander. And he cheats and bullies, too, does he?"

He turned to Shi Jin and Li Zhong. "You two wait for me here while I take care of the scoundrel. I'll be right back."

They grabbed him, pleading him to calm himself. They finally managed to restrain him.

"Come here, old man," said Lu Da to the father. "I'll give you some money. Tomorrow you can go back to the Eastern Capital. How about it?"

"If you can help us return home, you'll be giving us a new lease on life," said the old man and his daughter.

Lu Da pulled out five ounces of silver and placed them on the table. To Shi Jin he said, "If you have any silver, lend it to me. I'll give it back to you tomorrow."

Shi Jin extracted a silver bar weighing ten ounces from his bundle and put it down beside Lu Da's money. The major looked at Li Zhong. "You lend me some too."

Li Zhong produced two ounces of silver. The smallness of the offering annoyed Lu Da. "Big-hearted, aren't you?" he snorted. He handed all the silver to the old man. "This will cover the travelling expenses for you and your daughter. Go back to your inn and pack your things. Tomorrow at dawn I'll come to see you off."

Old Jin and his daughter thanked him and departed.

After the three men had finished their drinks they left the inn. Shi Jin and Li Zhong went their respective ways. Lu Da returned to his quarters in the garrison and went to bed still angry, without having any supper.

2

The night passed without incident. Father and daughter rose at dawn, lit a fire and cooked breakfast. When they finished eating, they collected their belong-

4

ings and paid their bill.

The sky was just turning light when Lu Da strode into the inn and asked for Old Jin and Jade Lotus.

"If you're going, go quickly," Lu Da ordered them. "What are you waiting for?"

Old Jin and Jade Lotus quickly left town and got the cart the old man had hired the day before.

Lu Da sat himself down on a stool at the door of the inn and remained there for several hours. Only when he felt sure that the old man and his daughter were far away did he leave the inn. He went directly to Zhuangyuan Bridge.

Zheng had a butchery there with two chopping blocks. The butcher was sitting behind a counter by the door, keeping an eye on his assistants as they cut and sold meat.

Lu Da came up to the counter. "Butcher Zheng," he shouted.

Recognizing him, Zheng came out rapidly from behind the counter and greeted him with respect. "Major, a pleasure. Please be seated, sir."

Lu Da sat down. "The garrison commander has ordered me to buy ten pounds of lean meat, chopped fine, to be used for filling. There mustn't be a speck of fat in it."

"Right," said Zheng. He turned to his assistants. "Pick out a good cut and chop up ten pounds."

"I don't want these dirty oafs touching it," said Lu Da. "You do it yourself."

5

"Certainly. Glad to." Zheng selected a cut of lean meat and started mincing. After chopping for an hour, Zheng wrapped the minced meat in lotus leaf.

"Now cut up ten pounds of fat. There mustn't be a speck of lean in it. This is also for filling."

Zheng selected ten pounds of fat and began mincing. When he had finished chopping the fat and wrapped it in a lotus leaf, it was time for lunch.

"Now I want ten pounds of gristle, chopped fine, also to be used for filling, and I don't want to see a speck of meat in it."

Zheng laughed awkwardly. "Are you making fun of me?"

Lu Da leaped up, one package of chopped meat in each hand, and scowled at the butcher. "That's exactly what I'm doing — making fun of you." He flung the contents of the packages right in Zheng's face.

The shower of meat stung the butcher into a rage. He grabbed a boning knife from the block and jumped down the shop steps. Lu Da was waiting for him in the middle of the street.

None of the assistants from Zheng's shop or passers-by dared interfere. The knife in his right hand, Zheng reached for Lu Da with his left. Lu Da seized the outstretched hand, closed in and sent the butcher sprawling with a swift kick in the groin. Another step forward, and he put his foot on Zheng's chest. Raising a huge fist, Lu Da thundered, "You lousy an mal! Who gave you the right to coerce and cheat Jin's daughter, Jade Lotus?" He landed a punch on Zheng's nose and another on his eyebrow, sending the blood streaming down his face.

Worsted, Zheng pleaded for mercy.

"You rotten bastard, "the major exclaimed scornfully. "If you had shown any guts I might have let you off. But since you're so lily-livered, I won't. " He struck the butcher a heavy blow on the temple. The butcher lay stretched out on the ground. He didn't move.

Lu Da pretended to be enraged. "Playing dead, eh? I'll bang you a few more! " He had observed that Zheng's face was changing colour. "I only wanted to give the bastard a beating, "he said to himself. "Who would have thought that three blows would kill him? They're sure to hold me for trial. I'd better get out of here."

He rose and strode away, pausing briefly to look back and shout, "Go on playing dead. I'll settle with you later."

Lu Da returned to his quarters and hastily packed. Carrying a staff as a weapon, he sped out the town gate.

3

Having failed to bring Zheng back to life, his wife and neighbours meanwhile went to the judge's official residence and filed a charge of murder. Court was called into session, and the document of accusation read out.

"That Lu Da is a major in the garrison," thought the judge. "I must mind my step." Instead of issuing an order for Lu Da's arrest, he went to the headquarters of the garrison commander. The two men exchanged greetings.

"What brings you here?" asked the commander. "I've come to inform Your Excellency that Major Lu Da has, without cause, beaten a butcher named Zheng to death. I wouldn't dare arrest him without reporting to Your Excellency first."

The garrison commander was startled. "That Lu Da is a skilled military man," he thought, "but he's rough and rude. Today he's committed a murder. How can I cover up for him? I must let him be taken and questioned." To the judge he said: "Since he has committed a capital offence you may arrest and question him according to law."

The judge bid farewell to the commander and returned to his office to resume court. He issued an order to the police inspector for Lu Da's arrest.

The inspector had Lu Da's room searched, but nothing was found except for some old clothes and bedding. He returned to the judge's office and reported.

"Major Lu Da has fled to escape punishment. No one knows where."

8

The judge ordered the police to have Lu Da arrested within a specified time, on pain of being beaten. An urgent proclamation offering a monetary reward for Lu Da's capture was posted everywhere, giving his age, birthplace and a description of his appearance.

4

After leaving Weizhou, Lu Da dashed about in panic, not knowing where to go. After many days of wandering he arrived in a bustling county town in Daizhou, with many people and thriving markets. On a street corner he saw a crowd gathered in front of a proclamation. Someone was reading it out loud. Illiterate himself, Lu Da pushed forward to listen. What he heard was the offer of a reward for the capture of Lu Da, former major in the Weizhou garrison, now wanted for the murder of Butcher Zheng.

As Lu Da stood there listening, a man threw his arms around him from behind and cried, "What are you doing here, brother Zhang?" Whoever it was drew Lu Da away from the street corner.

The man was none other than Old Jin from the Weizhou inn, the old man Lu Da had rescued. The old fellow didn't stop pulling Lu Da away till they reached an isolated spot. Then he said, "You are too rash, benefactor. That proclamation offers a reward for your capture. How could you stand there looking at it? If I hadn't spotted you, you might have been

9

nabbed by the police."

Lu Da told the old man what had happened in Weizhou after Old Jin and his daughter had left the town. "I thought you were returning to the Eastern Capital. What're you doing here?" asked Lu Da.

"Originally I intended to go back to the Eastern Capital," answered the old man. "But I was afraid that son—of—a—bitch would catch up with us, and you wouldn't be around to rescue us. So I changed my mind and headed north. On the way I met an old neighbour from the capital who was coming here on business. He took me and my daughter along. He was good enough to find her a husband, and she's now the mistress of a wealthy man, Squire Zhao. The squire has provided her with a house. Thanks to you, benefactor, we now have plenty to eat and wear. My daughter has often spoken of your kindness to the squire. He's said many times he'd like to meet you. You must come and stay with us a few days. We can talk about what you should do next."

Lu Da and Old Jin had walked less than half a *li* when they came to the door of the house. Pushing aside the bamboo portiere, the old man called, "Daughter, our benefactor is here!"

Jade Lotus emerged at once, attractively attired and made up. She begged Lu Da to be seated in the centre of the room. Then she curtsied before him six times. "If you hadn't rescued us, benefactor," she said, "we'd never possess what we have today." She invited

10

him upstairs to the parlour.

The old man took Lu Da's staff and bundles. To his daughter he said, "Keep our benefactor company. I'll arrange dinner."

When wine, food and fruit were served, father and daughter in turn filled Lu Da's cup. Then Old Jin dropped to his knees and bowed low.

"Please, dear elder, don't do that," said Lu Da. "You embarrass me terribly."

The three drank till almost nightfall. Suddenly they heard a commotion outside. Lu Da opened the window and looked out. Some twenty to thirty men, all armed with staffs, were gathered in front of the house. A gentleman on a horse cried, "Don't let the rascal get away!" "Bring him down!" the men with staffs were shouting.

Lu Da realized that he was in danger. He snatched up a stool and started down the stairs. Old Jin rushed down ahead of him, yelling. "Nobody move!" He ran over to the gentleman on horseback and said a few words. The mounted gentleman laughed and ordered the band to disperse.

5

When his men had gone, the gentleman got off his horse and entered the house. Old Jin asked Lu Da

11

to come down. The gentleman bowed as Lu Da descended the stairs.

" 'Meeting a man of fame is better than just hearing his name. ' Please accept my respects, righteous major. "

"This is Squire Zhao, my daughter's lord, " explained Old Jin. "Someone told him that a young man I had brought to his house was upstairs, drinking, so he came with his servants to fight. When I explained, he sent the servants away. "

Squire Zhao invited Lu Da to the upper chamber. Old Jin reset the table, and once more prepared food and drink. Zhao ushered the major to the seat of honour. Lu Da refused.

"How could I presume?"

"A small mark of my respect. I've heard much about the major's valour. What great good fortune that I could meet you today! "

" Though I'm just a crude fellow who's committed a capital offence, the squire doesn't scorn my lowliness and is willing to make my acquaintance. If there's any way I can be of service, you have only to say so. "

Squire Zhao was very pleased. He asked all about the fight with the butcher. They talked of this and that, discussed jousting with arms, and drank far into the night.

The following morning Zhao said, "I'm afraid this place isn't very safe. Why not come and stay at

12

my manor for a while?"

Lu Da assented willingly. He said goodbye to Old Jin and his daughter and set out with the squire.

Lu Da stayed at the manor for six or seven days. Every day he was wined and dined. One day, while Lu Da and the squire were chatting in the study, Old Jin entered hastily. He looked to see that no one else was around and then said to Lu Da, "You mustn't think me overly cautious, benefactor. But ever since the night the squire and his servants raised such a row in the street because they heard some man was drinking upstairs, people have been suspicious. Word has spread that is was you who were there. Yesterday three or four policemen were questioning the neighbours. I'm worried that they'll come here and arrest you."

"In that case, I'd better be on my way."

"Things might turn out badly if I kept you here, major," the squire admitted. "Yet if I don't, I'll lose face. I have another idea. It'll give you complete protection. But maybe you won't be willing."

"I'm a man with a death penalty waiting for him. I'll do anything to find refuge."

"Some thirty odd *li* from here, on Mount Wutai, there's a monastery. The abbot is my friend. If you agree to join the Buddhist order, I'll pay all the expenses. Would you be willing to shave off your hair and become a monk?"

Lu Da thought to himself, "Whom could I go to

for protection if I were to leave here today. I'd better accept the offer." Aloud he said, "I'll become a monk if you sponsor me, squire. I rely entirely on your kindness."

6

And so it was decided. That night everything was prepared. The next morning Lu Da and the squire set out for Mount Wutai, accompanied by servants carrying gifts and luggage. They reached the foot of the mountain before mid—morning. Squire Zhao and Lu Da went up in sedan—chairs, sending a servant ahead to announce them.

At the monastery gate, they found the deacon and supervisor waiting to welcome them. The abbot was notified of their arrival and soon emerged with his assistant and the elder. Squire Zhao and Lu Da hurried forward and bowed. The abbot greeted them in the Buddhist manner.

"I've something to ask of you, Great Abbot. It has long been my desire to sponsor a new member for this monastery. Although I have had the certificate ready for some time, until today I've not been able to do so. This cousin here is named Lu. He was formerly a military officer, but because of many difficulties he wants to have done with worldly affairs and become a monk. I earnestly hope Your Eminence will exercise mercy and compassion and, as a favour to us,

14

accept this man into your order. I'll pay all expenses."

"Gladly," said the abbot. "This will add lustre to our monastery."

A day or two later all was ready for Lu Da's ordination ceremony. Everyone assembled in the preaching hall. A barber shaved off his hair and his beard. The elder requested the abbot to select a name by which Lu Da would be known in the Buddhist order.

"Let him be called Sagacious."

The scribe filled out the certificate and handed it to Sagacious Lu. At the abbot's direction he was given his monk's garments and told to put them on. Then he was led to the dais. The abbot placed his hand on Lu's head and instructed him in the rules of conduct.

"Do not kill, steal, fornicate, drink, or lie. These are the five rules."

Squire Zhao invited all present into the assembly hall where he gave gifts to every member of the monastery staff. The deacon introduced Sagacious to various members of the monastery, and then conducted him to the rear building where the monks meditated. Nothing further happened that night.

The next day, Squire Zhao took his leave of the abbot and the monks, and set off down the mountain for home. Before leaving he urged Lu Da to be restrained in all things, and under no circumstances to be arrogant.

15

Lu Da promised to behave.

7

Before Sagacious Lu knew it, four or five months passed. It was early winter, and Lu's mind, which had been quiescent for a long time, began to stir. One clear day he put on his black cassock and strode from the monastery.

Halfway down the mountain he halted to rest in a pavilion. He sat down on a bench and said to himself, "In the old days I had good meat and drink every day. But now that I'm a monk I'm shrivelling from starvation. I have a terrible taste in my mouth. If only I could get a drink."

As he was mulling this over, he saw in the distance a man carrying two covered buckets on a shoulder-pole. The man approached, entered the pavilion, and put his load down.

" Hey, fellow, what have you got in those buckets?"

"Wine."

"How much a bucket?"

"Are you kidding, monk? This wine is for the monastery's cooks, janitors, caretakers and field labourers — no one else. The abbot has warned me that if I sell to a monk he'll take back the money and house the monastery loaned me for my winery. I daren't sell you any of it."

"You really won't?"

"Not even if you kill me."

The man didn't like the look of things. Picking up his shoulder—pole, he started to walk away. Sagacious Lu dashed out of the pavilion after him, seized the pole and kicked the fellow in the groin.

Sagacious Lu carried both buckets to the pavilion. He picked the ladle up off the ground, removed the covers, and began drinking. Before long, one of the buckets was empty.

The vintner recovered from his pain. Swallowing his anger, he shouldered what was left of his load and flew down the mountain.

Lu Da sat in the pavilion a long time. The wine had gone to his head. He pulled his arms out of his cassock and tied the empty sleeves around his waist. Bare chested he strode up the mountain, swinging his arms.

The monastery gatekeepers had been watching him from afar. They came forward when he approached and barred his way with their staffs.

"You're supposed to be a disciple of Buddha," they barked. "How dare you come here in this besotted condition." One of the gatekeepers sped back inside and reported to the supervisor, while the other tried to keep Sagacious Lu out with his staff. Lu flipped it aside and gave him a staggering slap in the face. As the man struggled to recover, Sagacious Lu followed up with a punch that knocked the man groaning to the ground.

The supervisor summoned the caretakers, cooks and janitors — nearly thirty men. Armed with staffs, they poured out of the cloisters and rushed to meet Sagacious Lu. Lu strode towards them with a thunderous roar. He sprang at them so fiercely that they fled in confusion to the preaching hall and closed the door. Sagacious Lu charged up the steps. With one kick he smashed the door open. The trapped men raised their staffs and came out fighting.

The abbot, who had been notified by the supervisor, hurried to the scene with four or five attendants.

" Sagacious, " he shouted, " I forbid you to misbehave."

Sagacious Lu was drunk, but he recognized the abbot. "I had a couple of bowls of wine, but I did nothing to provoke these fellows. They came in a gang and attacked me."

"If you have any respect for me, "said the abbot, "you'll go to your quarters at once and sleep it off. We'll talk about this tomorrow."

Helped by the abbot's assistants, Sagacious Lu staggered to the monks' hall, collapsed on his bed and slept, snoring loudly.

The next morning the abbot sent an assistant to summon Sagacious Lu. Lu went with him to the abbot's room.

"Although you were originally a military man, " said the abbot, " I ordained you because of Squire

18

Zhao's sponsorsnip. I instructed you: do not kill, steal, fornicate, drink or lie. But yesterday evening you came back drunk and beat up the gatekeepers, broke the door of the preaching hall and drove out the cooks and janitors. How could you behave so disgracefully?"

With many kindly words the abbot exhorted Sagacious Lu to reform. Sagacious Lu promised never to do such things again.

8

For three or four months after his drunken riot Sagacious Lu didn't venture to leave the monastery. Then one day the weather suddenly turned warm. Sagacious Lu came out of his quarters, strolled through the monastery gate and stood gazing in admiration at the beauty of Mount Wutai. From the foot of the mountain the breeze brought the sound of the clanging of metal. Sagacious ambled down the slope.

Passing through an archway inscribed with the words "Wutai, A Blessed Place", he saw before him a market town. Meat, vegetables, wine and flour were for sale. Again he heard the clang of metal. The sound came from an ironsmith's shop. He entered the shop and asked the smith to make him a sixty—two—pound Buddhist staff and a monk's knife of the best steel.

From the ironsmith's shop he went to a wine shop.

"Bring me some wine," he shouted. Knowing that

the abbot did not permit the sale of wine to the monks, the innkeeper refused to serve him. Sagacious Lu left the wine shop and walked on. Soon he saw another wine shop, walked in and again ordered some wine. Again the innkeeper refused to sell him any. Sagacious Lu went to four or five wine shops, but they all refused to serve him.

At the far end of the market he saw a small wine shop. He went in and called, "Host, bring some wine for a wandering monk."

"Where are you from, reverend? If you're from the Mount Wutai monastery, I'm not allowed to sell you wine."

Lu Da assured the host that he was a travelling monk who was just passing through. Lu consumed some twenty big bowls of wine and half a dog carcass, paid for what he had drunk and eaten, and headed towards Mount Wutai. Halfway up the slope, he sat down in the pavilion and rested. The wine began to take effect. He leaped up and said to himself, "I haven't had a good workout for a long time. What I need is a little exercise."

He swung his arms vigorously up and down, left and right, with increasing force. One arm accidentally struck one of the pavilion's posts. It snapped, and half the pavilion collapsed.

The gatekeepers heard the noise and climbed to a high vantage point for a look. They saw Lu staggering up the slope.

"Woe!" they exclaimed. "That brute is soused again!"

They closed the gate and bolted it. When Sagacious found the gate locked, he pounded on it for a while with his fists. But the gatekeepers didn't dare let him in. Suddenly he noticed a Buddhist guardian idol on the left side of the gate.

"Hey, you big worthless fellow. Instead of helping me knock at the gate, you raise your fist and try to scare me. I'm not afraid of you!"

He jumped on the pedestal, and seizing a broken post flailed the idol's leg, bringing down a shower of gilt and plaster. Lu paused, and then turned to the guardian idol on the right.

"How dare you open your mouth and laugh at me?" he yelled. He leaped on the pedestal and with a thunderous crash brought that idol down to the ground with two hard blows. Sagacious laughed uproariously.

The gatekeepers notified the abbot of what had happened. He merely said, "Don't provoke Sagacious. Go back to your gate. Let him do as he pleases. We'll ask Squire Zhao to make us new idols for the gate and repair the pavilion."

"If you lousy rats don't let me in," bellowed Sagacious, "I'll set fire to this stinking monastery and burn it down!"

"Remove the bars and let the beast in," the monks hastily called to the gatekeepers. "If we don't, he's really liable to do it!"

The gatekeepers tiptoed to the gate, pulled the bolt, then flew back and scattered. Lu pushed hard against the gate. Unexpectedly, it gave way, and he stumbled in and fell flat on his face. He crawled to his feet, rubbed his head, and hurried to his quarters.

He plunged into the meditation hall. The monks, who were sitting cross-legged on their pallets, looked up, startled. As Lu clambered onto his pallet and opened his cassock, the dog's leg he had brought along with him from the wine shop dropped to the floor. "Good," said Sagacious, "I was just getting hungry." He picked up the bone and began to gnaw at it. Four or five monks hurried over, pleading with Sagacious to desist. He flung the bone aside, and drummed his knuckles on the monks' shaven pates. The whole meditation room was thrown into an uproar. Monks got their cassocks and bowls from the closets and quickly left. There was a general exodus.

Cheerfully, Sagacious fought his way out. This time the supervisor did not notify the abbot. He summoned all the monks on duty, including every cook and janitor — nearly two hundred men in all. They armed themselves with clubs and staffs, and marched to the meditation hall.

Lu let out a roar when he saw the host of monks charging him. He ran into the preaching room, knocked over the altar table, tore off two of its legs, and bolted out again. He came at the attackers so

fiercely that they hastily retreated to the cloisters. Sagacious advanced, brandishing the table legs. He feinted
one way and struck another. Only those furthest away
escaped his cudgels.

Right to the door of the meditation hall the battle
raged. Then the voice of the abbot rang out.
"Sagacious, stop that fighting! You too, you monks!"

The attackers had suffered several dozen
casualties. They were glad to fall back. Sagacious
threw down the table legs.

"Sagacious, you're giving me too much trouble,"
said the abbot. "For centuries these hallowed grounds
have known only tranquillity and the fragrance of incense. It's no place for a dirty fellow like you. I'll
arrange for you to be transferred elsewhere."

The next morning the abbot conferred with the
elder. They decided to give Lu some money and send
him on. The abbot then summoned Sagacious.

"Sagacious," said the abbot, "the last time you
got drunk and made a disturbance in the monks' hall,
you didn't know any better. This time you got drunk
again, smashed the guardian idols, wrecked the pavilion, and caused a riot in the meditation hall. This is a
serious crime. Our monastery is a peaceful place. It's
impossible for us to keep you here. As a courtesy to
Squire Zhao I'm giving you a letter of introduction to
another place where you can stay."

9

"In the Eastern Capital, "said the abbot, "a Buddhist brother of mine, called Lucid Teacher, is the abbot of the Great Xiangguo Monastery. Take this letter to him and ask him to find you a job. " Lu bowed low to the abbot, shouldered his knapsack, bid farewell to the abbot and the monks, and left Mount Wutai. After getting his staff and knife from the ironsmith, he went on his way.

Lu travelled for more than half a month, not stopping at any monastery.

As he was walking along one afternoon he became so absorbed in the beauty of the hills and streams that he failed to notice the lateness of the hour. Where could he spend the night? He hastened on another twenty or thirty *li*. While crossing a wooden bridge, he noticed a manor house.

"I'd better put up in the manor for the night, " Lu said to himself.

As he drew near, peasants working at the entrance to the manor asked him, "What brings you to our manor at this late hour, monk?"

"I couldn't reach an inn before dark. I hope your manor will put me up for the night. I'll be moving on tomorrow morning. "

"We're busy tonight. You can't stay. "

"It's only for the night. "

"Hurry along, monk. Don't hang around here, if you value your life. "

Sagacious lost his temper. "Can't you oafs be civil?"

At this moment an old man of about sixty emerged from the manor. "What are you rowing about?" he shouted as he approached.

"I'm on my way from Mount Wutai to the Eastern Capital," said Sagacious. "I couldn't reach an inn so I asked to be allowed to stay one night in the manor. But these surly blockheads wouldn't let me in."

"Since you are a monk from Mount Wutai," said he old man, "come in with me." He led Sagacious into the main building of the manor.

"Our peasants didn't know you were from Mount Wutai. Don't hold it against them. Although we're busy tonight, we shall be glad to put you up."

Lu rested his staff against a chair and bowed respectfully. "Thank you, patron. May I ask your honourable name?"

"Our family name is Liu. Because this place is called Peach Blossom Village, the peasants refer to me as Grandpa Liu of Peach Blossom Village. May I ask what the reverend's name is and what he is called in the Buddhist order?"

"My surname is Lu. Our abbot gave me the Buddhist title of Sagacious."

Grandpa Liu invited Sagacious to have dinner with him. Lu didn't need to be coaxed. Not having any scruples, he finished off a pot of wine and a platter of meat.

When the table was removed, the old man said: "Please make yourself comfortable in the wing next door, reverend. If you hear any noise during the night, don't come out whatever you do."

"Would you mind telling me what's going on here tonight? Why are you looking so unhappy? Has my coming here put you to too much trouble?"

"The trouble is my daughter is getting married tonight, and bringing a son—in—law into the family."

Sagacious laughed. "Men and women all must marry. It's an important event in every person's life and perfectly normal. What's there to be upset about?"

"You don't understand, reverend. We don't want this marriage. I have no other children, and my daughter is only nineteen. Not far from here is a height called Peach Blossom Mountain. Two chieftains built a stronghold on it recently with six or seven hundred men. They pillage and rob. A few days ago they came to our manor to collect tribute, and one of the chieftains saw my daughter. He gave me silver and a bolt of red silk as an engagement pledge, and chose tonight for the wedding. I had no way of opposing him. I had to consent. That's why I'm upset."

"Suppose I reasoned with him and convinced him not to marry your daughter. How would that be?"

"How can you make him change his mind?"

"When I was on Mount Wutai I learned the Buddnist Laws of Logic from the abbot. Now I can talk a man round even if he's hard as iron. Tell your daughter to hide. I'll reason with the groom in her chamber and get him to call the marriage off. Just leave everything to me."

10

Sagacious quaffed more wine, finished off a goose, and then directed a servant to put his bundles in a guestroom. "Has your daughter hidden herself, grandpa?"

"I've sent her to a neighbour's."

"Let's go to the bridal chamber, then."

Grandpa Liu and his servants went out to prepare the wedding feast. Sagacious pushed aside all the tables and chairs in the room. He put his knife at the head of the bed and leaned his staff against the bedstead. Lowering the bed curtains, he stripped to the buff, jumped into the bed and sat there.

Around ten, the sound of drums and gongs was heard on the mountainside. Grandpa Liu, worried about the success of the ruse, went out of the manor gate with his servants to greet the brigands. In the distance forty or fifty torches turned the night as bright as day, revealing a troop of men, on horse and afoot, speeding towards the manor.

Grandpa Liu shouted for his servants to open the

gate wide, and went forward to welcome the party.
Four or five lanterns at the head of the procession
illuminated the brigand chieftain, mounted on a big
white horse with a curly mane.

At the manor gate, the chieftain dismounted.
Grandpa Liu hurried forward with a cup of wine on a
tray and knelt before the bandit chief. The chieftain
raised the old man to his feet.

"You are my father-in-law. You shouldn't kneel
to me."

"Don't say that," Grandpa Liu replied. "I'm
only one of the subjects in the great chief's domain."

The old man led the chieftain to a lamp-lit table
on the threshing ground. "You shouldn't have arranged such an elaborate welcome, father-in-law, "
the brigand protested courteously. "But where's my
wife?"

"She doesn't dare come out. She's too shy."

Grandpa Liu was anxious to have the monk
reason with the brigand. "I'll show you to her room."
He escorted the chieftain to the bridal chamber. "This
is it, "he said. "Please go in. "He departed with his
candle. Not at all sure that their plan would succeed,
he wanted to get out of the way, fast.

The chieftain pushed open the door. Inside it was
pitch dark. "That father-in-law of mine is a miserly
manager. He doesn't even light a lamp, but rather
leaves my bride sitting in the dark."

Sagacious, seated behind the bed curtains, muffled

his laughter. The brigand felt his way to the centre of the room.

"Wife," he demanded, "come out and greet me. Don't be shy." Calling to his 'wife', he groped forward until he touched the bed curtains. He opened them and thrust his hand inside. It brushed against Lu's belly. The monk promptly seized the chieftain by the head and pushed his struggling frame down on the bed.

"You dirty thief," shouted the monk, and struck the brigand a blow on the neck and ear.

He hauled the bandit off the bed, and pummelled and kicked him. "Help!" howled the bandit.

Hearing the cry for help, Grandpa Liu picked up a lamp and rushed into the bridal chamber, followed by a swarm of bandits. They saw a big stout monk seated astride the brigand chieftain, thumping him vigorously.

The bandits rushed at Sagacious, cudgels and lances in hand. The monk pushed the chieftain aside, snatched his staff from the bedstead, and charged. He attacked so fiercely that the bandits cried out and fled. In the excitement, the chieftain crawled out of the room, raced to the front gate, and groped his way to an unsaddled horse. Flailing the horse wildly, he dashed away, riding bareback at a gallop.

Grandpa Liu grasped Sagacious by the arm. "You've brought disaster on my whole family, reverend!" he groaned.

" Don' t worry, Grandpa. Two thousand men wouldn't scare me, to say nothing of a few piddling bandit chiefs. "

" You mustn' t leave us, reverend, " pleaded Grandpa Liu. "My family needs your protection. "

"That goes without saying. I wouldn't leave if my life depended on it. "

11

In the meantime, the Head Bandit, seated in his stronghold on Peach Blossom Mountain, was about to send a man down to see how his second-in-command was getting on, when a number of bandits, breathing hard and looking distraught, rushed in crying "Woe, woe! "

" What' s wrong? " demanded the Head Bandit quickly.

"Our Number Two chief has been beaten up! " The Head Bandit looked. His lieutenant had lost his red hat. His robe was ripped and tattered. Number Two dismounted and collapsed in front of the Head Bandit. " Save me, brother, save me, " he pleaded. Number Two told the Head Bandit what had happened to him at the manor.

"So that's how it was. You go inside and rest. I'll catch the lousy thief and bring him here, " said the chief brigand. He called to his men, " Get my horse ready at once. All of you come with me. "

With as many men as he could muster he rode

down the slope. Everyone was shouting and yelling.

12

To get back to Sagacious Lu. He was drinking in the manor when a servant announced, " The Head Bandit is coming down the mountain witn a big gang! "

Sagacious hung his knife at his belt. Staff in hand, he strode out to the threshing ground. " Dirty bastard! " swore Lu. " I' ll teach you to meddle with me! "Whirling his staff, he charged.

The chieftain parried his blow. " Hold off a minute, monk, "he cried. "Your voice is very familiar. What's your name?"

"I'm Lu Da, a former major in the Weizhou garrison, and nobody else. Now that I' m a monk, I' m called Sagacious Lu."

The brigand laughed delightedly and rolled from his horse, tossing his weapon aside. He clasped his hands together in salutation.

It was none other than Li Zhong. Grandpa Liu, watching the pair, was dismayed. "So the monk is one of them too, "he thought.

Lu led Li Zhong to the hall to talk over old times. He called to Grandpa Liu, but the old man didn't dare come forward.

" Don' t be afraid of him, Grandpa, " said Sagacious. "He's my brother. "Lu and Li Zhong had a lot to tell each other about what had happened since they parted. Li Zhong told Lu that the man Lu had thrashed in the manor was called Zhou Tong. He had a stronghold on Peach Blossom Mountain. Once, when Li Zhong was passing by the foot of the mountain, Zhou Tong had come down with a gang and attacked him. Li Zhong had defeated him and Zhou had asked him to stay on as lord of the stronghold. Li Zhong had been an outlaw from that day on.

"Since you're the leader, call off the marriage to Grandpa Liu's daughter. She's his only child. You can't take her and leave him alone."

Grandpa Liu was very pleased. He had food and wine placed before the two guests. Each of the lesser bandits was also served food and wine. All ate their fill.

"I'm putting the whole matter in your hands," Sagacious said to Li Zhong.

"I can arrange things," said Li Zhong.

13

But it is enough of Li Zhong, Zhou Tong, and Grandpa Liu and his daughter for the moment. Let us return to Sagacious Lu. On leaving the manor he travelled from morning till evening, covering fifty or sixty *li*. He was hungry, but there were no inns on the road. Suddenly, he heard the sounds of bells in the distance. "Good," he thought. "If it's not a Buddhist monastery, it's a Taoist temple. That's the place for me."

32

After crossing a number of ridges, Sagacious saw a path up the mountain. He followed it for half a *li*, crossed a bridge and arrived at a run—down monastery. It was from here that the tinkling of bells had come. Above an arch a faded sign read "Waguan Monastery". Lu proceeded another forty of fifty paces and entered the compound. He went directly to the guest—quarters. The front gate was gone and the surrounding walls had crumbled.

He went to the abbot's hall. It was filthy with swallow droppings. he cried, "A passing monk wants some food."

He shouted for a long time, but no one responded. He went around to some other rooms. In a small room at the rear of the kitchen, he found a few old monks squatting, their faces sallow and sunken. "You monks are very rude, "said Lu. "I have been shouting and shouting, but none of you answered."

"We haven't eaten ourselves for three days. How can we find food for you? All the other monks are gone, and we don't have a single grain of food. We have really been hungry for the past three days."

"Liars! I don't believe there isn't any grain in a big place like this."

"It's true that our monastery was once prosperous. Wandering monks came from all over. Then one of them brought a Taoist priest and the pair took control. They ruined everything. There's nothing those two won't do. Murder and arson mean nothing to them. They drove all our monks away. Only we, who are too old to move, remained. That's why we have nothing to eat."

The old monks told Sagacious that the monk was called Cui, and the Taoist priest, Qiu. They lived in a building behind the abbot's hall.

Outside, someone was singing. Lu took up his staff and went to take a look. On the other side of a crumbling wall he saw a Taoist priest with a carrying pole on his shoulder. From one end hung a basket containing a few fish and some meat wrapped in a lotus leaf. A jug of wine dangled from the other end of the pole.

Sagacious grasped his staff and followed the priest. Under a locust tree he saw a table laid with platters of food, three wine cups and three pairs of chopsticks. A fat monk sat in the middle chair. A young woman sat beside him. The Taoist priest set down the basket and joined them.

Lu walked up to them. Startled, the monk jumped to his feet. "Please have a seat, brother," he cried. "Have a cup of wine with us."

"What do you mean by ruining the monastery?" Sagacious demanded. "Who is this woman? Why is she here?"

"Please be seated, brother," the monk replied. "Allow me to speak."

"Let's hear it. Out with it."

"The monastery used to be a fine place. But those

34

few old monks living in the cloisters like to eat and drink and carouse and spend money on women. The abbot couldn't restrain them. They laid complaints against him and had him expelled. As a result, the monastery has fallen into decay, and the monks have all left. This priest and I came here recently to take over. As for this woman, she is the daughter of Wang Youjin in the village below. He often made contributions to the monastery. But he's fallen on hard times and has had to sell all of their family property. His daughter has no other relatives, and her husband is ill. She's come here to borrow some grain. That's all there's to it, brother. And don't listen to what those old animals say."

"Those old monks have been playing tricks on me," Lu muttered. He returned to the kitchen, staff in hand. Sagacious pointed at the old monks and said angrily, "So it was you who ruined the monastery. You lied to me!"

"Don't believe that monk, brother," the old men responded in a chorus. "He saw you had a knife and a staff, so he didn't dare quarrel with you. If you don't believe us, go back again and see how he treats you this time. Judge for yourself. They're drinking wine and eating meat, while we have hardly anything to eat."

"That's true," said Lu. Holding his staff by the

lower end, he went to the rear of the abbot's com
pound. Angrily breaking down the door with one kick,
he strode through. The monk Cui, now armed with a
staff, rushed forward to attack him under the locust
tree. With a roar, Lu sprang into the fray.

They fought for a long time, neither gaining
ground. The Taoist priest strode towards Lu from the
rear with another staff. Lu fought the pair for more
than ten rounds. But he was hungry and travel—weary,
and couldn't cope with their combined strength. He
executed a feint and ran, dragging his staff after him.
His adversaries chased him to the stone bridge outside
the monastery. There, they sat down and rested.

14

Sagacious Lu kept going for some time. When he
had caught his breath, he said to himself, "I left my
rucksack in the kitchen. Now I've no money for the
road. This is a pretty fix. I can't go back because
those two rascals are too much for me."

He dawdled along another few *li* until he came
to a large forest. Suddenly, he saw a man poke his
head out of the shadows.

"That bird is a robber, or I miss my guess. And
he's here waiting for business. My belly's full of
wrath and I've no place to get rid of it. I'll strip the
lout of his clothing and sell it for wine money."

Staff in hand, he hurried towards the forest,

crying, "You thug in the wood, come out, quick! "

When the man heard this, he laughed and said, "I'm down on my luck and in need of money, and he comes to pick a quarrel! "

"Jackass, " he shouted. "It's you who've come looking for trouble. I haven't sought you out."

"I'll show you who I am, " said Sagacious Lu. Brandishing his staff, he charged. The other fellow rushed forward with his staff. But even as he did so, he thought, "Where have I heard that voice before?"

"Your voice sounds familiar, monk, " he said. "What's your name?"

Sagacious attacked without answering. They fought a dozen rounds. " That monk is a grand warrior, "the man said to himself in admiration. After another five rounds he shouted, " Rest a bit. I've something to say! "Both contestants tossed aside their weapons!

"Really, what's your name? " the man queried "I'm sure I know your voice. "Sagacious Lu told him. "Don't you recognize Shi Jin? " the man said with a bow.

"So it's you, Master Shi! "Sagacious laughed. The two exchanged greetings and went into the forest and sat down. "Where have you been since we parted? " asked the monk.

"The day after I left you at the inn I heard that you had killed Butcher Zheng and run away. The police discovered I had helped you send off Old Jin and his daughter, so I decided I'd better flee too. I went to Yanzhou, then returned to the Northern Capital and lived there a while. But my money ran out, and I came to this place to pick up some more. I never thought we'd meet here. What made you become a monk, brother?"

Lu told his whole story from the beginning.

"You say you left your rucksack at the monastery. Let's go back and get it. If they don't give it up, we'll finish the creeps off."

They took their weapons and returned to Waguan monastery. As they neared the entrance, they saw the monk and the Taoist priest sitting on the bridge.

"Come on, you miserable scum," shouted Lu. "Let's fight to a finish."

He ran towards the bridge, twirling his staff. The monk Cui was annoyed. He charged down the bridge with his staff.

They fought eight or nine rounds. Gradually, Cui weakened, and began looking for a chance to escape. Qiu, the Taoist priest, saw that Cui was losing. He hurried forward to help him.

Shi Jin bounded out of the forest, shouting, "Don't any of you try to get away!" He attacked the priest.

Both pairs battled furiously. The fight between Lu and Cui was reaching its climax. Lu saw an opening. With one clout of his weapon he knocked Cui off the bridge.

Seeing the monk fall, the priest became unnerved. He feinted and ran. Shi Jin caught up with him and plunged his weapon into the priest's body. The man fell to one side.

Sagacious and Shi Jin tied the bodies of their victims together and threw them into a ravine. Then they reentered the monastery and collected Lu's rucksack from the kitchen. The old monks, having seen Lu routed, feared that the monk Cui and the Taoist priest would kill them, had all hung themselves. The kept woman had jumped into a well and committed suicide

They searched the eight or nine small buildings, but found no one else. In the kitchen they turned up some fish, meat and wine. They lit the stove, cooked the food and dined.

Then each shouldered his pack. They tied reeds together into torches and ignited them in the stove. Then they set fire to the small buildings in the rear. When these had burned almost to the ground, they lit more torches and set the main hall ablaze from behind. Sagacious and Shi Jin watched for a while. The whole monastery was burning briskly.

They set out and travelled all night. Soon they came to a fork in the road. "We part here, brother, " said Lu. "I'm going to the Eastern Capital. You are going to Huazhou. We'll meet again some day." Shi Jin bowed and bid Sagacious farewell. Each went his separate way.

15

We'll now go on with our story of Sagacious Lu.

After eight or nine days on the road he caught sight of the Eastern Capital. He entered the city. In the centre of the city he asked a passer—by, "Could you tell me where the Great Xiangguo Monastery is?"

"There, ahead, by the bridge."

Sagacious went on to the monastery and proceeded to the guesthouse. A servant went in to announce him. Soon the reception monk came out. He was somewhat startled by Lu's fierce appearance, the iron staff in his hand, and the knife at his waist.

"Where are you from, brother?" he asked.

"I'm from Mount Wutai. I have a letter from my abbot requesting Lucid Teacher, the venerable abbot of this monastery, to give me a position as a working monk."

"In that case, please come with me."

To make a long story short, Lucid Teacher, after reading the letter from Mount Wutai and consulting the deacon, decided to put Sagacious Lu in charge of a large vegetable garden next door to the Temple of the Sacred Mountain. A notice of appointment was issued and posted in the compound, effective the following day.

The next morning Lu bid the abbot farewell, shouldered his pack, hung his knife at his waist and took up his staff. With two monks as escorts, he went directly to the vegetable garden to assume his duties.

In the neighbourhood of the monastery's vegetable garden there . . . hung out twenty or thirty thugs and gamblers. They made their living by selling the vegetables they stole from the monastery's fields. That day, when some of them went to raid the fields, they saw a notice posted on the gate of the overseer's compound. It read:

> The monastery has appointed the monk Sagacious Lu overseer of these vegetable fields. Starting tomorrow, he will be in charge.

The roughnecks called a conference of the entire gang. "This monk is new to the job. This is a good chance to pick a quarrel with him and beat him up — teach the lout to respect us," they decided. After devising a plan for picking a quarrel with Sagacious Lu, they went to seek him out.

As for Sagacious Lu, on arriving at the overseer's compound, he put his belongings in the house, leaned his staff against the wall and hung up his knife. The lay brothers who worked in the fields came to greet him, and he was handed the keys.

Sagacious made a tour of the garden. He saw twenty or thirty hoodlums coming towards him bearing a platter of pastries and ceremonial wine.

"We neighbours have heard that you've been put

41

in charge," they said, grinning broadly, "and we've come to offer our congratulations."

Not knowing a plot was afoot, Sagacious walked forward until he reached the edge of the ordure pit. Two of the gangsters advanced, one of them intending to seize his left leg, the other his right, and toss him in.

Noticing their strange pose Sagacious grew suspicious. "This gang is a queer-looking lot. They're up to no good. Can they be planning to dump me in the ordure pit?"

Sagacious strode up to the pair. Before either of them could even lay a finger on him, he lashed out with his right foot and kicked one of them into the ordure pit. The other began to take off, but a quick thrust of Lu's left leg sent him into the pit too.

Startled, the rest of the gang turned to run. "Whoever moves goes into pit," bellowed Sagacious. The riffraff froze, not daring to take a step.

The two who had landed in the ordure pit stood in the filth wailing, "Forgive us, reverend!"

Sagacious roared with laughter. "Fools! Go and wash off in the pond. Then I want to talk to all of you. Come into the compound."

When they returned he sat down in their midst, pointed his finger at them and scoffed, "You nincompoops! Did you think you could fool me? How could scum like you hope to make sport of me?"

The whole gang dropped to their knees. "Our families have lived here for generations," they said, "supporting themselves by gambling and robbing these vegetable fields. From now on, we'll be happy to serve you." The hoodlums thanked Sagacious Lu for his mercy and withdrew.

16

The next day, after talking things over, the gangsters scraped some money together and bought ten bottles of wine. Leading a live pig, they called on Sagacious and invited him to join them in a feast. Sagacious sat at the head of the table, with the twenty or thirty thugs lining both sides. Everyone drank, and the party grew lively. There was singing and talking and laughing.

That night the roughnecks departed. But they came again the next day, and every day thereafter, bringing meat and wine to feast Sagacious. They begged him to demonstrate his skill with weapons.

He went into the house and brought out his solid iron staff. He tossed up the heavy staff and flourished it effortlessly, making it whistle through the air. The roughnecks cheered and applauded.

Just as Sagacious was warming up, a gentleman appeared at a gap in the compound wall. "Truly remarkable," he commended the monk. Sagacious stopped his exercise and turned to see who had spoken.

The gentleman was about thirty-five years old; he

was dressed in an officer's robe.

"Remarkable indeed," he said. "What wonderful skill!"

"Who's that officer?" queried Sagacious.

"An arms instructor of the Mighty Imperial Guards. His name is Lin Chong."

"Invite him in. I'd like to meet him."

Hearing this, the arms instructor leaped in through the gap in the wall. The two men greeted one another, and sat down beneath an ash tree.

"Where are you from, brother monk?" asked Lin Chong. "What is your name?"

"I am Lu Da, from west of the pass. Because I killed many men, I had to become a monk. In my youth, I spent some time in the Eastern Capital. I know your honourable father, Major Lin."

Lin Chong was very pleased, and adopted Sagacious as his sworn brother on the spot.

"What brings you here today, Arms Instructor?" asked Sagacious.

"My wife and I have just arrived at the Temple of the Sacred Mountain next door to burn incense..."

Just as they were talking, a female servant, agitated and flushed in the face, rushed up and cried: "Hurry, master! Our lady is being molested by a man in the temple!"

Lin Chong quickly took his leave of Sagacious. "I'll see you again, brother. Forgive me!" Lin Chong leaped through the gap in the wall and raced with the

44

servant to the temple.

When he reached the temple, he saw a young man blocking his wife's path. "Let's go upstairs," the young man was urging her. "I want to have a talk with you."

Lin pushed forward, seized the young man by the shoulder and spun him around. "I'll teach you to insult a good man's wife," he shouted, raising his fist. Then he recognized Young Master Gao, adopted son of Marshal Gao Qiu, commander of the Imperial Guards.

The young hooligan made full use of his foster father's influence in the Eastern Capital. His favourite pastime was violating other men's wives. When Lin saw that he was Young Master Gao, strength left his arms.

"This has nothing to do with you, Lin Chong," said Gao. "Who asked you to interfere!" He didn't realize that the lady was Lin Chong's wife. Had he known, the thing would never have happened.

Some of the bystanders soothed Lin Chong, while others persuaded Gao to leave the temple grounds, get on his horse and depart.

Lin Chong was turning to go with his wife and her servant when Sagacious Lu, staff in hand, came charging into the temple compound, leading his vagabonds.

"I've come to help you fight," said Sagacious.

"The man turned out to be the son of our Marshal Gao. He hadn't recognized my wife and behaved discourteously. I was going to give the jerk a good drubbing, but then I thought it would make the marshal lose too much face," Lin Chong explained, "so I decided to let the young hooligan off this time."

"The next time you have any trouble, just call me and I'll take care of it!" With these words Sagacious Lu left the temple compound.

17

We'll skip over some of the story of Lin Chong and his troubles for the moment, and continue to talk about Sagacious Lu.

When Sagacious was in charge of the Great Xiangguo Monastery's vegetable garden, Marshal Gao decided to put Lin Chong out of the way because of Young Gao's passion for Lin Chong's wife. A plan was evolved, whereby Lin Chong was arrested and sentenced to exile in Cangzhou. His escorts were instructed to kill Lin Chong on the way to his destination.

When Sagacious Lu heard of this, he wouldn't stand for such injustice. He followed Lin Chong along the road to Cangzhou, and just as the two guards were about to do Lin Chong in, he leaped out from behind a pine tree, brandishing a staff. After cutting Lin Chong's bonds and helping him to his feet, Sagacious Lu wanted to kill the guards, but Lin Chong wouldn't allow it.

The two escorts went back and reported to Marshal Gao that just as they were going to dispatch Lin, he had been rescued by a monk from the Great Xiangguo Monastery.

Furious, Marshal Gao made the abbot of the Great Xiangguo Monastery dismiss Sagacious Lu, and sent men to arrest him.

Lu, however, was tipped off and was able to flee in time. He burned down the vegetable garden buildings and took to the road. But nowhere could he find a refuge.

In Mengzhou Sagacious stopped at an inn and was nearly done in by the innkeeper's wife, who drugged his wine. Luckily, her husband came home unexpectedly early. He quickly gave Sagacious Lu a drink that revived him.

After four or five days at the inn, Sagacious heard that he would be safe in the Precious Pearl Monastery on Two—Dragon Mountain. He went there intending to join the band of outlaws who held the mountain. But their chieftain, Deng Long, wouldn't have him.

Sagacious fought him, and Deng Long saw that he was no match for Sagacious, so he fled up the mountain, closing and bolting the three big gates at its foot. No matter how Sagacious cursed the chieftain, he wouldn't come down and fight.

18

Sagacious returned to the inn and related the story of his unsuccessful attempt to join Deng Long's band.

"The stronghold can be conquered only by guile, not by force," said the innkeeper. The innkeeper suggested that Sagacious Lu dress like a local peasant. The innkeeper would take away his staff and knife and bind him, using only slip-knots. Then he would take him up the mountain to the gates and shout, "We're from the neighbouring inn. This monk drank so much he got tipsy, but he refused to pay. He kept muttering that he was going to muster his men and attack your stronghold. We tied him up and now present him to your chieftain."

Sagacious thought the scheme was shrewd, and so that's just what they did. Deng Long ordered his men to let the innkeeper and Sagacious Lu up the mountain. When Sagacious was brought before Deng Long, he slipped his bonds, and the innkeeper handed him his staff. Deng Long was finished off in a moment. With him out of the way, the five or six hundred brigands occupying the mountain all submitted. Deng Long's body was burned. Taking all the money and grain with him, Sagacious Lu set out for the Mount Liangshan fortress.

On his arrival several days later, he was met by the fortress chieftains. A big feast was laid on to celebrate the addition of a new chieftain to the Mount Liangshan forces.

But of this we'll say no more.

19

We'll not relate in detail all the valourous deeds by which Sagacious Lu distinguished himself after becoming a chieftain of the Liangshan Marsh outlaws.

He was finally ordered to return to the capital with some of the other chieftains. On the way there they took quarters in a monastery near Hangzhou.

One night, when the moon was bright, Lu awoke. He felt his time had come. He said to the monks, "I'll have to round out my circle and rest in silence." In religious parlance this means to die.

He asked for hot water to bathe in. When this was brought, he cleansed himself and changed into fresh monk's vestments. He then went into the temple, pulled a hassock to the centre of the meditation hall and lit some fragrant incense in a burner. Then he seated himself cross-legged on the hassock and, quite naturally, transcended into space.

Sagacious Lu's remains were cremated behind the monastery.

BOOK ONE

CHAPTER TWO — LI KUI

1

We will now talk of Li Kui, known on account of his swarthy complexion as Black Whirlwind.

Li Kui was honest and straightforward. The slightest injustice drove him wild. He loved to drink and to gamble. When he got drunk he would brawl and get into scraps.

Li Kui came from Yishui County. He had beaten a man to death in his native village and had had to flee home. He had wandered to Jiangzhou and remained there, even though later there was an amnesty. He was on the staff of the prison in Jiangzhou. Because he was nasty when drunk, everyone was afraid of him.

Now it so happened one day that just as Li Kui was wrangling with a waiter in an tavern in town, he was overheard by Song Jiang, a clerk of the Yuncheng County magistrate's court, of whom we'll hear more later.

On enquiring Song Jiang was told that Li Kui was a guard at Jiangzhou prison who often misbehaved, but had his good points. He was straight and righteous. The slightest injustice enraged him, and he would tear into bullies. He was raising a row just then with the innkeeper, who had refused to lend him money.

The superintendent of the prison, with whom Song Jiang was having dinner at the inn, was the only man who could handle Li Kui when he was drunk, so the waiter hurried over to ask the superintendent to help pacify Li Kui. The superintendent soon returned with Li Kui. He introduced the two men to one another. Learning that the man before him was Song Jiang, whose reputation for righteousness and generosity was renowned, Li Kui bowed. Song Jiang returned the courtesy.

"What angered you?" asked Song Jiang.

"I wanted to borrow ten ounces of silver from the host here, but the knave wouldn't lend me a thing."

Without a word, Song Jiang pulled out ten coins and handed them to Li Kui. Li Kui picked up the money, pushed the portiere aside and went off.

"I'll be right back."

Having obtained the money, Li Kui thought, "What luck! Brother Song Jiang has never met me before, but he lends me ten ounces of silver. I'll gamble with the money. If I win something I'll be able to wine and dine him to repay his kindness."

Li Kui hurried to a gambling den outside the town run by a man called Zhang Yi. Entering the den, Li Kui threw his ten ounces on the gambling floor and asked for the toss coins. " Tails, " he shouted and tossed. The coins came up heads. "Tails,"he shouted. Again the coins turned up heads.

Li Kui snatched up his money from the floor as well as the money belonging to other gamblers, and put it all in the pocket of his gown.

"Brother Li, you gamble honestly as a rule. Why are you behaving so badly today?"

" I usually play straight, but today' s an exception."

Zhang Yi rushed up to wrest back the money. A dozen gamblers swarmed against Li Kui. Li pounded them until they had no place to hide, and then he headed for the gate.

He thrust the gatekeepers aside, kicked open the gate and went through, pursued by the other gamblers. As he was striding away, a man ran up from behind, seized his arm and shouted, "How dare you grab other people's property, you bastard! "

"What frigging business is it of yours? " Li Kui spun around to find himself facing the superintendent. Standing to his rear was Song Jiang. A look of embarrassment spread over Li Kui's face.

" Don' t blame me, brother. Black Whirlwind usually plays fair. But I lost your silver and had no money to invite you out. I got excited and behaved badly."

Song Jiang laughed. "Any time you need money, just ask me. You obviously lost, so give them back their money."

Li Kui had no choice but to take the silver from his pocket and hand it over to Song Jiang. Song Jiang called Zhang Yi over and gave him the money.

2

The three men proceeded to a restaurant overlooking the Xun—Yang River. The superintendent invited Song Jiang to be seated, sat himself opposite, and placed Li Kui at his side. They ordered vegetables, fruit and seafood delicacies. The waiter produced two jugs of wine.

Six or seven rounds of drinks were consumed. Song Jiang was pleased with his two companions. After drinking several cups of wine, he suddenly got a craving for hot pepper fish soup. "Is there any fresh fish around here?" he asked the superintendent.

"Don't you see all those fishing boats on the river? The whole region teems with fish and rice."

"Some hot pepper fish soup would be just right for sobering up."

The superintendent called the waiter and ordered fish in hot pepper soup. Not long after, the soup arrived. Li Kui didn't bother with chopsticks. He pulled the fish out of the bowl by its head and ate it, bones and all.

"This is preserved fish, brother," said the superintendent. "I'm sure it's not to your taste."

"I thought a little fresh fish soup would go well after wine," said Song Jiang. "But this fish isn't really very good."

"We'll get some fresh fish for our brother," said Li Kui jumping up. Before Song Jiang and the superintendent could stop him, Li Kui left.

Li Kui went down to the river. Eighty or ninety fishing boats were moored in a row to willow trees along the river bank. "You've got some fresh fish on board?" yelled Li Kui to the fishermen sprawled on the boats.

"We can't open the hatches till the catch—master comes," answered one of the fishermen.

"Who cares about your frigging catch—master! Just let me have some fish."

Before the fishermen could stop him, Li Kui jumped into one of the boats. He didn't understand anything about these craft. The catches of fish were kept alive in large holds under the sterns, trapped in by porous bamboo gates. Li Kui groped around, but couldn't find any fish. When he pulled up the gate, all the fish in the boat escaped.

He leaped over to the adjoining craft and hauled up its bamboo gate. Seventy or eighty fishermen rushed on board and attacked Li Kui with punting poles. Enraged, he snatched up a dozen of the punting poles with both hands and snapped them like so many chopsticks. The startled fishermen left hastily, untied the moorings of their boats and shoved off.

54

Li Kui angrily seized a broken pole and charged up the bank to continue the battle. In the midst of this turmoil, a man was seen approaching along a path. "You've come at last, master," several fishermen called. "That big dark fellow has been grabbing fish."

The man sped towards Li Kui, shouting, "How dare you mess up my business, bastard!"

Without a word, Li Kui whirled his pole and swung. Had Li Kui known anything about the man who had challenged him, he would not have ventured to get into a scrap with him. The man the fishermen addressed as "master" was the catchmaster. His name was Zhang Shun. Because of his prower in swimming, he was nicknamed White Streak in the Waves. Taunting Li Kui with a poke in the legs delivered by his pole, he jumped aboard a boat. His enraged opponent leaped in immediately to pursue him.

When Li Kui swung at Zhang Shun, the latter dodged and seized the pole. With a few shoves of the pole, Zhang Shun sped the craft like an arrow to the middle of the river. With his feet he tipped the boat over, turning it bottom up and dumping both men in the river. "I'm not going to fight you yet. I want you to drink some water first," Zhang sneered.

Li Kui knew how to swim, but not very well. He was confused and alarmed. Zhang seized Li Kui by the arms. The river parted and Li Kui was lifted up, only to be shoved down under. Fiercely interlocked, the two men battled in the waves. Li Kui was ducked so often that his eyes became white. Again and again he was lifted, again and again pushed under. He was clearly getting the worst of it.

In the meanwhile, the superintendent and Song Jiang had run up to the bank of the river. The superintendent called out, "Brother Zhang, stop fighting. That big dark fellow is my friend. Let him go. Come ashore and talk."

Zhang Shun recognized the superintendent. He released Li Kui, hurried to the shore, climbed the bank and greeted the superintendent respectfully.

"For my sake, rescue that brother of mine and bring him here, "the superintendent pleaded.

Zhang Shun dived into the river and swam swiftly to where Li Kui was floundering about, his head in the water. Zhang grasped him by his hand and hauled him towards the shore. Between gasps Li Kui vomited up a lot of water.

3

One day — this was some time after he became one of the gallants of Mount Liangshan — Li Kui burst into tears.

"What's the trouble, brother?" Chao Gai, the supreme leader of the Liangshan stronghold, inquired hastily.

"You and the other chieftains have been so considerate of me for so long. My old mother is home alone.

56

My elder brother is a hired hand. How can he support her? I want to bring her to Mount Liangshan, so she can have a few years of peace and happiness."

"You're absolutely right," said Chao Gai. "We'll send a few men with you to bring her back here. An excellent idea."

"It can't be done," Song Jiang interjected. "Brother Li is too irascible. If he goes home, he's sure to get into trouble. Even if we send men with him, that won't be any good either. He's too hot-tempered. He'd quarrel with them on the road. Besides, he's killed a lot of people in Jiangzhou. Everybody there knows Black Whirlwind. For sure his native village has been alerted. Better wait till things quiet down, brother Li. There will still be time."

"Should my mother stay in her village and suffer? Do you want Black Whirlwind's belly to burst with rage?"

"Calm yourself, brother. We'll let you go, but on three conditions."

"What are they?"

"The first condition is that you don't drink on the way," said Song Jiang. "The second condition is that you go alone and fetch your mother quietly. The third condition is that you leave your battle-axes here. Be careful during the journey. Go soon and return quickly."

"Nothing hard about these conditions. Don't worry, brother. I'll take off today and I won't remain long at home."

Li Kui tied up his belongings, hung a dagger at his waist, and took a pike and some silver ingots. He drank a few cups of wine and after respectfully bidding the chieftains farewell, went down the mountain.

"Brother Li is bound to get into a scrape,"Song Jiang said. "Is there anyone among us who comes from his parts?Someone who could go there and keep tabs on him?"

"Zhu Gui is an Yishui County man. They're from the same township."

Song Jiang sent for Zhu Gui.

"Brother Li Kui has gone home to get his mother,"Song Jiang told him. "Because he's nasty when drunk, we didn't ask anyone to go along. But we're afraid he'll get into trouble. I hear you're from the same parts. I'd like you to go and keep an eye on him."

"I can go, easy enough. I haven't been back in a long time either. I'll be glad to see my people again."

Zhu Gui bid the leaders farewell and set out for Yizhou.

4

On leaving Liangshan Marsh, Li Kui travelled alone and reached the border of Yishui County. As promised, he did no drinking, and kept out of trouble. Outside the gate of the county town he saw people crowded around a proclamation board. He pushed among them and listened to a man who was reading aloud. The proclamation offered a large reward for the capture of Song Jiang and his accomplice Li Kui.

Li Kui seethed inwardly, his control melting away. A man hastened up from behind and locked him in a restraining embrace "Why, brother Zhang, " cried the man. "What are you doing here?"

Black Whirlwind turned his head and looked. It was Zhu Gui. "What about you?" Li Kui demanded.

"Come with me and I'll tell you."

The two went to a nearby inn inside the town gate and sat down in a quiet room in the rear. Zhu Gui pointed his finger at Black Whirlwind.

" You' re very rash, brother. That proclamation offers a reward for Song Jiang and Li Kui. And you stand there looking at it! Suppose some sharp—eyed fellow saw you and hauled you off to the authorities? What would you do then? Because brother Song Jiang was afraid you' d quarrel, he didn' t send anyone along with you. But he was also worried you' d get into trouble. So he ordered me to catch up with you and keep an eye on you. Where have you been all this time?"

"He told me not to drink any wine. That's why I couldn' t walk very fast. How do you know this inn? Do you live around here?"

"The inn belongs to my brother. I used to live in these parts. I was a travelling merchant. But I went broke and became a bandit in Liangshan Marsh. This is the first time I've been home."

Zhu Gui introduced his brother to Li Kui, and the innkeeper treated them to wine.

"Brother Song Jiang instructed me not to drink. But now I've reached my home territory. If I drink a bowl or two, what's the frigging difference?"

Zhu Gui didn't venture to stop him, and they drank until late night. Food was then served, and Li Kui ate. When dawn was brightening the sky, he started for the village.

"Don't take the narrow path," Zhu Gui advised. "Follow the main road east from the big oak tree, straight to the village. Fetch your mother and return quickly to the mountain stronghold."

"It's nearer if I go by the path. Who's got the patience to take the main road?"

"There are robbers along that path who'll steal your bundle."

"That doesn't worry me." Li Kui picked up his pike, hung on his dagger, bid farewell to Zhu Gui and his brother, and headed for the village.

By the time he had travelled a dozen *li* or so, the sky had turned dark. Ahead was a grove of about thirty large trees. When Li Kui reached the edge of the grove a big fellow suddenly emerged. "Shell out money for a safe passage, if you know what's good for you," the man shouted.

Li Kui looked him over. His head was bound in a

red silk kerchief. He grasped a battle—axe in each hand. A black substance was smeared all over his face.

"Who the hell are you, daring to play the robber in this place?" Li Kui roared.

"When you hear my name you'll tremble. I'm Black Whirlwind! Leave your money and your bundle and I'll spare your life and let you pass."

Li Kui laughed. "No such frigging thing. Who are you, oaf? Where are you from? How dare you use my name and play the fool here?"

He charged, pike in hand. The man realized he had met his match and turned to flee. Li Kui stabbed him in the thigh, felling him, and planted a foot on his chest.

"Recognize me?"

"Master, spare your servant's life!"

"I'm Li Kui, the Black Whirlwind, a man among bold men. You've abused my name, you nincompoop!"

"My family name is also Li, but of course I'm not Black Whirlwind. You're so famous in the gallant fraternity that the very mention of your name frightens demons. So I borrowed it when I became a robber here. I've made some tidy profits that way, but actually I've never harmed anybody. My real name is Li Gui, and I live in that village over there."

"So you've got your frigging nerve, robbing and ruining my reputation!" Li Kui raised his weapon.

"If you kill me, master, you'll be destroying two,"

Li Gui hastily cried.

Li Kui stayed his hand. "What do you mean by that?"

"I didn't want to become a robber. But I've a ninety-year-old mother at home, without anyone to support her. So I've been using your renowned name to scare lone travellers and snatch their bundles. That's how I've been able to take care of her. If you kill me, my old mother will surely starve to death!"

Although Li Kui killed people without batting an eye, these words gave him pause. "I've come home specially to fetch my mother," he thought. "If I kill a man who's supporting his own mother, Heaven and Earth will not forgive me." And he said, "All right, you jerk, you can live." He released Li Gui. Still holding his axes, Li Gui dropped to his knees and bowed.

"Just remember that only I am the true Black Whirlwind," Li Kui cautioned him. "You're not to give my name a bad reputation from now on."

"Today my life has been spared. I'm going home and changing my profession. I'll never again use master's name here to rob."

"You're a dutiful son. Here are ten ounces of silver to give you a start in your new business."

5

Li Kui trudged up the mountain path. By midmorning he was hungry and thirsty. There wasn't an inn or restaurant in sight. Then, in the hollow ahead, he saw a number of thatched cottages. As he hurried towards one of them, he saw a woman coming out the rear door. A wild flower was tucked into the bun of hair on the back of her head, and her face was rouged and powdered.

" Sister—in—law, " Li Kui said to her, " I' m a traveller who's passing by. I'm hungry, but I can't find an inn. If I pay you some silver, will you give me some food and wine?"

The woman saw how tough he looked, and dared not refuse. "We haven't any wine, "she said, "but I can cook some rice for you. "

"That will do. I'm frigging hungry. "

The woman lit the fire in the kitchen, washed the rice in the stream, and set it on to cook.

Li Kui went to the slope behind the house to relieve himself. He saw a man approaching stealthily around a bend of the mountain. Li Kui returned to the rear of the house. The woman, who was about to go up the slope to pick some vegetables, opened the rear door and saw the man.

"Brother, "she exclaimed, "how did you hurt your leg?"

"I had a close call. I've been waiting for a lone traveller for half a month, but business has been bad. Then today one came along, and who do you think it was? The real Black Whirlwind! Of all the frigging luck! Of course I was no match for him. He brought me down with one in the thigh from his pike and wanted to kill me. I put on an act and cried, 'I have a ninety—year—old mother, without anyone to support her. If you kill me, she'll starve to death, for sure.' The fool believed me. Not only did he spare my life, he gave me silver to start a new business and look after my mother.'"

"Keep your voice down," said the woman. "A big swarthy fellow arrived just now and asked me to cook some rice. I'll bet he's the one. Take a look at him. If it's him, find me some drug and I'll put it in the vegetables. After he passes out, you and I will dispose of him."

Li Kui had heard every word. He said to himself, "The bastard! I gave him silver and spared his life, and now he wants to kill me!"

He came around to the back door as Li Gui was about to leave and grabbed him by the hair. The woman ran towards the front door. Li Kui threw his captive to the ground, pulled out his dagger and cut off his head. He hurried round to the front door, looking for the woman, but she had disappeared.

The rice on the stove was steaming hot, but he had no vegetables to go with it. He scooped the rice into a bowl and ate. When he was full, he dragged Li Gui's body into the house and set the place on fire. Pike in hand, Li Kui continued along the mountain path.

The sun was already low on the western horizon

by the time Li Kui reached home. He pushed open the door and entered.

"Who's there?" his mother called. Li Kui saw that she was blind. She was sitting on the bed, murmuring something.

"It's Black Whirlwind, ma. I've come back."

"You've been gone so long, son! Where have you been all these years? Your brother is working as a hired hand. He scarcely gets enough to feed himself. He can't really take care of me. I've thought of you often and wept till my tears ran dry. That's why I've become blind. What have you been doing with yourself?"

Li Kui thought, "If I tell her I'm a brigand in Liangshan Marsh, ma won't be willing to go with me. I'd better make up a story." Aloud he said, "Your Black Whirlwind is now an official. I've come to fetch you."

"That's fine, son. How are you going to take me?"

"I'll carry you on my back to the road, and there we'll find a cart to travel in."

"Wait till your brother comes home. Talk it over with him first."

"What for? We'll just go."

Li Kui took a big ingot from his pouch and placed it on the bed for his brother. He hoisted his mother onto his back, picked up his pike, left the house and strode forth along a secluded path.

6

Night had fallen when they reached the foot of a slope. Li Kui's mother, being blind, couldn't tell whether it was morning or evening. Li Kui knew that the height ahead was called Yiling Mountain. Only on the other side was there human habitation. He trudged upward with her in the starlight.

"Son," she said, "could you ask someone for some water?"

"After we cross the ridge, ma, we'll find a house where we can rest and eat."

"I had only dry rice at noon. I'm very thirsty."

"My throat is burning, too. After I've carried you to the top, I'll look for water."

"Save me, son. I'm dying of thirst."

Li Kui plodded to the summit. He set the old woman down on a large rock beside a pine tree.

"Be patient, ma. I'll fetch you some water."

Li Kui heard the gurgling of a brook, and went in the direction of the sound. He found it finally, after crossing two or three hillocks. He drank several mouthfuls.

"How can I bring the water to my mother?" he pondered. He stood up and gazed around. High on a ridge above he saw a temple. "Good," he thought. Grasping hanging vines and shrubs he clambered up. He walked to the temple, pushed open the courtyard gate and entered. In front of the chapel stood a large stone incense burner

Li Kui tugged at the vessel, but it and its base were carved from a single block. He couldn't budge it. He lifted it up, base and all, and clanked it down on the stone steps, knocking the urn free. This he took to the stream and scrubbed clean with bunches of grass. He then filled it half full with water and, holding it in both hands, retraced his path to the summit.

His mother was not on the big rock beside the pine tree. He called to her to come and drink. There was no sign of the old lady anywhere. He shouted a few times, without response.

Then, on the grass, about thirty paces away, he saw bloodstains. He began to tremble. Casting aside the incense vessel, he followed the trail of blood to a large cave. Two tiger cubs were outside licking a human leg. Li Kui couldn't stop shivering.

"I came all the way from Liangshan Marsh to fetch my old mother," he thought. "Did I carry her here on my back, in spite of hardships, just for you to eat?"

Li Kui was in a fury. He prodded the two cubs with his pike till they snarled, bared their claws and attacked. Then he stabbed one to death. The other ran into the cave. Li Kui chased it inside and killed it. Crouching in the cave, he looked out. A savage tigress was returning to her lair.

"You are the beast who ate my mother!" he thought. He lay down his pike and pulled out his dagger.

The tigress sat down at the mouth of the cave, her hindquarters and swishing tail inside the entrance. Using all his might Li Kui drove his dagger into her with such force that blade and hilt penetrated her stomach. With a roar the tigress leaped over a chasm, the dagger still in her. Li Kui snatched up his pike and gave chase. The tigress, in great pain, charged down the cliff.

Li Kui was about to follow, when a gust of wind sprang up among the trees, bringing down a shower of leaves and branches. From the place where the wind arose, a roaring tiger leaped out and charged directly at Li Kui.

Coolly, Black Whirlwind thrust his pike into the neck of the hurtling beast. It halted abruptly, staggered six or seven paces, then fell and expired on the bluff. Li Kui went into the den to see whether there were more tigers, but there was no sign of any.

Very weary, he made his way to the chapel and slept till daylight.

7

Li Kui rose early, collected his mother's leg and what remained of her other bones, wrapped them in his robe and buried them in a grave he dug behind the chapel. He wept bitterly. Finally, hunger and thirst impelled him to gather his bundle, take up his pike, and proceed slowly across the ridge.

He met half a dozen hunters armed with bows and arrows. When he told them that he had killed four tigers they didn't believe him.

"You, one man, killed four tigers? You might have done in the two cubs, but two full—grown tigers — impossible! You must be kidding."

"Why should I kid you? Come up and see for yourself."

"We'll be very grateful if it's true. A wonderful thing!"

The hunters whistled shrilly. In a few minutes forty or fifty men, armed with barbed spears and cudgels, were following Li Kui up the trail. When they reached the summit, sure enough, there were two dead cubs at the cave; the body of a female tiger lay at the foot of the cliff; a dead male tiger was sprawled before the chapel.

Overjoyed, the hunters carried the tigers down, slung on poles. They sent a man ahead to inform the village head and the gentry.

When word spread that four tigers had been killed on Yiling Mountain, excitement in the village ran high. Everyone, men and women, young and old, flocked to see the dead beasts and to peer at the hero.

Among the spectators was Li Gui's wife. She had fled to this village of Yiling where her parents lived. When she went to view the tigers, she recognized Li Kui. She rushed home and told her parents.

"That big swarthy fellow who killed the tigers is the man who murdered my husband and burned our home. He's known as Black Whirlwind of Liangshan Marsh."

Her parents immediately informed the village head. "If he's Black Whirlwind," the official thought, "then he's Li Kui, who killed a man in the village on the other side of the mountain and ran away to Jiangzhou. He made trouble there too, and a large reward has been offered for his capture. And here he is!"

The village head quickly sent for Squire Cao, at whose house Li Kui was just then being feasted. "That tiger killer is none other than Li Kui, the Black Whirlwind," he told Squire Cao. "There's a notice out for his capture."

A retired petty official, Cao was a nasty, unscrupulous type. Through various crooked deals he had recently become very rich.

"We'll ply him with wine and ask him whether he wants to go to the county town to claim the reward for the tigers," he suggested. "If he's unwilling to go to the county town, then we'll know he's Black Whirlwind. We'll keep toasting him in relays till he's drunk. Then we'll tie him up, inform the county authorities and have them send the sheriff to come and get him. We can't go wrong."

"Very good," the village head agreed.

Squire Cao returned home to set the plan in ac

tion. He ordered a large platter of meat and a big jug of wine. The gentry, the village head and the hunters toasted Li Kui with large bowls and flagons of wine.

"Will you be going to the authorities to claim the reward for the tigers, or would you prefer to receive some recompense here?" asked the squire.

" I' m a traveller passing through, and I don' t have much time. I happened to have killed a few tigers. There's no need to claim any county reward. If you have a little money here, that will do. If you don't, I'll go on without it."

8

Of how Squire Cao duped Li Kui by getting him drunk and then tying him up securely until the sheriff and some soldiers could reach Yiling Village, we'll say no more. We'll speak rather of how Zhu Gui and his brother Zhu Fu rescued Li Kui as he was being conveyed to the county town under escort.

Zhu Fu suggested that when the sheriff and his party came to his inn with their prisoner, the brothers would offer them wine to celebrate the killing of the tigers. A sleeping draught would be mixed in the wine, and they would all fall unconscious. Then Li Kui could be set free.

The problem was that the Sheriff did not drink much. Even if he passed out, he would recover quickly.

They finally decided to cook twenty or thirty

pounds of meat, sprinkle some knock-out medicine over it and, since the sheriff did not drink, press him to eat the meat. He would then keel over.

Everything went off as they planned. When the sheriff and the soldiers saw the meat and the wine, they tucked in. Li Kui watched with shining eyes. The moment he saw Zhu Gui and his brother he knew it was a ruse.

"Let's march, quickly, " the sheriff ordered. But the men were unable to stir. Lips trembling, legs numb, one by one they fell to the ground. His own head grew heavy and his legs light, and he melted into a heap, completely out.

With a roar Li Kui burst his bonds. He grabbed a pike and charged towards Squire Cao. He ran him through, and then dispatched Li Gui's wife and the village head. His blood lust aroused, he wanted to slaughter the hunters and all the county soldiers. Zhu Gui and Zhu Fu had difficulty restraining him.

9

Zhu Fu and Li Kui sat by the roadside. In less than an hour the sheriff, who had recovered more quickly than the others from the effects of the sleeping draught, came flying down the path, his pike tightly grasped in his hands.

"Robbers, stay where you are! " he shouted. He rushed forward fiercely.

Li Kui jumped up and advanced to meet him with levelled pike. The two men fought six or seven rounds, with neither besting the other. "Stop, "cried Zhu Fu, separating them with his pike. "Listen to me." The contestants paused.

"Please hear me. " Zhu Fu said to the sheriff. "The problem is my brother Zhu Gui is one of the chieftains on Mount Liangshan. He was ordered by his leader Song Jiang to look after brother Li Kui. You were taking him to the authorities. How could Zhu Gui go back and face Song Jiang?We had to play that trick on you. Brother Li Kui wanted to finish you off, but I wouldn't let him, and he killed only the soldiers. Today, scores of men have been killed and Black Whirlwind has escaped. How can you report back to the magistrate?You're sure to be put on trial, and there's no one to rescue you. Wouldn't it be better if you went with us up the mountain and joined Song Jiang's band?What do you say?"

The sheriff thought for several minutes. "Suppose they won't have me?"he finally said.

Zhu Fu laughed. "Surely you've heard of Song Jiang! He welcomes bold men from all over. "

The sheriff sighed. "I've become a man without a home or country. Luckily I have no wife or children, so I don't have to worry about the authorities arresting them. I suppose I'll just have to go with you. "

Li Kui chuckled. "Brother, why didn't you say that earlier?"He gave the sheriff a deep bow

Since the sheriff had no family or property, the three men set off together. Halfway, they caught up with Zhu Gui, who was delighted. They had an uneventful journey. As they neared Mount Liangshan, they were met by two bandits who had been sent down to inquire about them. But of what happened after they reached the stronghold, we'll make no mention now.

10

We'll now tell of how Li Kui got implicated in the abduction and killing of the little son of the magistrate of Yuncheng, and of the consequences of the death of the child.

Now in Yuncheng Town there was a sheriff called Lei Heng. One evening he went to the theatre where a travelling singer was performing. Having sung and danced, the girl took up a platter and went around for a collection. When she approached Lei Heng, he wanted to put some coins in the platter too, but discovered that he hadn't a penny with him. He told the singer that he had forgotten his money that day, but would bring her some the following day.

The singer and her father began to make jokes at Lei Heng's expense. In the end the sheriff could not contain himself. With a punch and a kick Lei Heng puffed up the old man's lips and knocked out a couple of his teeth. People rushed to separate them.

Lei Heng was persuaded to go home.

It so happened that the singer had been intimate with the magistrate when he had been in the Eastern Capital. After Lei Heng gave her father such a drubbing, she went directly to the magistrate and complained.

"Draw up a complaint, immediately," the magistrate exclaimed heatedly.

Lei Heng's friends tried to intercede for him. But the girl pouted and flounced until the magistrate gave in. Lei Heng was arrested, brought before the court, and beaten till he confessed. The magistrate ordered him collared with a rack and paraded in the streets.

Lei Heng was committed to a prison, the warden of which was a man called Zhu Tong, a friend of Lei Heng's. One day, Zhu Tong selected a dozen guards and left Yuncheng with Lei Heng. After marching ten *li* they came to an inn.

"Let's have a few bowls of wine," Zhu Tong suggested.

Everyone went into the inn and drank. Zhu Tong took Lei Heng out the back door. In a secluded spot, he opened the rack and freed him.

"Go home, brother, quickly, and get your mother. Travel all night, and find refuge elsewhere. I'll take the consequences."

Lei Heng bowed his thanks. He hurried home along a path by the rear door. He gathered his valuables and departed with his mother. They travelled

75

through the night to Liangshan Marsh, where Lei Heng joined the band.

11

For letting Lei Heng escape, Zhu Tong was confined in prison in Cangzhou. When he was delivered to Cangzhou, the magistrate was favourably impressed with his demeanor and said, "Don't take this man to prison. I want him here in my office as my attendant."

From then on Zhu Tong served in the magistrate's office.

Now the magistrate had a four-year son, whom he loved better than gold or jade. One day, as the magistrate was talking with Zhu Tong, the child went directly to Zhu Tong and asked to be picked up.

"I want this bearded man to carry me. No one else," piped the little boy.

"I'll take him outside for a stroll," Zhu Tong suggested. "We'll be back soon."

"All right," said the magistrate, "since that's what he wants."

Zhu Tong carried the child to the street and bought him some sweets. When they came back, the magistrate ordered wine for Zhu Tong.

"Any time the child wants you to take him to play, you can take him out for a walk."

"Your wish is my command, Excellency."

Thereafter, Zhu Tong took the little boy for a stroll every day. Half a month went by, and it was the fifteenth day of the seventh month — the Driving Out of Devils Festival. That evening, the nursemaid spoke to Zhu Tong.

"The child wants to see the lanterns on the river. Madam, his mother, says you can take him."

It was early evening. Zhu Tong strolled around the temple grounds with the little boy. A man behind Zhu Tong tugged him by the sleeve.

"Brother, would you come away for a moment so we can talk?"

Zhu Tong looked around. To his surprise, there was Lei Heng. Zhu Tong told the child he was going to buy him some candy, and went off with Lei Heng.

"What are you doing here?" Zhu Tong asked.

"After you saved me, I had no other place to go with my old mother, so I joined the Liangshan Marsh band. I told them of your kindness to me, and the chieftains were extremely moved. They deputed me to invite you up our mountain to join our band. Please come to our fortress and satisfy the wish of our chieftains."

"Brother, what are you saying? You haven't given the matter thought. I let you escape because your mother was old and your family poor. Now you suggest that I should become a bandit."

They walked towards the bridge. There was no sign of the little boy. Zhu Tong groaned. He searched high and low. Grasping his arm, Lei Heng said, "Don't bother to search, brother. When the two men who came with us heard you say you wouldn't go, they probably took the child away."

"This is no time for jokes. That little boy is the magistrate's very life. I'm responsible for him."

They went outside the town. Zhu Tong was quite upset.

"Those two who came with us are ignorant fellows," said Lei Heng.

"What're their names?"

"I heard one of them being called Black Whirlwind."

Zhu Tong was shocked. "Not the fellow who killed those people in Jiangzhou?"

"That's the man."

Zhu Tong stamped his feet in anguish and groaned. Then he hurried on. When they were about twenty *li* from the town, they saw Li Kui, the Black Whirlwind ahead. Zhu Tong hastened up to him. "Where's the magistrate's son?"

"The child is here."

"Bring him out, then, and give him to me."

"I put a potion in his mouth and carried him out of town. He's sleeping in that grove."

Zhu Tong plunged in among the trees. He saw the little boy lying dead on the ground. Zhu Tong rushed out of the grove, enraged. The three men were gone. He peered in every direction. Then he saw Black Whirlwind standing in the distance.

Wild with fury, Zhu Tong tore after him. Li Kui retreated, with Zhu Tong in pursuit. Soon Zhu Tong was gasping for breath.

Ahead of him, Li Kui called, "Come on. Come on."

The seething Zhu Tong wanted to swallow him down in one gulp. But he couldn't get near him. The chase dragged on through the night. Gradually, the sky brightened.

12

To escape Zhu Tong's wrath, Li Kui was forced to seek refuge in the manor of a personage called Chai Jin, known also as Small Whirlwind. He stayed in Lord Chai's manor for over a month.

One day, a messenger delivered an urgent letter to the manor. Lord Chai read it and said, "In that case I'll have to go."

"What's the trouble, Excellency?" asked Li Kui.

"I have an uncle who lives in Gaotang. The magistrate's brother—in—law Yin Tianxi has taken over his garden. My uncle is so infuriated that he's taken ill, and may not live. He has some dying words he wishes to impart. My uncle has no children. I'll have to hurry to his side."

"Would you like me to keep you company?"

"I'd be glad if you would."

Lord Chai packed some luggage, selected a dozen good horses, and told a number of servants to get ready. The next day at dawn Lord Chai, Li Kui and their company climbed into their saddles, left the manor and headed for Gaotang.

On arriving there, Chai Jin dismounted in front of his uncle's residence. Chai Jin left Li Kui and the others in the outer hall and went to his uncle's bedroom. Once seated beside his uncle's bed, he wept. Chai Jin asked his uncle's wife what had happened.

"The new magistrate is also the military commander here," she told him. "Because Marshal Gao in the Eastern Capital is his cousin, he feels he can do anything he pleases. He brought with him Counsellor Yin. Although very young, Yin knows he has the magistrate's backing, and he inflicts harm on people with his outrageous behaviour. One of his toadies told him that we have a pretty garden in the rear with a pavilion overlooking a pool. He broke in with twenty or thirty hooligans the other day and inspected the garden, wanting to drive us out of our home and move in himself. Your uncle protested, but the despicable fellow wouldn't listen. He insisted that we leave. Your uncle tried to push him away, but got beaten for his pains."

Chai Jin stayed a while with his uncle, and then came out and told Li Kui and the others about the dispute. Li Kui jumped to his feet.

" That unreasonable bastard! I'll give him a

couple of licks with my axes first. Then we can start discussions! "

At that moment a servant hurried out to ask Lord Chai to go to his uncle. His uncle addressed him with tears in his eyes.

"I die today because of the humiliation imposed on me by Yin Tianxi. You owe it to me as one of the same flesh and blood to write a complaint to the emperor and obtain redress. Take care of yourself. I have no other bequests."

Having said this, Chai Jin's uncle died.

A coffin was prepared, and a memorial tablet set up in keeping with the rites. The whole family dressed in deep mourning, and young and old lamented.

Two days went by. After Yin Tianxi and twenty or thirty cronies had been carousing outside the town, they staggered up to the residence of Chai Jin's uncle. Yin reined in his spirited horse and shouted a demand to see the person in charge.

Lord Chai hastily emerged. Yin addressed him from his saddle.

"I gave orders the other day that the family were to move out. Why haven't I been obeyed?"

"Uncle was sick in bed. We couldn't disturb him. He died in the night. We'll move when the forty—nine—day mourning period is over."

"I give you three days more. If you're not out by then, I'll put a rack around your neck and let you taste a hundred blows of my staff!"

81

"You mustn't persecute us like this, Counsellor!"

"Men, give this fellow a drubbing, "Yin said angrily.

The gang started towards Chai Jin. Li Kui had been watching and listening through a crack in the door of the house. At this juncture he pushed it open, dashed up to Yin with a roar, and dragged him from his horse. With one punch he knocked him sprawling. The thirty ruffians rushed to Yin's aid. Li Kui promptly knocked out a dozen. Yelling, the remainder turned and fled.

Li Kui picked Yin up and pummelled him with his fists and feet. Lord Chai couldn't restrain him. It wasn't long before Yin lay dead on the ground.

Chai Jin groaned. He led Li Kui to the rear hall and said, "They'll be sending men here very soon! You can't stay! You've got to go back to Liangshan Marsh, quickly. "Li Kui gathered his battle-axes, took some travel money, and set out for the mountain fortress.

Not long after, more than two hundred men armed with swords, spears and staves surrounded the manor. Chai Jin came out and said, "I'll go with you to the authorities and explain."

They bound his arms and went in to look for the big swarthy culprit. He was gone. They took Chai Jin to the magistrate's office and flung him down at the magistrate's feet.

"How dare you kill my Yin Tianxi!" shouted the

magistrate.

"I called to visit my uncle, who was gravely ill. Unfortunately, he died, and we are now in mourning at his residence. Counsellor Yin came with thirty men and wanted to drive us out. He wouldn't listen to my explanations and ordered his men to beat me. While defending me, one of my servants, Big Li, killed him in the heat of battle."

"Where's Big Li?"

"He panicked and ran away."

"He's your servant. Would he have dared kill a man without orders from you? You deliberately let him escape, and now you try to delude the court. Take him, guards, and give it to him hard."

They pounded Chai Jin till his flesh was a pulp and his blood streamed in rivulets. A twenty-five-pound rack was placed around his neck, and he was cast into prison.

13

Li Kui travelled through the night to get back to Liangshan Marsh. On arriving at the fortress he reported to the leaders. Zhu Tong was filled with rage the moment he saw him. He rushed at Li Kui with his staff. Li Kui, brandishing his axes, clashed with him in combat. Chao Gai and others exhorted them to stop.

"Tell brother Zhu Tong you're sorry you killed the magistrate's little boy."

Li Kui couldn't very well refuse. He said to Zhu Tong, "I'm not afraid of you, but the brothers insist. I have no choice. I apologize."

Only then was Zhu Tong appeased. Chao Gai ordered that a feast be laid on to cement the reconciliation.

"Lord Chai went to Gaotang because his uncle was ill. The magistrate's brother-in-law, Yin Tianxi, wanted to take over the house and gardens, and cursed Chai Jin. I knocked the lout around and killed him," said Li Kui.

"You escaped, but they're sure to prosecute Lord Chai," Chao Gai cried in alarm.

One of the chieftains was sent down the mountain to make enquiries about what had happened to Lord Chai. He soon returned and reported.

"I went to Lord Chai's manor and learned that he and Li Kui had left for Gaotang. I hurried after them. In Gaotang, the whole town was agog. Everyone said that Yin Tianxi tried to seize the residence of Lord Chai's uncle, and a big dark fellow beat him to death. Lord Chai was implicated, tied up and cast into prison. All the property of Lord Chai's uncle and his family has been confiscated. There's no guarantee that Lord Chai's life will be preserved!"

"Lord Chai has always been benevolent to our fortress," said Chao Gai. "Today he's in danger. We must rescue him. I'll go personally."

"You're our leader, brother. You shouldn't

84

make a move lightly," said the other chieftains. "We'll
go on your behalf."

14

Gaotang was a small town, but it had a large
military force, so a regiment of five thousand men
with a support force of three thousand was organized
for the assault under the command of twenty–two
chieftains.

The Liangshan Marsh forces finally bested the
troops defending Gaotang. The magistrate was killed
by Lei Heng.

The first thing that was done when the men of
Liangshan Marsh entered the town was to go to the
prison to release Chai Jin. But Chai Jin was not
among the prisoners. The chieftains were worried and
puzzled. In one of the buildings they found the family
of Lord Chai's uncle, in another the family of Chai
Jin himself. Only Lord Chai could not be found. Then
one of the warders said, "The magistrate instructed me
that if luck went against him I should finish Lord
Chai off. But I didn't have the heart to do it, because I could see he was a good man. So I took him
to a dry well in the rear courtyard, removed the fetters
and pushed him in to hide him. Then I reported to the
magistrate that he was dead. I don't know whether
he's dead or alive."

The warden hastily led the chieftains to the well.

85

They peered down into its black maw. They called, but no one responded.

"He doesn't seem to be there."

"Let's not get upset," said the chieftains. "We won't know for sure until we send someone down to see."

Before the words were out of his mouth, Li Kui pressed forward and shouted, "Let me go."

A long rope was tied to a large basket. Li Kui stripped to the buff, grasped his battle—axes, and sat down in the basket, which was lowered into the well.

Eventually, the basket reached bottom. Li Kui crawled out and felt around. Finally he touched a man crouching in a puddle.

"Lord Chai," he called out.

But the man didn't move. Li Kui stretched out his hand in front of the man's face. He felt only a faint breath coming from his mouth.

"Thank Heaven and Earth! He can still be saved!"

He put Lord Chai into the basket, and the basket was hauled up. Then the basket was lowered again for Li Kui, and he was also pulled up.

When they examined Lord Chai, they found that he had gash on his forehead, the flesh on both legs had been beaten to a pulp, and his eyes were half open and half closed. He was a sorry sight. A doctor was called to treat him.

A cart was ordered for Chai Jin to lie on. Li Kui and Lei Heng were instructed to escort him to the

Liangshan stronghold.

15

On the Ninth day of the Ninth Lunar Month Festival some of the Liangshan Marsh chieftains decided to go to the Eastern Capital to see the lantern show. Among them was Li Kui. At first it had been decided not to take him along, for fear he would make trouble. But he stubbornly insisted, and there was no refusing him. Sure enough, no sooner had the chieftains entered the city, than Li Kui got into a scrap. When the other chieftains heard the sounds of yelling and shouting, they decided to leave the city immediately lest the gates be closed before they could escape.

In the meanwhile, Li Kui returned to his inn for his battle axes. The other chieftains wanted to collect him and return to the stronghold. But they saw no sign of Li Kui anywhere. Li Kui, axes in hand, was proceeding to the county town of Shouzhang.

The court had just adjourned for the noon recess when he walked up to the gate of the government headquarters. " The Lord Black Whirlwind of Liangshan Marsh is here! "he shouted.

The staff of the county office was paralyzed with fright. Theirs was the closest town to the outlaw stronghold, and mothers had only to say "Black Whirlwind Li Kui" to scare crying children into silence. And there he was, right then, in person.

Li Kui went in and sat down on the magistrate's official chair. "A few of you had better come out and talk," he called. "otherwise I'll set fire to the place."

The people in the corridor held a hasty conference. They decided they'd have to comply. "He might really do it, " they said. Two of their number were selected and sent into the hall.

They bowed four times, and spoke, still on their knees. "Since you've come, chieftain, you must have some instructions."

"I don't want to disturb your county. I was passing by and thought I'd stop a while and fool around. Call your magistrate. I want to see him."

"When he heard you'd come, he left through the back door. We don't know where he's gone."

Li Kui didn't believe them. He wandered through the rear chambers looking for the magistrate, and came upon the clothing wardrobe. He twisted open the lock, took out the official hat and put it on. Next, he slipped into the green robe of office, tied on the belt, exchanged his hemp sandals for elegant boots, and walked back into the hall.

"All you officers, " he called, "come in here and see this! " They had no choice but to obey. "How does this outfit look on me?"

"Very appropriate."

"Now I want you to summon court for me. If you don't, I'll level this town to the ground."

The officers were afraid of him. They called a

number of functionaries, who beat three rolls on the big drum with bone and ivory sticks. Then all advanced and hailed Li Kui respectfully.

Li Kui laughed heartily. "Now let two litigants argue their case."

"No litigant would dare appear before the chieftain."

"Then a couple of you can act the parts. I won't hurt you. It's just for fun."

The functionaries conferred, and picked two jail keepers to play the roles. Local people crowded the gate of the county office to watch. The two litigants knelt at the front of the hall.

"Pity me, magistrate," said the plaintiff. "That man struck me."

"He cursed me first," retorted the defendant. "That's why I hit him."

"Who is the one who was hit," Li Kui queried.

"I, sir," said the plaintiff.

"And who is the one who hit him?"

"He swore at me," said the defendant, "so I clouted him."

"The man who gave the beating is a good fellow," said Li Kui. "Let him go. The other is a spineless lout. Why did he allow himself to be struck? Put a rack around his neck and parade him before the populace in the street outside the office."

Li Kui rose, fastened the green official robe, tucked the elmwood tablet in his belt, grasped his big axes, and went out to supervise the affixing of the rack around the neck of the plaintiff. Only after the man was put on exhibition at the county office gate did Li Kui stride on. He was still wearing the magistrate's splendid clothes and boots.

In the street he ran into one of the chieftains who had been looking for him everywhere.

"Everyone has been worried stiff about you, and here you are playing the fool! Come back to the mountain at once!"

The chieftain dragged Li Kui off without any ceremony. Li Kui was compelled to leave Shouzhang County and return to Liangshan Marsh.

15

We are nearing the close of our narrative of the adventurous life of Li Kui, the Black Whirlwind.

We find frequent mention of him in the annals of history of the period. When the Liao Tartars invaded and pillaged Shandong, Shanxi, Henan and Hebei, Li Kui joined other chieftains of Liangshan Marsh in repulsing them. Leading a thousand men, Li Kui distinguished himself in battles against the hordes of Liao Tartars at Tanzhou, Stony Valley and Bazhou.

It was Li Kui and his men who took Tanzhou, a vital entry to Liao territory, dealing the Tartars a heavy blow. In the battle at Stony Valley, Li Kui killed the Vice-Commander-in-Chief of the Great

Liao Army, He Zhongbao. Unfortunately, in the battle of Bazhou Li Kui was captured by the enemy after being pinned down by hooked poles. To get him back, the Liangshan brigands exchanged a young Tartar general who had been captured previous day for him

16

After the decisive victories over the Liao Tartars, the Liangshan Marsh forces returned to the fortress. A count of the chieftains showed a total of twenty-seven still alive. They were all given high posts and presented with valuable gifts.

This profoundly disturbed the emperor's ministers, Marshals Gao and Yang.

"They are our enemies," said Gao. "Now they've been made high officials and honoured by the imperial court. We ministers have become laughing stocks!"

"I have a plan," said Yang. "Let's send an emissary to Song Jiang with imperial wine in which we'll put a slow-working poison. In half a month he'll be beyond saving."

"An excellent idea," said Gao.

In brief, an emissary was directed to take two bottles of imperial wine to Song Jiang in Zhushou, where Song had been appointed governor. Gao and Yang put a slow-acting poison in the wine.

One day, Song Jiang was informed that an emissary had arrived from the capital with imperial wine. Accompanied by other officials he went out of the city to welcome him and escort him in.

In the public hall the emissary read the emperor's greeting, presented the wine and urged Song Jiang to drink. When Song Jiang requested the emissary to join in, the man refused, saying that he was a teetotaler. Song Jiang ceremoniously drank and the emissary returned to the capital.

Song Jiang's stomach began to pain him soon after, and he suspected that something had been added to the wine. He quickly made enquiries and learned that the emissary had in fact done some drinking while stopping at a hostel for officials along the road. Song Jiang realized that he had been tricked. He was positive the wine had been poisoned by the emperor's ministers. He sighed.

"It doesn't matter if I die, but Li Kui, who is today the commandant of Hunzhou, will certainly take to the hills again when he hears about this dirty trick the imperial court has played. There's only one thing I can do."

He dispatched a man that same night to Hunzhou with a message for Li Kui to come to Zhuzhou immediately.

When Black Whirlwind received the message from Song Jiang, he said to himself, "Big brother has sent for me. It must be important." He embarked by boat at once with an aide. On reaching Zhuzhou, he went directly to Song Jiang in his offices.

"From the time we broke up I've done nothing but think of you, brother, "said Song Jiang. "Many of the chieftains are in far—off districts, and I've had no news of them. Only you, brother, are relatively near. So I've asked you to come and discuss a very serious matter."

"What is it?"

"First have some wine."

Song Jiang escorted Li Kui into a rear hall, where wine and a goblet were waiting. Li Kui drank for some time until he was half intoxicated.

"I must tell you, brother, "said Song Jiang, "I hear the imperial court is sending me poisoned wine. If I die what will you do?"

"Rebel, brother, "Li Kui shouted. "Let's rebel!"

"Our army is gone. Our brothers are scattered. How can we rebel?"

"I've got three thousand men in Zhenjiang. You have soldiers here in Zhuzhou. We'll muster them, and as many of the local people as we can get to join us, raise more troops, buy horses and fight! We'll be happy back in Liangshan Marsh. At least we won't have to take any more crap from these stinking ministers!" "Slowly, brother. We must talk this over."

Li Kui of course didn't know that the wine he imbibed contained a slow poison. That night he drank more. The next day Song Jiang saw him off to his boat.

"When will you start your revolt, brother?" Li

Kui asked. "I'll come with my troops and reinforce you."

"Brother, don't blame me!" said Song Jiang. "The emperor sent me some poisoned wine the other day, and I drank it. I'm going to die soon. Though I am innocent, the imperial court is causing my death."

"I was afraid that after I died you would rebel and spoil our reputation for righteousness. And so I asked you here and gave you the poisoned wine also. When you return to Hunzhou you'll surely die." As he spoke, Song Jiang's tears fell like rain.

Li Kui also wept. "Enough, enough, enough!" he cried. "I took care of you in life, Big Brother, and I'll serve you after death as well!"

His body felt heavy. Weeping, he bid Song Jiang farewell and boarded his boat. When he reached Hunzhou, sure enough, the poison took effect.

As Black Whirlwind lay dying, he instructed his attendants, "After I'm gone you must take my coffin to Zhuzhou and bury me beside Big Brother." Later, his wishes were carried out.

BOOK ONE

CHAPTER THREE — WU SONG

1

Wu Song was from Qinghe County, the second son in his family. This Wu Song got drunk one day in his county town and got into a brawl with an official in the local government office. With one blow of his fist he knocked the man senseless to the ground. Wu thought he had killed him, and ran away. For a year he took refuge in the manor of Lord Chai, a squire in Henghai County. Later Wu Song learned that the official had not died. He intended to go home and see his elder brother, but then caught malaria and wasn't able to leave.

While staying in the squire's manor, he often got drunk. He would lose his temper and beat up the servants, who complained about him to the squire.

Wu Song was homesick. He was concerned about his brother, from whom he had not heard in a long time. The squire urged him not to leave, but Wu insisted. At last he wrapped his belongings into a bundle, tied on his staff, bade goodbye to the squire, and left.

He travelled for several days and came to Yanggu County. He was hungry and thirsty from walking.

Seeing an inn ahead, he went inside, sat down and called for some wine. The innkeeper brought three bowls. Wu Song asked for some meat, and then for more wine. The innkeeper pointed to the pennant hanging by the door which read "Three bowls and you can't cross the ridge".

"What does that mean?"

"Any traveller who drinks three bowls of our wine gets drunk and can't cross that ridge there."

"Poppycock! I'm paying, aren't I? Pour me three more bowls!"

Seeing that the wine had little effect on Wu Song, the innkeeper kept serving until Wu had had eighteen bowls in all.

Wu Song rose to his feet. "I'm not a bit drunk!" He went out the door and started walking away.

The innkeeper ran after him. "Come back. I want to tell you about a proclamation issued by the authorities. It says that there's a fierce tiger on Jingyang Ridge. It comes out at night, and has already killed nearly thirty people. The authorities have ordered travellers to go in groups and cross the ridge only between late morning and early afternoon. No one is permitted to travel alone. It's already late. Why not spend the night at my place? And then tomorrow you can get together a band of twenty or thirty travellers and cross the ridge in safety."

Wu Song laughed. "I've crossed that ridge at least twenty times, and have never seen any tiger.

Don't try to scare me with that crap."

2

Staff in hand, Wu Song strode off towards Jingyang Ridge. It was late afternoon when he reached the foot of the ridge and began to ascend the slope. The sun was setting in the west.

Soon he came upon a dilapidated temple. A notice was posted on the door. It warned that a tiger had been killing people on Jingyang Ridge; travellers were permitted to cross the ridge only in bands, and only between late morning and early afternoon.

So there really was a tiger! Wu Song thought of going back to the inn, but he was afraid that if he did so, the host would take him for a coward. He decided to keep climbing and see what happened. He walked on.

The wine in him made him pleasantly warm. His gait was unsteady and, he staggered into a thicket. In front of him was a large smooth rock. He clambered onto it, and prepared to sleep. Suddenly there was a thunderous roar and a huge tiger bounded out of the thicket.

Wu Song jumped down, seized his staff, and slipped behind the rock. The big animal clawed the ground with his front paws, sprang high and came hurtling forward. Wu Song dodged, and the tiger landed beyond him. With a roar, the huge animal tried to lash at Wu Song. Wu Song dodged, and the tiger missed.

Not waiting for the beast to swirl around, Wu Song raised his staff high and swung with all his might. There was a loud cracking. In his haste, Wu had struck a tree instead of the tiger. The staff had snapped in two, leaving him holding only the ramaining half.

The beast charged furiously, landing in front of Wu Song. Wu threw away the stump of his staff, seized the tiger by the ruff, and exerting all his strength, kicked the animal in the face and eyes, again and again. The tiger floundered frantically, clawing wildly at the yellow earth before it.

Relentlessly clutching the tiger by the ruff with his left hand, Wu Song freed his right and with all his might pounded the tiger's muzzle.

After sixty or seventy blows, the tiger lay motionless in a pool of blood, panting wearily. Wu Song got up. Finding the stump of his broken staff, he beat the tiger till it breathed no more.

Tossing the staff aside, he tried to lift the beast, thinking he would drag it down the mountain. But he was so exhausted from the struggle that he couldn't move it. He decided to go down the ridge first in case another tiger came, and then consider what to do in the morning.

3

As Wu Song was descending the ridge, two hunters with tiger pelts bound tightly around their waists appeared before him. They were amazed to see him crossing the ridge at dusk, alone and unarmed. They were even more amazed when he told them that he had encountered a tiger on the ridge and punched and kicked it to death. If it hadn't been for the blood on his clothes, they wouldn't have believed his story.

Wu Song led the hunters to where the tiger lay dead in a great heap. They shouted to the band of peasants who had been lying in ambush, waiting to catch the beast. Astonished and joyous, the peasants crowded around, gaping at Wu Song and the fierce beast. Five or six of them finally trussed up the tiger and carried it down the ridge slung from a pole.

When the party reached the foot of the ridge, a large crowd of peasants, led by the village head and prominent township families, were waiting to welcome the hero. The tiger was placed in front of a hall.

A guest room was prepared for Wu Song's use. Exhausted from his battle with the tiger Wu Song was soon asleep. He rose at daybreak. The next day he was wined and dined, and congratulated by everyone. Then he was escorted to the county town. There the magistrate wanted to know how Wu Song had been able to kill the huge tiger. Wu Song told the story. All present listened in stupefaction. The magistrate gave him several cups of wine and rewarded him handsomely.

Wu Song distributed the money among the hunters.

The magistrate, impressed by Wu Song's generosity, decided to make him a police inspector in the county. The same day the appropriate documents were drawn up. Who would have thought that Wu Song, who had wanted to go home and see his elder brother, would become an officer in the police force in Yanggu?

4

A few days later, when Wu Song was leaving the county office in search of amusement, a voice hailed him from behind. It was none other than his elder brother.

Wu Song was overjoyed to see him, as he hadn't seen his brother for over a year. Wu the Elder took him to his house.

Now, Wu the Elder, in contrast to the handsome, stalwart Wu Song, was very short and ugly. He made a living out of peddling buns. His wife was young and quite pretty. Nothing about her husband pleased her, and she was not averse to merrymaking with the dandies that were always hanging around outside her house. She was quite ready to take a lover.

When Golden Lotus — that was what Wu the Elder's wife was called — saw Wu Song and heard that he was the man who had killed the tiger on Jingyang Ridge, she thought to herself, " If I could

100

have a man like that I wouldn't have lived in vain. Who would have thought that I was fated to meet my love here? Why not get him to move in?"

Her face wreathed in smiles, Golden Lotus said to her brother-in-law, "It can't be very convenient to stay in the county office compound. Why don't you move over here? I'll be glad to make you anything you want to eat or drink."

While they were talking, Wu the Elder returned home with the food and wine he had bought. He asked Mistress Wang from next door to come over and prepare the meal.

When everything was ready, Golden Lotus raised her cup and asked Wu Song to drink with her. Wu the Elder was busy warming the wine and refilling the cups. He had no time for anything else.

After a few cups had been downed, Golden Lotus openly ran her eyes over the younger man's body. Embarrassed, Wu Song kept his head down and avoided her gaze. Finally, he rose to leave. As his hosts were seeing him out of the house, Golden Lotus repeated her suggestion that Wu Song move in with them. "Otherwise, the neighbours will laugh at us. After all, you're our own brother." Wu the Elder also pressed Wu Song to move in.

5

And so, Wu Song came to live in his brother's

house. Every morning he signed in at the magistracy and performed his duties. Whenever he returned home, Golden Lotus had food ready, and would serve him with obvious pleasure. She was always dropping hints, but being a moral man he paid no attention.

One winter morning a month later, Wu Song came home a little later than usual. Golden Lotus asked her next—door neighbour Mistress Wang to buy some wine and meat for her. She then lit the charcoal brazier in Wu Song's room.

"I'm really going to tempt him today," she said to herself. "I don't believe he can't be aroused...."

Wu Song sat down to warm himself by the fire. Golden Lotus bolted the front door, closed the back door, brought in the wine and food, and placed them on the table.

"Why isn't brother back yet? Hadn't we better wait for him?"

"Let's have a few cups of wine, just the two of us."

Golden Lotus too pulled a stool over to the brazier and sat down near the table on which was a tray with wine cups. She raised a full one and handed it to Wu Song. He drained it. Golden Lotus refilled it. Wu Song finished this one, too. He poured a cup and handed it to the girl. She drank it.

Her bosom slightly exposed, her hair hanging down in a soft cloud, Golden Lotus smiled bewitchingly. She poured Wu Song three or four cups in succession, and had the same number herself. She talked more and more freely. She went out and got some more wine. Holding the container in one hand, she placed the other on Wu Song's shoulder and squeezed. He was poking up the fire in the brazier. She took the poker from him.

"You don't know how to stir up a fire," she said provocatively. "I'll show you. The idea is to get it good and hot." Wu Song, embarrassed, did not reply.

Warmed by a rising, uncontrolled passion, Golden Lotus put down the poker, poured a cup of wine, drank a mouthful and offered Wu Song the rest.

"Finish this, if you have any feeling for me."

Wu Song flung the cup with the wine on the floor.

"Have you no shame!" he cried. He gave her a push, nearly knocking her off her feet.

But we'll say no more of this.

6

The next day when Wu the Elder came home, he found Golden Lotus in tears. She told him that that nasty brother of his had tried to get fresh with her when no one was around. Wu the Elder didn't believe her: he knew that his brother had always been well behaved.

He went to Wu Song's room to call him to have something to eat. Wu Song didn't say anything. He put on his clothes and headed for the door. Wu the Elder tried to stop him, but he silently continued on his way.

When Wu the Elder tried to question Golden Lotus, she called him a dolt and said that Wu Song had left because he was ashamed to face his brother. She swore that she would not let Wu Song live in the house ever again. Wu the Elder didn't dare open his mouth. At that moment Wu Song arrived with a soldier. He packed his belongings and left again.

"Good riddance!" Golden Lotus cursed. "He's moved, thank Heaven and Earth! Now we don't have an enemy right under our noses!"

The simple-minded Wu the Elder couldn't understand her rage. Unhappiness over his brother's departure gnawed his heart.

From then on, Wu Song stayed in the county office compound. Wu the Elder more than once wanted to go and see him, but his wife wouldn't have it, and in the end Wu the Elder gave up the idea.

Time passed by, and soon the snow was gone. One day the county magistrate summoned Wu Song and said, "I have a load of gifts and a letter to send to a relative in the capital. But I'm afraid there may be trouble on the road and I need a hero like you to deliver them. Do this for me, and I'll reward you well when you return."

Wu Song couldn't refuse. He went to his quarters, gathered up some silver, bought a bottle of wine and some food, and proceeded to Wu the Elder's home.

When Golden Lotus saw Wu Song arrive with food and wine, she thought, "The knave must have me on his mind, so he has come back! I'm too much for him!"

She went upstairs, put on fresh make-up, fixed her hair and changed into more alluring clothes.

"Have we offended you in some way? You haven't been here for days! But now, happily, today you have come!"

"I've something to say," replied Wu Song. "I've come specially to speak to you both."

The three sat down, Wu the Elder and Golden Lotus at the head of the table, Wu Song on a stool at the side. Wu Song filled a cup with wine, and holding it, faced his brother.

"I've been given a mission to the capital by our magistrate. I'm leaving tomorrow, and will be gone for forty of fifty days, maybe longer. There's something I must say before I go. You've always been weak and timid, and people may try to take advantage when I'm not around. From tomorrow on leav: the house late and come back early. Don't drink with anybody. And when you get home, lower the curtain and bolt the door. If anybody insults you, don't quarrel. I'll take care of him when I come back. Pledge me this, rother, with this cup."

Wu Song poured a second cup and turned to

Golden Lotus.

"Sister—in—law is clever. There's no need for me to say much. My brother is a simple, honest fellow. He needs you to look after him. With you running the house properly, he'll have nothing to worry about. As the ancients put it, 'When the fence is strong no dogs get in.'"

Golden Lotus turned in a fury on her husband. "What rumours are you spreading — slandering me? I'm not a wife to be ashamed of. Ever since I married you, not so much as an ant has dared enter your house! What's this talk about fences not being strong and dogs getting in?"

Wu Song smiled. "Since that's how you feel, sister—in—law, that's fine. Just make sure your deeds correspond to your words. I'll remember what you have said. I ask you to drink to it."

Golden Lotus thrust the cup aside and ran out of the room weeping, putting on a big show of injured innocence.

Wu Song rose to leave. Wu the Elder walked down the stairs with him and saw him to the door.

"Don't forget what I've told you, brother, "Wu Song said.

He returned to the county office compound and prepared for the journey. The magistrate gave him private instructions. Accompanied by soldiers and trusted servants Wu Song left Yanggu Town for the capital.

7

Our story now divides into two parts. We'll talk
of Wu the Elder first. His wife reviled him for days on
end after Wu Song departed. Wu the Elder took her
abuse in silence. He remembered his brother's words:
he came home early, lowered the bamboo curtain and
bolted the front door; Golden Lotus fumed with resent-
ment, but Wu the Elder only said, "I'm going to do
what Wu Song said. His advice is good. It'll prevent
all sorts of trouble."

For another two weeks she rowed with him. But
then she became accustomed to his unvarying
schedule, and when he was due to come home she
lowered the curtain and bolted the door herself. Wu
the Elder was relieved.

Then one day it so happened that a man was
passing by Wu the Elder's house just when a pole she
was holding slipped and landed right on his head.
Angrily, he halted and turned around, ready to blow
up. But when he saw the winsome creature standing
there, he promptly cooled down and smiled.

Golden Lotus clasped her hands and curtsied
apologetically.

"I was careless and you've got hurt!"

The man bowed. "It doesn't matter. Think nothing of it."

The man's name was Ximen Qing. When he

became wealthy, people called him the Right Honourable Ximen. He was smooth and cunning, and skilled with fists and staves.

Shortly after his encounter with Golden Lotus, Ximen, who had been entranced with her, entered the tea shop kept by Mistress Wang, Golden Lotus's next—door neighbour. Without beating about the bush, he told Mistress Wang he wanted her to arrange a meeting for him with Golden Lotus.

But no more need be said about how Mistress Wang arranged for Ximen and Golden Lotus to meet and become lovers.

8

In less than half a month, everyone in the neighbourhood, except Wu the Elder, knew that Golden Lotus met Ximen Qing every day at Mistress Wang's tea house.

Quite by accident a boy called Yunge, who earned a living by selling fruit, was wandering one day along the streets looking for Ximen to try and get a few coppers from him. He learned that Ximen could be found every day in Mistress Wang's place, where he spent his time philandering with Wu the Elder's wife.

Yunge went to the tea shop in search of Ximen. Mistress Wang seized him as he entered, gave him two lumps on the noggin, and pushed him out of the door, throwing his basket after him.

"Dirty old whore monger! Hitting me for no reason at all! Just wait, old bawd, I'm going to tell Wu! See if I don't!"

Cursing and weeping, the boy set out in search of Wu the Elder. After taking a turn through a couple of streets, he encountered the man carrying his hampers of buns. The aggrieved boy could not refrain from telling Wu the Elder about Golden Lotus' affair with Ximen.

9

Enraged, Wu the Elder rushed into Mistress Wang's tea shop. "Wu the Elder is here," the old woman loudly exclaimed. Golden Lotus, hearing her shouts, became frantic. Ximen, who had dived under the bed, crawled out. Wu tried to grab him, but Ximen lashed out with his right foot and caught the short man right in the centre of the chest, knocking him flat on his back. Ximen then fled.

With Golden Lotus's help, Mistress Wang picked Wu the Elder up. Blood was flowing from his mouth, and his skin was waxy yellow. They brought him round, and supporting him under his arms, helped him up the stairs of his house, where they put him to bed.

On enquiring the next day Ximen learned that there were no repercussions. He continued to meet Golden Lotus as usual. They hoped Wu the Elder would die.

Wu called Golden Lotus to him and said, "You got your lover to kick me in the chest, and I'm more dead than alive. Yet you two are still carrying on with your affair! I may die — I'm no match for you. But don't forget my brother Wu Song! Sooner or later he is coming back. Do you think he's going to let you get away with it?"

Golden Lotus went next door and told Mistress Wang and Ximen what her husband had said. Ximen felt his blood run cold.

"Save us, godmother!" he groaned.

"If you want to be long-term lovers, without having to be frightened every day, I have a clever scheme. Of course, you may not want to go through with it."

"What's this scheme?"

"The wretch is very ill. Take advantage of his misery and do him in. Get some arsenic from the drug store. Then let this lady buy medicine for heart pains, mix the two together and finish the man off. She can have him cremated, so there won't be any traces. When Wu Song comes back, what will he be able to do? What do you think of my plan?"

"It's a frightful crime, godmother! But never mind, we'll do it! All or nothing!"

10

When the deed was done, Mistress Wang wiped around Wu's mouth, and cleaned up the blood that had spewed from all the openings in his body. She tied a kerchief round his head, put on his clothes, spread a piece of fine white silk over his face, and covered the body with a clean quilt. Then she and Golden Lotus set the bedroom in order. When all this was done, Golden Lotus commenced bewailing the demise of her provider.

The sky was not yet light when Ximen came to hear the news. He gave Mistress Wang money to buy a coffin and other funerary articles.

"There's only one more difficulty," the woman said. "He, the local coroner, is a clever man. I'm afraid he may notice something and not agree to the encoffining."

"Don't worry about that. I'll have a few words with him. He wouldn't dare go against me."

11

When Coroner He inspected the body of Wu the Elder, what he saw caused him to fall over backwards. His lips turned purple, his eyes clouded over. His assistants carried him back to his house, where his wife put him to bed.

When he saw that his assistants had gone and that he and his wife were alone, he said softly, "I'm all right. On my way to inspect Wu's body for

encoffining I met Ximen Qing, who treated me to wine
and gave me ten ounces of silver. 'Put a cover over
everything when you inspect the corpse, ' he said. I
went to Wu's place. I could see that his wife was
not a good person, and I became suspicious. I
uncovered the shroud. Wu's face was purple. There
was blood in his ears, eyes, nose, and mouth.
Obviously, he had been poisoned. I was going to
announce this, but then I thought — he has nobody to
stand up for him. If I offend Ximen Qing I'll only be
stirring up a hornets' nest. I was going to let the
matter go and approve the encoffining. But then I
remembered that Wu has a brother who beat a tiger
to death on Jingyang Ridge. Sooner or later he's
coming home, and then this whole thing is going to
blow up! "

"Just the other day, "his wife reported, "I heard
someone say, 'Yunge went with Wu the elder to Mistress Wang's tea shop to nab adulterers. There was a
terrific row! ' So that's what it was! You get your
assistants to approve the encoffining, and find out
when the funeral will be. If they keep the body at
home till Wu Song returns and then bury it, there
won't be any complications. But if they're going to
cremate it, something surely is wrong. You attend the
ceremony and take a couple of bones from the pyre
when no one is looking. These, plus the ten ounces of
silver, will be conclusive proof. "

"You're a good wife and a very clever woman! "

112

The coroner did as his wife advised.

12

It was the end of winter when Wu Song departed. When he returned it was spring. He had felt uneasy in his mind all the time he was away, and he was anxious to see his brother.

He first reported to the magistrate on the success of his mission. The official was very pleased. He rewarded Wu Song with a large silver ingot, and wined and dined him.

Wu Song then went to his quarters, changed his clothes, and hurried to his brother's house. The sight that met his eyes when he entered stunned him. The first thing he saw was a tablet with the inscription "In Memory of Wu the Elder, My Departed Husband."

"Sister—in—law, "he called. "I'm back. It's me, Wu Song."

Golden Lotus was just then frolicking upstairs with Ximen. At the sound of Wu Song's voice, Ximen scooted out the back door and left via Mistress Wang's tea shop.

Golden Lotus, who hadn't worn mourning since poisoning her husband, hastily washed off her make—up, removed her ornaments, and exchanged her red skirt and figured tunic for drab mourning garments. Then, sobbing, she descended the stairs.

"Sister—in—law, don't cry. When did my brother

die? What was wrong with him? What medicine did he take?"

Weeping, Golden Lotus replied, "About twenty days after you left, he had severe pains in the heart. He was ill for eight or nine days. I prayed, I gave him every kind of medicine, but nothing helped and he died! Now I'm miserable and alone!"

"My brother never had this ailment before. How could his heart have killed him?" said Wu Song. "Where is he buried?"

"I was all alone. How could I go looking for a suitable burial place? After three days, I had him cremated."

Wu Song was silent for several minutes. Then he left and returned to his quarters.

13

There is no need to tell how Wu Song vainly tried to see justice done in the court. The magistrate and other county functionaries all had connections with Ximen. When he complained that his brother Wu the Elder had been poisoned and murdered by his wife and Ximen Qing, who had been having adulterous liaisons, the magistrate said, "Since ancient times the rule of proof has been: 'For adultery catch the pair, for robbery find the loot, for murder produce the body.' Your brother's body is no more, and you didn't catch them in the act. You haven't got a case."

Wu Song had to think of something else.

14

Wu Song returned to his quarters and fetched some ink, a pen and four or five sheets of paper, which he concealed on his person. He ordered the soldiers who were with him to buy meat, two casks of wine and some fruit, and bring them to his brother's house.

"Tomorrow is the last day of the mourning period for my brother," he told Golden Lotus. "The neighbours have gone to a lot of trouble for you. I've bought some wine to thank them on your behalf."

Golden Lotus already knew that Wu Song had failed to have his accusation entertained by the court, and no longer feared him.

Wu Song went first to Mistress Wang next door and invited her over. He then invited four other neighbours. These, plus Mistress Wang and Golden Lotus, made a total of six. Some of the guests, sensing that something was brewing, tried to leave, but there were soldiers at the doors, front and back, standing guard.

After the guests had had several rounds of wine, Wu Song courteously addressed one of the neighbours who could write: "Permit me to trouble you." He rolled up his sleeves and from inside his garments whipped out his knife. His eyes glared round and fierce. "In the presence of you honourable neighbours, 'the culprit must pay for his crime, the debtor repay his debt'. I ask only that you be witnesses!"

With his left hand he grasped his sister—in—law, with his right he pointed at Mistress Wang. "Please don't reproach me, "said Wu Song. "There's no need to be alarmed. My motto is 'an eye for an eye, a tooth for a tooth'. No harm shall come to any of you. I request only that you witness this."

Wu Song glared at Mistress Wang. "Now listen carefully, you old bitch! You're responsible for my brother's death! I want you to answer my questions!"

He turned and faced Golden Lotus. "Trollop! How did you scheme and kill my brother? Tell the truth and I'll spare you!"

"Your brother died of pains in the heart. It has nothing to do with me!"

Before the words were out of her mouth, Wu Song rammed the knife into the table, grabbed her hair, kicked the table over, lifted her effortlessly across it, placed her on her back before the altar table, and stood on her. Again he seized his knife and pointed at Mistress Wang.

"Speak, old bawd! And make sure that it's the truth!"

Wu Song directed a soldier to bring the pen, paper and ink and lay them before the guest who could write. "Write this down, please, word for word!"

The old woman tried to lie her way out of it. "It has nothing to do with me. What shall I say?"

"Old bitch, "Wu Song grated. "I know everything!

If you don't talk, first I'll carve up this harlot, and then I'll kill you, old dig!"

He flashed the knife close to Golden Lotus's face. The girl was scared out of her wits. "Spare me, brother-in-law! Let me up! I'll speak!"

Wu Song picked her up and set her kneeling in front of the altar table. "Speak, wanton, and be quick about it!"

Golden Lotus had no choice but to tell the whole story. Wu Song made her pause after every sentence so that it could be written down.

The old woman also confessed. Then both women were compelled to impress their thumb prints and make their marks. The four neighbours signed their names and made their marks also.

Wu Song had the soldier tie Mistress Wang's hands behind her back. He rolled up the confessions and put them inside his robe. He then pushed the two women to their knees in front of the memorial tablet.

"Brother, today I shall avenge you!"

Golden Lotus could guess what was coming. She opened her mouth to scream. Wu Song yanked her over backwards by the head. Quicker than it takes to tell, he plunged the knife into her breast. With another slash of the knife he cut the girl's head off. Blood gashed all over the floor.

Wu Song sent the soldier upstairs for a quilt, and wrapped Golden Lotus's head in it. He spoke respectfully to the four neighbours, "I hope you won't

117

mind, but I must ask you to wait upstairs. I'll return shortly."

Terrified by Wu Song's savagery, the neighbours could only obey his commands. They went upstairs and sat down. Wu Song instructed the soldier to take Mistress Wang upstairs too and keep her under guard. He locked the door to the upper story and told the other two soldiers to stand watch below.

With the head of Golden Lotus wrapped in a quilt, Wu Song went directly to Ximen's place. He was told that Ximen had gone with an acquaintance to an inn at the foot of Lion Bridge.

Arriving at the inn, Wu Song inquired who Ximen was drinking with. "He's drinking with an acquaintance upstairs in the room overlooking the street," the waiter told him.

Wu Song charged up the stairs. Ximen was sitting there with a guest in the company of two singsong girls.

Wu Song shook open the quilt and rolled out the gory head, which he then threw in Ximen's face.

Ximen saw that it was Wu Song. With a scream he leaped on a bench and swung one leg over the window-sill, intending to flee. But he was too high above the street and didn't dare jump.

Wu Song vaulted onto the table and came at Ximen in a wild rush. Ximen tried to fight him off. With his left hand Wu Song seized Ximen between the head and shoulder, and with his right grabbed

Ximen's right leg. Then he lifted him high.

Down Ximen went into the street. Wu Song picked up Golden Lotus's head and leaped through the window after him. Taking out his knife, he approached his foe. Ximen was lying flat, already half dead. Wu Song pressed down on him and with one sweep of the knife cut off his head.

Tying the two heads together by the hair, he hurried back to his brother's house. He placed the heads as sacrifices before the memorial tablet. "Brother," he said, weeping. "Go up to Heaven. I've avenged you! I have killed the adulterous pair!"

He told the soldier to ask the neighbours upstairs to come down, and instructed him to bring down Mistress Wang. He confronted the neighbours. "Please listen. I still have something to say. The crime I committed to avenge my brother was proper and reasonable. Though it may mean my death, I have no regrets. I'm going to give myself up now. I don't know whether I'll live or die. May I trouble you to sell my possessions to raise money for my trial? Today I shall surrender to the magistrate. All I want you to do is to testify and tell the truth, regardless of the consequences."

15

Wu Song, carrying the two heads, set out for the magistracy with Mistress Wang. The whole county town was in an uproar. Countless watchers lined the streets.

When the magistrate heard who was coming and why, he immediately called his court into session. After examining the evidence, the magistrate ordered that Wu Song and Mistress Wang be committed to jail. The witnesses were lodged in the gate house.

The magistrate considered Wu Song a gallant, principled man. He remembered the mission Wu Song had undertaken for him to the capital and his various good qualities. He wanted very much to help him, and so instructed the court officers to mitigate the indictment so that it read:

"Wu Song, wishing to sacrifice to the memory of his brother, was prevented from doing so by his sister—in—law, and for this reason they quarrelled. She tried to knock down the memorial tablet, they fought, and in the course of the fight he killed her. Ximen Qing, her adulterous lover, intervened. The two men battled, all the way to Lion Bridge, and there the lover was killed."

The magistrate directed that Coroner He's cremation record, the silver Ximen had given him, the charred bones, the confessions, and the murder weapon be taken under guard to Dongping for disposition of the case by a higher—ranking magistrate

Chen Wenzhao, the Dongping magistrate, was an intelligent official. He already knew about the case. When the county officers arrived, he looked over the record of the testimony and questioned each of the witnesses. He had Wu Song's heavy rack exchanged for a light one, and committed him to jail. A heavy rack was placed around Mistress Wang's neck, and she was locked up in a cell for the condemned.

Chen sympathized with Wu Song, and thought him a gallant, highminded person. He frequently sent people to inquire after him. Chen lightened the charges against Wu Song still further. The final decision read:

"Wu Song cannot be completely exonerated. He is to be given forty strokes on the back, tattooed with the mark of a criminal and exiled to a place two thousand *li* distant...."

Wu Song was brought from jail, and the decision was read to him. He was given forty strokes, but the jailers saw to it that only six or seven actually cut his flesh. A light rack was fastened around his neck and the mark of a criminal was tattooed on his face. The magistrate exiled him to the district town of Mengzhou.

Mistress Wang was sentenced to death, and the sentence was carried out at once.

16

Wu Song and the two guards assigned by the court to take him to Mengzhou set out. They reached Mengzhou a few weeks later. They went to the magistrate's office and presented the documents from Dongping. Wu Song was taken to the prison. The local guards put him in a room by himself, turned over his papers and got a receipt.

A dozen or so prisoners came over. "If you have a letter of introduction or any silver in your pack, take them out, and when the head keeper comes, give them to him. It's decreed that all exiles, when they first arrive, shall be beaten a hundred blows to break their spirit. It'll be cruel if you have no present for the head keeper."

Wu Song thanked them for telling him. But when the head keeper came, Wu Song refused to give him a copper. "I've got money, but I'm keeping that to buy myself wine," he said. "What are you going to do about it?"

The head keeper stamped off in a rage. A few minutes later, three or four guards came and shouted for the new prisoner. They escorted him to the examination room, where the warden was formally seated. Half a dozen soldiers pushed Wu Song forward.

Wu Song was about to receive the Spirit—Breaking Beating, when a young man standing beside the warden whispered something in the official's ear. The warden gave Wu Song a break. "You were sick on the way, and you must still be running a high fever. We'll put the beating off for the time being. Guards, take him back to the single room."

From that day on, an army man brought him a

hamper with fried meat, a bowl of soup, a large bowl of rice and a measure of wine thrice a day, collecting the dishes after Wu Song had had his fill. "What's going on here?" Wu Song wondered.

Wu Song had been in the prison for several days, during which time he was continually wined and dined. He was quite puzzled. At last he could restrain himself no longer.

"Whose household are you from?" he demanded of the man who brought him the meal. "Why do you keep serving me food and wine?"

"I'm acting on the orders of the warden's son."

"Very peculiar. I can't figure it out. If I don't know what's behind this food and wine, I can't consume them in peace. What's his name?"

"Shi En. He's skilled with fists and staves, and everyone calls him Golden—Eyed Tiger Cub."

"Sounds like a good man. Ask him to come and see me. Otherwise I won't touch a morsel of your food."

The servant was very reluctant to do so, but Wu Song grew angry, and so he had no choice but to comply.

Shi En hastened over. He dropped at Wu Song's feet and bowed low. Wu Song at once returned the courtesy.

"I have never had the honour of meeting you. Yet you saved me from a beating the other day, and now you send me food and wine. And you haven't asked me to do a single thing for you. Such unmerited kindness disturbs my sleep. What exactly do you want with me?"

17

"As a child I learned how to joust with spear and staff," said Shi En. "I became known around here as Golden—Eyed Tiger Cub. Outside the East Gate of this town is a market village called Happy Grove. Since I was a skilled fighter, I went to Happy Grove and opened an inn. There are over a hundred large inns in the village and twenty or thirty gambling houses. Every enterprise had to pay me regular tribute. Money kept coming in. "But then Zhang, the stockade garrison commander, came from Luzhou, bringing with him a man called Jiang Zhong, known as Jiang the Gate Guard Giant because he's so huge and strong. He simply moved in and took over my territory. When I tried to stop him, he gave me such a drubbing I couldn't get out of bed for two months. My wounds still haven't fully healed.

"Originally, I was going to take my men and have it out with him. But he has the backing of Commandant Zhang's garrison. So here I've been, burning with rage but unable to get revenge. I've known for a long time what a great fighter and man of justice you are, brother. If only you can help me to square accounts with that thug, I'll be able to close my eyes

124

peacefully when I die. But you've had a long hard journey, and I was afraid you hadn't regained your strength. I wanted to wait several months till you recovered completely, and then tell you about it. That's the whole truth of the matter."

"I'm not bragging,"Wu Song began, "but all my life I've been beating tough guys and worthless bums. If the situation is what you say, what are we doing here?Get some wine and we'll drink it on the way. I'll go with you. You can watch me pummel him like I did the tiger!"

Just then, Shi En's father, the old warden, entered. "I'm glad to meet you,"he said to Wu Song. "Please join me in the rear hall for a while."

Wu Song followed him, and the old man invited him to have some food and wine. The warden personally handed Wu Song a filled cup. "Everyone has great respect for your courage, warrior. My son was doing business in Happy Grove. Then that Jiang the Gate Guard Giant, relying on the garrison's backing, muscled in and openly took over. Only a hero like yourself can avenge this insult. Don't refuse my son."

Wu Song drank freely. He became very drunk, and had to be helped to his room.

18

The next day, Shi En said to Wu Song, "We'll start tomorrow morning after breakfast."

As they were setting out after breakfast, Wu Song said, "There's one thing I must ask. If you want me to beat up Jiang the Gate Guard Giant, you've got to invite me to three bowls of wine at every inn we pass. You're afraid I won't be able to fight. Actually, I'm no good without wine. The more I drink, the better I am. It's only when I'm really drunk that I have my full strength."

"I didn't know, brother. Since drink makes you stronger, I'll send a couple of servants on ahead with some wine and something to eat, and have them wait for us on the road."

Shi En and Wu Song left the Anping Stockade through the East Gate. On the way there were a number of inns. At every inn Wu Song downed three bowls of wine.

"How much further to Happy Grove?" asked Wu Song.

"Not much. It's just over there, where those trees are."

"When we get there, go somewhere and wait. I'll find him myself."

Shi En told the servants to accompany Wu Song, and he himself departed. As Wu Song neared the Happy Grove, one of the servants pointed. "That's Jiang's inn at that crossroads."

Wu Song skirted around the back of the grove. A big tough fellow was seated in a folding armchair in the shade of locust tree. Feigning drunkenness, Wu

Song glanced at him. "That must be Jiang the Gate Guard Giant."

19

There's hardly any need to describe blow by blow the battle between Wu Song and Jiang the Gate Guard Giant. What chance did Jiang stand against a man who had killed a huge tiger on Jingyang Ridge with only some punches and kicks?

When Wu Song had finished with the hoodlum, Jiang could only piteously beg for mercy.

"If you want me to spare you, you must promise me three things. One, you must return all equipment to its original owner Shi En the Golden-Eyed Tiger Cub. Two, you must round up all the head toughs in Happy Grove and have them apologize for you to Shi En. And three, you must leave Happy Grove, go directly back to your native village and never return to Mengzhou. Do you promise?"

"Oh yes, I do. I agree completely!"

20

One day about a month later, three military men arrived at the inn looking for Wu Song. Shi En recognized them; they were adjutants of General Zhang who commanded the garrison in Mengzhou.

"The general has heard of Wu Song's gallantry

and has sent us to fetch him," they said. "Here's His Excellency's invitation."

Wu Song was a straightforward fellow who never beat about the bush. "Since the general has sent for me, I'll go," he said, "and see what he has to say."

The general was cordial. "I've heard that you're a splendid man, a hero without peer, a fearless, fighter who stands by his friends to the death. I need someone like you. Would you be willing to serve under me as an adjutant?"

Wu Song agreed and remained in the general's residence. He was quite happy. "The general seems keen on advancing me," he thought. He wouldn't have been so pleased had he known what Zhang had in mind.

In the eighth lunar month General Zhang laid on a feast to celebrate Mid—Autumn Festival, to which he invited Wu Song.

Wu Song drank a dozen cups of wine, one after another. Fearing that he might do something discourteous under the influence of liquor, he rose, thanked the general and his wife, and went to his room in the wing.

He was starting to undress when he heard voices in the courtyard shouting, "Thief! Thief!" He grasped his staff and went to the courtyard in search of the thief. As he was searching among the flower beds someone threw a stool beneath his feet. He stumbled and fell. Six or seven soldiers, yelling "Catch the thief!"

pounced on Wu Song and tied him up.

"It's me!" Wu Song cried in agitation. But the soldiers paid no attention.

What followed needs no great powers of imagination. Despite all his denials, the general accused him of ingratitude. "Your crooked heart hasn't changed!" he cried with fury. "How could you do such a thing?"

He ordered Wu Song's room searched. To Wu Song's amazement, the soldiers discovered about two hundred ounces of gold and silver in his trunk.

21

The next morning, police brought Wu Song to the courtroom. The magistrate had Wu Song beaten. A long rack was affixed around his neck and he was locked up in prison. His legs were in fetters day and night and his wrists manacled. He wasn't allowed the slightest freedom.

When Shi En was informed of what was happening, he hurried into town to confer with his father. "Commandant Zhang is behind this," the old warden said, "getting revenge for Jiang the Gate Guard Giant. I'm sure he wants to have Wu Song killed. We have to bribe a few clerks and bailiffs so that we can protect Wu Song while he is in prison. Then we can see what else can be done."

The bailiff, a man named Kang, was a good

friend of Shi En. Shi En went to Kang's house and presented him with a hundred ounces of silver. The bailiff politely refused several times before finally accepting.

The next day, Kang took Shi En to the big jail where Wu Song was confined. "You've been framed by General Zhang to avenge Jiang the Gate Guard Giant," Shi En told Wu Song. Wu Song had been thinking of attempting a jailbreak, but Shi En's information caused him to abandon the idea.

22

At the conclusion of the preliminary detention period of sixty days, Wu Song was brought before the magistrate. The magistrate ordered a punishment of twenty blows and exile to Enzhou. The prisoner and his escorts left immediately.

Before they had gone many *li*, Wu Song heard one of the escorts whisper to his companion, "Any sign of the other two?"

Wu Song laughed coldly to himself. "So there are more of you thugs coming to get tough! Don't rejoice too soon!"

When they were about eight *li* from their destination, two men appeared on the road ahead, waiting with staves and swords. They joined the prisoner and his escorts, and walked along with them. A bit further on, they came to a place with many fish ponds. As the five men began crossing a wide-planked bridge, Wu Song halted. The two with the staves started closing in on him.

" Down you go! " Wu Song cried. With two powerful kicks he sent the two tumbling into the water below. The two guards fled from the bridge in panic.

Wu Song wrenched open his rack, tore it in two, and raced after the guards. He caught up with one, and grasping a sword he retrieved from the water, finished him off with a few stabs. He then dispatched the other guard in the same way.

The two men Wu Song kicked into the stream had struggled out and started to flee. Wu Song hacked one to the ground and seized the other.

"Tell the truth and live! "

"We two are apprentices of Jiang the Gate Guard Giant. He and Commandant Zhang told us to join forces with the guards and murder you! "

"Where's your master now?"

" When I left he was in the Duck and Drake Bower in the rear courtyard, drinking with the commandant and the general. He's waiting for us to return and report! "

"So that's how it is. In that case I won't spare you! "

Wu Song's hand rose and his blade descended, killing the man. He rolled all the bodies into a pond, stood on the bridge and surveyed the carnage.

"Although I've finished off these four bastards, "

he thought, "my hatred won't be appeased until I've killed General Zhang, Commandant Zhang and Jiang the Gate Guard Giant!"

He made up his mind to go back to Mengzhou Town.

23

Wu Song went back to Mengzhou Town. As a result, the ornate hall of General Zhang's residence became carpeted with corpses, and the red festive candles shone on blood-steeped floors. After Wu Song destroyed the greedy men, he could breathe freely again.

Having consummated his gory deed, Wu Song clambered over the town wall, waded across the moat, and made his way toward a small ancient temple nestled in a grove. It had been a hard night for him, he was weary, and the wounds from the beating he had received before being sent into exile were painful. He badly needed a rest.

After he had rested four or five days, he began to consider where to find a good refuge. It was obvious that the temple was not a safe place for him.

Friends suggested that he go to a monastery on Two-Dragon Mountain, Sagacious Lu and a man called Yang Zhi had turned robbers there and taken control over that territory. It would be the best refuge for Wu Song. His friends offered to write a letter to

Lu telling him all about Wu Song.

Wu Song's friends made him up to look like a monk. They cut his hair in long bangs that would cover the tattoo on his face. They furnished him with a black robe, a metal clasp to bind his long hair, a rosary of a hundred and eight beads, and a monk's certificate, so that no one would presume to question him closely on the road.

Wu Song packed his bundle, thanked his friends, listened carefully to their parting advice, and went off with a stately gait, the very picture of a pilgrim monk.

24

We would gladly continue the story of Wu Song, recount how he became one of the chieftains of the Liangshan Marsh outlaws, and extol his heroic exploits in battles against tyrants and despots. But that would form a sizable volume by itself. We'll therefore break off our story here and mention briefly how Wu Song lived out his last years.

After inflicting a crushing defeat on the Liao Tartars, the Liangshan Marsh outlaws, whom Wu Song had joined, were ordered to cross the Yangtze River to suppress a revolt against the imperial court.

In a battle against one of the rebel generals, the foe's sword bit into Wu Song's arm so deeply that he fainted from loss of blood. When he regained consciousness, with one slice of his knife he cut off the useless left limb. He was carried back to camp to recuperate.

Thus ended Wu Song's heroic martial career. Wu Song became a monk in a monastery and lived to the ripe old age of eighty.

BOOK TWO

CHAPTER FOUR — YANG ZHI

1

Yang Zhi, also known as Blue—Faced Beast, was a descendant of three generations of generals.

When he was younger, he passed a military examination, and was appointed an aide in the palace. When Longevity Hill was being built, he was sent along with some other aides to Lake Taihu to collect ornamental rock formations and coloured stones, and bring them back to the capital to decorate the hill. As they were crossing the Yellow River, on their return trip, their boat capsized and the rocks they were transporting were sunk. Yang didn't dare report back to the capital, and ran away. Later, he was pardoned. When our narrative of his adventures begins, he was wandering around Guanxi, on his way back to the Eastern Capital with money and valuables which he intended to use to see whether he could arrange another position for himself. The peasant he hired was carrying them on a shoulder pole when Lin Chong and others who had turned robbers in these parts snatched the valuables away.

Yang Zhi, halberd in hand, shouted, "You dirty robbers! Where have you taken my luggage and valuables?"

Yang Zhi and Lin Chong began to fight. They attacked each other with murderous fury. Just as the struggle was reaching its climax, high in the mountain a voice rang out "Stop fighting, brave fellows! " Yang Zhi and his opponent stayed their hands. Down the mountain came the bandit chieftain Wang Lun, accompanied by many of the bandits.

"Beautiful technique, both of you, " Wang Lun commended. "You with the blue face, sir, would you tell me your name?"

Yang Zhi told Wang Lun who he was.

" Aren't you also called Blue-Faced Beast? " asked Wang Lun.

"That's correct."

"So that's who you are! We'd be very pleased if you'd come to our stronghold for a few cups of wine. We'll return your belongings there, "said Wang Lun. "I was in the Eastern Capital a few years ago, and heard of your fame. Today, I've been fortunate enough to meet you. Please rest a while in our stronghold. That's all I ask."

Yang Zhi went with Wang Lun, Lin Chong and the others to the fortress on the top of the mountain. Wang Lun ordered a feast of mutton and wine to be laid on in Yang Zhi's honour. When the assembled diners had drunk several cups, Wang Lun said to himself, "If we keep Lin Chong the new recruit here, we won't be able to manage him for long. Why not put on a show of kindness and keep Yang Zhi as well? Then we can play one off against the other."

Pointing at Lin Chong he said to Yang, "This brother has also just come here. I won't detain you if you're set on going to the capital. You've committed a crime. Although you've been pardoned, you'll never attain your former rank, especially now that shyster Gao Qiu holds military authority. Do you think he'll forgive you? You'd better stay on in our small stronghold, sharing our loot and meat and wine, and be an outlaw just like the rest of us."

"It's very considerate of you leaders. I still think I'd better go. I hope you'll return my luggage."

Wang Lun laughed. "Please set your mind at rest. Spend the night here. You can go tomorrow morning."

Yang Zhi was very pleased. They drank late into the night, and then all retired. The next morning, farewell toasts were drunk to Yang Zhi. After breakfast the chieftains directed a bandit to carry Yang Zhi's belongings. They went with him down the mountain and bid him farewell. Yang departed and the outlaws returned to the stronghold.

2

Yang Zhi set out down the road. He found a peasant to carry his luggage, and told the bandit to go back. After a number of days, Yang arrived in the

137

Eastern Capital. He took quarters in an inn, paid off the peasant, removed his weapons and ordered something to eat and drink. A few days later, he sent someone to the Council of Military Affairs with money and gifts to try, by bribes, to get himself reinstated as a palace aide. It cost him a lot, but finally he was granted an audience with Marshal Gao Qiu.

Gao read all the documents concerning Yang Zhi's case. "Ten of you aides are sent to transport ornamental rock. Nine deliver their cargo. Only you, you clod, lose yours," the marshal said angrily. "You don't even report back. Instead, you run away. Now you want a job again. You may have been pardoned, but you still have a criminal record. We can't use you!" He scrawled a refusal on Yang's application, and had him expelled from the headquarters.

Yang Zhi returned to the inn dejectedly. "Wang Lun was right," he thought. "I hoped for a chance to distinguish myself with spear and sword in a border post. I never expected to get such a rebuff."

Yang was quite depressed. A few days more at the inn and his money was gone. "What am I going to do?" Yang fretted. "I'll have to sell the ancestral sword. There is no alternative. I should be able to get a couple of thousand for it. That will keep me in expense money till I find a place for myself."

The same day he took the sword to the marketplace. But though he stood there all morning, no one asked about the sword.

Around noon he went to the busy Tianhanzhou Bridge to try his luck there. He hadn't been waiting long when he saw a hulking, swarthy fellow come staggering in his direction. He recognized the notorious rowdy Niu Er, known throughout the city as a trouble-making bully. He lumbered up to Yang and took the sword from his hand. "How much do you want for this?"

"Three thousand."

"All that money for this shitty thing! For thirty coppers I can buy a knife that will slice meat and cut bean-curd. What's so good about your sword?"

"This isn't one of those iron blades they sell in the shops. First, it can cut copper and pierce iron without curling the edge. Second, it can slice a tuft of hair blown against it. Third, it can kill a man and come away clean."

"Would you really dare cut copper coins?"

"Bring them out and I'll show you."

Niu Er went off and at once returned with twenty three-cent coins. He piled these on the bridge railing and said to Yang, "If you can cut through these, I'll give you three thousand for your sword."

Many people watched from a distance. "Nothing to it," said Yang Zhi. He rolled up his sleeves, grasped the sword and took aim. With one downward chop he cleaved the pile of coins neatly in two. The onlookers sent up a cheer.

"What did you say the second thing was?"

"Take a tuft of hair and just blow it against the blade. It'll cut right through it."

'I don't believe you!" The bully pulled a few hairs from his head and handed them to Yang Zhi. 'Go on, blow. I want to see."

Yang held the hairs in his left hand and blew them with one hard puff against the sword edge. The two halves of the tuft floated to the ground. Again a loud cheer broke out from the crowd:

"What was the third thing?"

"Kill a man without staining the blade."

No matter how the bully tried to provoke Yang Zhi to show him how he would do that, Yang refused to kill a man in the imperial city.

The bully wanted Yang to sell him the sword, and so Yang asked him to produce the money. But instead of paying, Niu Er butted Yang in the chest, and followed up by swinging his right fist in a wild punch.

Yang Zhi dodged and chopped a furious blow at Niu Er's forehead. The scoundrel collapsed. Yang closed in and finished off the bully with two thrusts in the chest. Blood gushed copiously. Niu Er lay dead.

3

"I've killed the wretch," Yang exclaimed to the bystanders. "I don't want to implicate you, but the man is dead. Please come with me to the authorities and be my witnesses."

They quickly rallied round and accompanied Yang Zhi to the magistrate's office. They all presented themselves and knelt where the magistrate was holding court. Yang laid the sword before him.

" I was formerly an aide in the palace, but because I lost a cargo of ornamental and coloured stones, I was dismissed. Now I have no money, and I took my sword to the street to sell it. The rascal Niu Er grabbed for it and started to punch me. I killed him in a moment of rage. These people from the neighbourhood all saw what happened."

Many spoke on his behalf.

"Since he has come forward voluntarily, "said the magistrate, " let him be spared the preliminary beating. " He ordered that a long wooden rack be fitted around Yang Zhi's neck, and that two inspectors and a forensic expert take Yang and his witnesses back to Tianhanzhou Bridge for an examination of the scene of the crime. The magistrate drew up the appropriate documents.

After the witnesses submitted formal statements in writing they were released under guarantee to produce themselves whenever the court summoned them. Yang Zhi was locked up in the jail for condemned prisoners.

4

Yang Zhi served a term of sixty days. Then he

was brought before the magistrate, who ordered that he be exiled to the garrison in the Northern Capital.

Documents were drawn up and two escorts appointed. After the escorts were given final instructions, the three set out.

Before long they reached the Northern Capital. That night the governor of the Northern Capital, Liang Zhongshu, was holding court. The two escorts entered with Yang Zhi and presented the documents from the Eastern Capital. Liang had met Yang in the Eastern Capital. He questioned him closely, and Yang related how Marshal Gao had refused to reinstate him, how he had tried to sell his sword, and how he had killed Niu Er. Liang ordered his attendants to remove the rack, and said he would keep Yang Zhi in his service.

Yang attended Governor Liang in his mansion from morning till night. Liang was impressed with his diligence. He wanted to make him a lieutenant, but he thought the other army men would be against it. He therefore ordered that a military tourney be held among all junior and senior officers at the training field outside the East Gate.

That night Liang summoned Yang and said to him, "I'm thinking of making you a lieutenant with a fixed salary. How good are you with weapons?"

"I attained my original position by passing arms tests. I'm familiar with all eighteen forms of the fighting arts."

Liang was delighted. He presented Yang with a set of armour.

The next morning at the tourney Yang had to display his military prowess against Lieutenant Zhou Jin first with lances, then with bow and arrow. Yang defeated Zhou with both weapons. Then Captain Suo Chao offered to joust with Yang Zhi. The battle raged for more than fifty rounds with no sign of a winner. Both Yang and Suo were eager to win glory and neither would desist.

Finally the flag officer galloped up shouting, "Stop, good warriors! His Excellency wants to issue an order!" Only then did they lower their weapons. They cantered back to their original starting points, and halted by their respective pennanted gates, facing Governor Liang and awaiting his command.

Liang presented each of them with a set of fine clothes, and bestowed on them the rank of major. Yang and Suo bowed and expressed their thanks.

5

Liang became very fond of Yang Zhi after the tourney, and they were together every day.

Time passed quickly. One day Liang's wife reminded him that her father, to whom he owed so much, would be celebrating his birthday on the fifteenth of the sixth lunar month.

"I've already sent out stewards to buy ornaments

of gold and precious stones to present to him as birthday gifts, " Liang told her. "They've been gone a month and have bought nine-tenths of what I want. When everything is ready, I'll have the gifts delivered to the Eastern Capital."

"Only one thing is troubling me. Last year, the ornaments and jewels we dispatched as gifts were snatched by robbers on the road. Whom should we choose to deliver them this time?"

"There'll be time enough to pick a man we can trust when you've got all the gifts ready."

The reader needs no great powers of imagination to guess whom Governor Liang entrusted with the mission of delivering the gifts to the premier in the Eastern Capital.

6

While this was going on in the Northern Capital, in Yuncheng, a county seat in Shandong Province thousands of *li* away, a band of gallant men were plotting how to lay their hands on the gifts on the road.

The band consisted of Chao Gai, ward chief of East Lake Village, a man who had always fought injustice and liked nothing better than befriending gallant men and helping the needy; Liu Tang, a young fellow who had furnished the information concerning the dispatch of birthday gifts by Governor Liang to the Eastern Capital; Wu Yong, a village school teacher, whom they called Teacher, or Wizard; and finally three fishermen, all brothers from the Ruan family. Six bold men in all, enough to ensure the success of the venture.

According to Liu Tang's information, the route by which the gifts were to be sent had already been chosen. All that was needed was a careful plan. Liu Tang had no hesitations about seizing the gifts which, he said, had been purchased with unclean money.

Later a Taoist priest named Gongsun Sheng, who had also heard that Governor Liang intended to send valuable gifts to Premier Cai in the Eastern Capital, joined the band, bringing the number up to seven.

After the man had introduced themselves and exchanged courtesies, they had a few rounds of drinks in Chao Gai's manor. Gongsun Sheng contributed the important information that the gifts were coming by way of the big road over Yellow Earth Ridge. Chao Gai suggested that Bai Sheng, an idler living in the village of Anlo not far from the ridge, also be employed on the job. Wu Yong then proposed a method for dealing with the convoy. He outlined his proposal, which was greeted enthusiastically by all present. They drank until dark, and then retired to rest in the various guest rooms.

7

But let's return to Yang Zhi, the Blue-Faced

Beast, who had by then become a trusted member of Governor Liang's retinue.

After buying all the valuable gifts for the premier, Liang chose a date to start them on their way. Lady Cai, the governor's wife, suggested that Yang Zhi be entrusted with the mission of delivering the gifts to her father. Liang summoned Yang Zhi and told him that if he could safely deliver the gifts to the Eastern Capital, he would be raised in rank. Yang readily agreed to comply with Liang's wishes.

Liang told Yang Zhi that he proposed to send ten extra-large carts, each fitted with a yellow banner reading "Convoy of Birthday Gifts to the Premier", and accompanied by a member of the city guard and a strong soldier.

Yang flatly refused. He explained that the roads were infested with brigands, and if they heard that the carts were loaded with precious cargo, they would certainly attempt to seize it.

In the end, Governor Liang agreed not to send any carts, but to have the gifts disguised as merchandise and packed into containers to be carried on shoulder poles by the ten soldiers. The escort would travel quietly day and night until the Eastern Capital was reached and the gifts delivered to the premier.

At the last moment, Governor Liang decided to send along Chief Steward Xie and two captains of the guards. Yang agreed to let them come along on the condition that he would be fully responsible for the mission and that the three of them would not cross him in anything.

8

Before dawn next morning the loads were lined up outside the main hall. Eleven strong soldiers selected from the guard were disguised as porters.

Yang Zhi and the old steward was dressed as merchants. The two captains were disguised as servants. Governor Liang handed over the official documents and watched the soldiers raise the carrying poles on their shoulders and set forth. Marching out of the city gate, the procession went down the highway in the direction of the Eastern Capital.

It was then the middle of the fifth lunar month. Although walking was difficult in the broiling sun, Yang Zhi pushed the march on briskly. During the first week after the convoy left the Northern Capital, they set out every day before dawn to take advantage of the morning cool, and rested in the heat of noon.

By the sixth or seventh day, the road began climbing into the mountains. Yang Zhi now started the marches well after sunrise and didn't stop until late in the afternoon. The eleven guards were all carrying heavy loads and weather was hot. Walking was a strenuous effort. Whenever they saw a grove they wanted to rest, but Yang Zhi drove them on. If they halted, the least he did was curse them, and often he flogged them with his switch, forcing them to continue on.

The two captains gasped for breath, and kept falling to the rear. Yang Zhi berated them harshly. His switch in his hand, Yang urged on the convoy.

"That murderous Yang is only a major in His Excellency's guard," the two captains complained to the old steward. "What right has he to act so mighty?"

"The governor ordered us not to cross him. That's why I haven't said anything. We must be patient."

That day they again marched until late afternoon. Then they stopped at an inn. Sweat was pouring from the eleven porters. Groaning and sighing, they addressed the steward.

"For the past two days we've been carrying these heavy loads in the burning sun, instead of starting early when it's cool. On the slightest excuse we're given a taste of the switch! We're flesh and blood too. Why should we be treated so cruelly?"

"Don't complain," the steward urged them. "When we get to the Eastern Capital, I'll reward you personally."

To make a long story short; after they had marched for fifteen days, there wasn't a man in the convoy who didn't hate Yang Zhi.

9

On the fourth day of the sixth month they again
rose late and set out. The heat was simply unbearable.
Yang Zhi hurried the convoy along a path skirting the
mountain. The column hastened on until they
mounted an earthen ridge. Then the porters lowered
their carrying poles and threw themselves down beneath the pine trees.

Yang Zhi seized his switch and lashed their heads
and shoulders. The old steward saw Yang Zhi belabouring the porters. " It's really much too hot to
march, Major, "he said, "Forgive them."

" You don't understand, Chief Steward. This is
Yellow Earth Ridge, a favourite haunt of bandits.
Even in peaceful times they have robbed here in broad
daylight, to say nothing of what they do in times like
these! Stopping here is very dangerous! "

"What's dangerous about today?"

Yang Zhi was going to reply when a shadowy
figure poked his head out of a grove opposite and
peered at them.

" Insolent thug! How dare you spy on our
convoy?"shouted Yang Zhi, charging into the grove.

In the grove he found seven wheelbarrows lined
up in a row and six men, stripped to the buff, resting
in the shade. One of them grabbed a halberd when he
saw Yang Zhi advancing.

"Who are you?"Yang yelled.

"Who are you?"the six countered.

"Aren't you robbers?"

"That's what we should be asking you! We're only small merchants. We haven't any money to give you!"

"Who are you really?"

"We six are from Haozhou. We're bringing dates to sell in the Eastern Capital. Please have some dates, sir."

10

Just as Yang returned to the convoy to let them know that those fellows were date merchants, another man appeared in the distance. Carrying two buckets on a shoulder pole, he sang merrily as he mounted the ridge. He walked to the edge of the pine grove, rested his buckets and sat down in the shade of a tree.

"What have you got in those buckets?" the soldiers asked him.

"Wine."

"Where are you going with it?"

"To the village, to sell."

The soldiers talked it over. "We're hot and thirsty. Why not buy some?" They began chipping in.

"What are you men up to?" Yang shouted.

"We're going to buy a little wine."

Yang Zhi flailed them with the switch. "What gall! How do you know the wine is not drugged?"

The wine vendor looked at Yang and laughed coldly. "What a dirty thing to say about a man s

150

wine! I wasn't going to sell you any wine in the first place."

As they were quarrelling, the date merchants emerged from the grove. "What's the trouble?" they asked.

"I was carrying this wine to sell in the village when these fellows asked if they could buy some," the vendor said. "I didn't let them have any. Then this gentleman claimed my wine was drugged. Is he trying to be funny, or what?"

"So that's what all the row was about. Suppose he did say so — so what? We were just thinking of having some wine ourselves. If they're suspicions, sell us a bucket."

"I don't mind selling you a bucket, but they said my wine was drugged. Besides, I don't have a dipper."

"We have our own dippers."

Two of the date merchants brought out two coconut ladles, while a third scooped up a big handful of dates. Then the six gathered around the bucket and drank. Before long the bucket was empty.

11

When the soldiers saw this, their throats felt even drier. All were longing to drink.

The old steward conferred with Yang Zhi. "Those date merchants have already finished a bucket of that vendor's wine. Only one bucket is left. Why not let the porters buy some wine and ward off heat stroke?"

"Since the chief steward suggests it," Yang Zhi said, "you rogues can have some wine. Then we'll march on."

The porters asked the date merchants for the ladles. The first two ladles of wine were presented to Yang Zhi and the chief steward. Yang refused, but the old man drank his. the next two ladles were consumed by the two captains. Then the soldiers swarmed around the bucket and imbibed heartily.

Yang Zhi wavered. The soldiers showed no ill effects. He scooped up half a ladle of wine and drank it while munching on a few dates.

The soldiers gave the wine vendor his money. The vendor then picked up his shoulder pole and the empty buckets, and swung off down the ridge, singing a folk song.

Standing at the edge of the pine grove, the date merchants pointed at the men in the convoy and said, "Down you go! Down you go!" The porters, the steward and the two captains, weak in the knees and heavy in the head, stared at each other as one by one they sank to the ground. Then the merchants pushed the wheelbarrows out of the grove and dumped the dates. They placed the loads of jewels and art objects into the barrows and covered them over.

"Sorry to trouble you," they called out, and trundled off down the ridge.

Yang Zhi, too weak to move, could but groan

inwardly. The porters couldn't get up. They had only been able to goggle helplessly while the merchants had loaded the barrows with the precious cargo.

12

There is no need to ask who those date merchants were. None other than Chao Gai, Wu Yong, Gongsun Sheng, Liu Tang and the three Ruan brothers. And the wine vendor was Bai Sheng. How was the wine drugged? When the buckets were carried up the ridge, they contained pure wine. After the date merchants finished the first bucket, Liu Tang removed the cover from the second, and deliberately drank half a ladleful in order to dull suspicious. Next, inside the grove, Wu Yong poured the drug into the other ladle. Then he came out and spilled it into the wine while taking a free scoop. As Wu pretended to drink, Bai Sheng grabbed the ladle and dumped the wine back in the bucket.

That was the ruse, planned entirely by Wu Yong.

13

Yang Zhi had not drunk much, and he recovered first. He crawled to his feet, but could hardly stand up. He looked at the others. Saliva was running from the corners of their mouths. None of them could move.

"They have made me lose the birthday gifts," Yang Zhi muttered in angry despair. "How can I ever face Governor Liang again? I've become a man without a name or country. Where can I go? Better that I should die here on this ridge!" Clutching his tunic, he staggered to the edge of the ridge and prepared to jump.

14

But he came to his senses and halted just in time. "This is no way to die. I can at least wait until I'm captured, and then decide."

He gazed at his companions. They could only stare at him, unable to move. Yang Zhi swore. "It's all because you wretches wouldn't listen to me that this has happened." He picked up a halberd that lay by the stump of a tree, buckled on his sword, and looked all around. There was nothing else that belonged to him. He sighed, and went down the ridge.

"You didn't take Yang Zhi's good advice," said the old steward to the porters. "You have ruined me!"

"What's done is done," the porters replied. "We'd better come to an understanding."

"Do you have any suggestions?"

"The fault is ours. If Yang Zhi were here, we'd have nothing to say. But since he's gone, no one knows where, why not put the blame on him? We can go back and say to Governor Liang, 'He abused and beat us all along the road. He drove us till we were too exhausted to stir another step. Yang Zhi was in cahoots with the robbers. They drugged us, bound us hand and foot, and made off with the treasure.'"

"That's an idea. We'll report the theft to the local district authorities the first thing tomorrow, and leave the two captains of the guard behind to help .n the capture of the robbers. The rest of us will travel day and night till we reach the Northern Capital. We'll tell the governor what we agreed upon, and he will inform the premier and direct the local authorities to apprehend the brigands. And that will be that."

Early the next morning the steward and his company advised the local authorities of the robbery.

15

We'll now talk of Yang Zhi as, halberd in hand, he gloomily left Yellow Earth Ridge. He travelled southward half the night, and then rested in a grove. "I've got no money and there's no one around here I know,"he brooded. "What am I going to do?"

As soon as the sky turned light, he set out again. After covering some twenty *li*, he stopped in front of a tavern. He went in, sat down and leaned his halberd against the wall. A woman who was standing beside the stove came over and spoke to him.

"Can I cook something for you, sir?"

"First let me have two measures of wine. Then

155

cook me some rice. If you have meat, I'll have some of that too."

The woman called a young fellow to pour the wine. She cooked the rice, fried some meat, and set them before Yang Zhi. When he had finished eating, he rose. picked up his halberd and headed for the door.

"You haven't paid yet, "the woman said.

"I'll pay you when I come back. Just give me credit for now."

The young fellow who had poured the wine rushed after him and grabbed his arm. With one blow, Yang Zhi knocked him to the ground. Yang continued on his way. He heard another voice shouting at him from behind.

"Where do you think you're going, hoodlum?" He turned and saw a big fellow running towards him, twirling a staff. A number of young waiters armed with pitchforks and some servants carrying cudgels were racing behind.

The first man met him head on. They fought twenty or thirty rounds. Of course the man was no match for Yang. He could only parry and dodge. Suddenly, the staff—twirling fellow jumped from the combat circle.

"You, big fellow with the halberd, "he shouted, "what's your name?"

Yang Zhi struck his chest. "It is and always has been Yang Zhi, the Blue—Faced Beast!"

"Not Yang Zhi, the military aide in the palace of the Eastern Capital?"

The man tossed aside his staff and bowed low. "I have eyes but didn't recognize Mount Taishan!"

Yang Zhi raised him to his feet. "And who are you, sir?"

"I was originally a pupil of Arms Instructor Lin Chong in the Imperial Guards. My name is Cao Zheng. A rich man in my district gave me some money and sent me here to Shandong to do business for him. I lost his entire capital. After that, I couldn't go back. I married a local country girl and moved in with her family. The man with the pitchfork is her young brother. When we fought just now I recognized your moves. They were the same as my arms instructor used to teach me. I knew I couldn't beat you."

"So you were one of Lin's pupils. Your teacher was ruined by Marshal Gao, and had to take to the hills. He's in Liangshan Marsh today."

"Please come to my home, Military Aide, and rest a while."

Yang Zhi returned with Cao Zheng to the inn The host told his wife to bring them food and wine While they were drinking, Cao Zheng asked, "What brings you here, Military Aide?"

Yang related in detail how he lost the birthday gifts he was delivering for Governor Liang.

"In that case, why not remain with me for a time?" Cao Zheng proposed. "Then we can discuss what to do."

"That's very kind of you."

16

Yang Zhi spent the night at Cao Zheng's house. The next morning he borrowed some travelling money, picked up his halberd, bid farewell to his host, and set out for Two-Dragon Mountain.

He travelled all day. Towards evening, he came within sight of a high mountain. "I'll sleep in this grove tonight, "he said to himself, "and climb up tomorrow."

When he entered the grove, he received a shock. Seated in the cool of a pine was a big fat monk, stripped to the buff. The monk, on seeing Yang Zhi, grabbed a staff and leaped to his feet.

"Hey, creep, "he shouted, "where are you from?"

"He has the same accent as I do. We're probably from the same part of the country, "thought Yang Zhi. "Tell me where you're from, monk, "he called out.

Instead of replying, the monk came charging forward, twirling his staff.

"That surly skinhead!" Yang swore under his breath. "I'll let out some of my anger on his hide!"

He rushed at his foe, halberd in hand. They battled up and down the grove until they had fought forty or fifty rounds, with neither the victor. The monk executed a feint and jumped from the combat circle.

"Rest!" he roared. Both men stayed their hands.

"You blue—faced fellow," yelled the monk, "who are you?"

"I'm Yang Zhi, a military aide from the Eastern Capital."

"The one who was selling his sword and killed that loafer Niu Er?"

"Don't you see the tattoo on my face?"

The monk laughed. "Who would have thought that we'd meet here?"

"May I ask your name, reverend? How did you know about my selling my sword?"

"I used to be a major in the Yen'an garrison under Old General Zhang. Then I killed a butcher who was bullying an old man and his daughter, and had to become a monk on Mount Wutai. Everyone calls me Sagacious Lu."

"I've heard a lot about you in the fraternity of gallant men," said Yang Zhi. "But I thought you were at the Xiangguo Monastery. What are you doing here?"

Sagacious Lu related in detail what had happened to him when he was at the Xiangguo Monastery and subsequently.

"In Mengzhou I heard that I would be safe in the Precious Pearl Monastery on Two—Dragon Mountain, and I went there intending to join Deng Long's band.

But the wretch wouldn't have me. Now I can't find a refuge anywhere."

Yang Zhi was very pleased to have met Sagacious Lu. The two bowed to each other there in the grove and then sat together the entire night.

"Here we are," mused Yang Zhi, "but Deng Long has closed the gates to his stronghold. Let's go to Cao Zheng's place and talk it over."

The two men left the grove and returned to the inn, where Yang introduced Sagacious Lu to Cao. Cao Zheng hastily poured out wine, and they discussed how to take Two—Dragon Mountain.

"If he's really shut the gates," said the innkeeper, "an army of ten thousand couldn't get up there. The stronghold can be conquered only by guile, not by force."

"Since it's such a good place," said Yang, "why don't you and I go all out and take it?"

"I have an idea for getting up there, but don't know whether you two will approve," said Cao Zheng

"Let's hear it."

17

"You, Military Aide, will have to change your clothes and dress like a local peasant. I'll take the staff and sword of the reverend, here. My wife's younger brother and a few servants will go with us to the foot of the mountain, and there we'll bind the reverend. I'll attend to that personally, using nothing but slipknots. Then I'll shout up, 'We're from the neighbouring inn. This monk drank so much he got tipsy, but he refused to pay. He kept muttering that he was going to muster his men and attack your stronghold. We took advantage of his drunkenness to tie him up and present him to your chieftain.'

"These clods will certainly let us up the mountain. When we get into the stronghold and are brought before Deng Long, the reverend will slip his bonds and I'll hand him his staff. Once you two fellows get to work, Deng Long will be finished. With him out of the way, his underlings won't dare resist. What do you think of my idea?"

"Shrewd, shrewd,"said Lu and Yang.

That night they all ate and drank heartily and made preparations for the coming expedition. They rose at dawn the following morning. Lu stored his pack and luggage at Cao's house. Then the party set out for Two-Dragon Mountain. They reached the grove after noon and changed their clothes. Sagacious Lu was bound tightly, but the knots were fake. Yang put on a straw sun hat and a tattered cloth shirt. He retained his halberd, but held it shaft forward. Cao Zheng carried the monk's staff. The others were armed with cudgels.

They halted outside the first gate. It was bristling with bows and lime flagons and ballista stones. When the guards at the gate saw the trussed-up monk, they sent a messenger flying to the summit to report.

Not long after, two junior officers came down to the gate and demanded, "Who are you people? What do you want here? Where did you get that monk?"

"We're from the village below. I run a small inn," Cao Zheng replied. "This fat monk came and drank himself silly, and then refused to pay. He kept saying, 'I'm going to get a thousand men from Liangshan Marsh and blast Two Dragon Mountain and wipe out this village of yours too!' I plied him with good wine until he was dead drunk, and then tied the rogue up and brought him here to hand over to your chieftains as a token of our filial respect. It will save our village from disaster."

The junior officers were delighted. "Excellent," they said. "Just wait here a while." They returned to the stronghold and reported that the monk had been captured.

Deng Long was overjoyed. "Bring him up," he cried. "I'll eat the bastard's heart and liver with my wine to slake a bit of my hatred!"

The brigands were ordered to open the gates and send up the prisoner. Yang Zhi and Cao Zheng escorted the bound Sagacious Lu up the trail. After passing through the three gates, they came to the Precious Pearl Monastery.

Lu didn't utter a sound as he was brought into the temple. A few minutes later Deng Long entered, and seated himself on his throne. Cao Zheng and

162

Yang Zhi pushed Sagacious Lu forward to the foot of the dais.

"Wretch!" cried Deng Long. "The other day you knocked me down! My groin is still swollen. Today it's my turn!"

The two servants yanked the rope binding Sagacious and the slipknots vanished. Lu took his staff from Cao Zheng and whirled it fiercely. Yang Zhi turned his halberd upright and grasped its shaft. Cao Zheng brandished a cudgel. Together the group charged.

Deng Long struggled to escape, but Lu's staff split his skull and smashed the throne. Yang Zhi ran his halberd through four or five of the bandits.

"Surrender, all of you!" yelled Cao Zheng. "If you don't, we'll kill every last one of you!"

All the brigands about the monastery as well as their officers were frightened stiff. They all submitted. Men were directed to carry Deng Long's body to the rear of the mountain and burn it.

An inventory was taken of the food supplies and of the items stored in the back of the monastery. Lu and Yang became the stronghold's leaders, and they feasted in celebration. Not long after, Wu Song joined them.

Later, together with Lu and Wu Song, Yang Zhi led the Two−Dragon Mountain band co−operated with the heroes from the Peach Blossom Mountain and Liangshan Marsh, launched an attack against

Qingzhou and took it. After the battle, Yang Zhi with the chieftains of Peach Blossom Mountain and the Two-Dragon Mountain colleted their men, horse's, and as much money and grain as possible, then burned down their strong holds and went to settle down in the Liangshan Marsh.

BOOK TWO

CHAPTER FIVE — LIN CHONG

1

We have already made our acquaintance with Lin Chong, Arms Instructor of the Imperial Guards, in our story of Sagacious Lu. We'll now continue to talk of Lin Chong.

The reader will recall how Young Master Gao, adopted son of Marshal Gao Qiu, Commander of the Imperial Guards, had become enamoured of Lin Chong's wife and was racking his brains for ways of getting her.

One day as Young Master Gao was sitting in his study fretful and unhappy, Fu An, one of his ne'er-do-well friends, having guessed what was troubling Gao, called on him with a scheme that would put Lin Chong's wife right into Gao's hands.

Gao thought Fu An's scheme excellent. He immediately began to put it into action.

2

To get back to Lin Chong. For several days he had been brooding at home. One morning he heard someone shouting at his front door, "Is the arms instructor in?"

Lin Chong went to the door, and there was his best friend, Lu Qian. "What brings you here, brother Lu?" Lin asked quickly.

"I'm concerned about you. I haven't seen you in the streets these past few days, brother. Come and have a few cups with me, and forget about whatever is troubling you."

They had some tea and then rose to go out. "Sister-in-law," Lu Qian called to Lin Chong's wife as they were leaving. "I'm taking brother Lin over to my place for a few cups of wine."

"Don't let him drink too much, brother Lu," Lin's wife admonished. "Send him home early."

The two men strolled down the street. "Let's not go to my home, brother Lin," Lu Qian said. "We can have our drinks in a wine shop."

They went to a wine shop, selected a small room and ordered some good wine and tidbits to go with it. Lin Chong sighed.

"What's the matter, brother?" asked Lu Qian.

Lin told Lu Qian about his encounter with Young Master Gao a few days previously.

"The Young Master didn't realize she was your wife," Lu said soothingly. "It's not serious. Forget it. Let's drink."

Lin Chong downed eight or nine cups. He wanted to wash his hands. As he was going down the stairs, he met his wife's servant. She said to him, "You had just left then a man came running over to our house and

166

said to the mistress, 'I'm a neighbour of Captain Lu. While drinking with him, Arms Instructor Lin suddenly gasped for breath and fell to the floor. You'd better go and look after him.' Our lady and I hurriedly followed the man to a place one street past the marshal's residence. When we got upstairs we saw a table laden with food and drink, but there was no sign of you, master.

"As we turned to leave, that young fellow who pestered the mistress at the temple the other day came out and said with a leer, 'Stay a while, lady. Your true husband is here!' I flew down the stairs. Our lady was screaming for help. I couldn't find you anywhere. Finally I met Doctor Zhang, who told me that he had seen you going into this wine shop. So I hurried over here. Go quickly, master!"

Shocked, Lin Chong ran at triple speed to Lu Qian's house without waiting for the servant and raced up the stairs. "How dare you hold a good man's wife prisoner!" he heard his wife exclaim. "Have pity on me, mistress," Young Master Gao entreated. "Even a woman of iron and stone couldn't be so coldhearted!"

"Wife, open the door," thundered Lin Chong.

Hearing her husband's voice, Mistress Lin rushed to comply. The terrified Young Master Gao pushed open a window, climbed out and fled along the top of a wall. He was gone before Lin Chong entered the room.

In a fury, Lin Chong smashed Lu Qian's furniture to bits, and then led his wife downstairs where her servant was waiting for them. The three of them went home together.

Lin Chong armed himself with a sharp knife and sped directly to the wine shop in search of Lu Qian. But his treacherous friend was gone.

"He didn't harm me. Don't do anything foolish," Lin Chong's wife argued.

"Who would have thought that Lu Qian could be such a bastard," fumed Lin Chong. "Calling me 'brother' while plotting against me all the time. Even if I don't catch that Young Master I won't let Lu Qian off."

3

Meanwhile, Lu Qian hid in the marshal's residence, afraid to return to his own home.

A few days later, Sagacious Lu came to Lin Chong's house. "Where have you been keeping yourself these past few days, Arms Instructor?" the monk asked.

"I've been too busy to call on you, brother," replied Lin Chong, apologetically. "Since you've honoured me with a visit in my humble home, I ought to offer you a few cups of wine. But we don't have anything decent to drink in the house. Why not go out for a stroll together and have a cup or two in the marketplace?"

They went out and drank together all day. Lin then began to drink with Sagacious every day.

4

As for Young Master Gao, after receiving that fright in Lu Qian's house and having to flee over the wall, he became ill and took to his bed. He didn't dare say anything to the marshal about what had happened.

Lu Qian and Fu An called on the young master at the residence. When they inquired what was ailing him, he said that now that he had failed in both attempts to get Lin Chong's wife, he felt worse than ever.

The sycophants urged him to be of good cheer. "There's only one way Young Master can get over things," they said privately. "The marshal should be told everything and asked to order the death of Lin Chong. Then the young master would be able to get Lin Chong's wife."

That night the marshal was informed of the matter. "The question is how to get Lin Chong out of the way," mused the marshal. "Let me think."

Lu Qian and Fu An told the marshal their plan. "Very well," said the marshal. "You may take action tomorrow."

To get back to Lin Chong. He drank every day and finally forgot about the matter.

One day as Lin and Sagacious Lu were walking in the streets, they saw a big fellow standing on a corner, dressed in an old military robe. He was holding a fine sword in his hand.

"No one recognizes its value," he was muttering. The two men paid no attention and continued walking. The man trailed behind them, saying, "A big city like the Eastern Capital, and not a single person knows the worth of military weapons."

At this, Lin Chong looked around. He was fated for trouble. "Let me see it," he said abruptly.

The fellow handed him the sword. Lin and Sagacious Lu examined the weapon. "An excellent blade! How much do you want for it?"

"The price is three thousand, but I'll take two."

"If you're willing to accept one thousand, I'll buy it from you," said Lin Chong.

"I need money quickly. If you really want the sword I'll let you have it for a thousand. But it's like selling gold at the price of iron."

Lin Chong brought the sword seller to his home, counted out the purchase price and gave it to him. The fellow took the money and departed.

Some time before noon two lieutenants came to Lin's gate and shouted, "Arms Instructor Lin, an order from the marshal! He's heard that you've bought a fine sword and wants you to bring it to compare with his. The marshal is waiting for you in the residence."

Lin Chong wondered who was the gossip that had reported the news so fast. He got dressed, picked up his sword and set off with the two lieutenants. Soon they reached the residence. In the reception room Lin Chong halted.

"The marshal is waiting in the rear hall," said the lieutenants.

Lin Chong went with them into the rear hall. But there was still no sign of the marshal, and he halted once more.

"The marshal is awaiting the arms instructor in the rearmost court. He directed us to bring you there," said the lieutenants.

Lin followed them to a courtyard lined on all sides with green railings. The lieutenants led him to the entrance of a large hall and told him to wait there while they reported to the marshal.

Lin stood there while the two men went inside. Some time passed, but they did not return. Growing suspicious, Lin pushed aside a hanging awning, poked his head in and looked. There, above the door, was a placard with four words written in green: White Tiger Inner Sanctum.

"This is where the highest military affairs are discussed," thought Lin Chong, startled. "How dare I go in there! "

He turned hastily. Behind him he heard the tread of boots. Another man had entered the courtyard. Lin recognized him. It was none other than Marshal Gao. Lin Chong proferred his sword with both hands and greeted him respectfully.

"Lin Chong, " the marshal barked. "I didn't summon you. How dare you force your way into the White Tiger Inner Sanctum! And carrying a sword! You must have come to kill me! Your intentions are surely evil! "

"Benevolent Lord, " Lin Chong replied with a bow, "two of your lieutenants brought me here saying you wanted to compare your sword with mine."

"Lies! Lies! No lieutenants would dare enter my official halls. Hey, guards! Seize this lout! "

Before the order had left the marshal's mouth, over thirty stalwarts came rushing into the courtyard and knocked Lin Chong to the ground.

The marshal ordered his men to send Lin Chong to Kaifeng, get the truth out of him, and then have him executed. Following the marshal's orders, the guards escorted Lin Chong to Kaifeng.

6

"Lin Chong, " said the Kaifeng magistrate, "you are an arms instructor in the Imperial Guards. You must know the law. How could you enter the Inner

Sanctum holding a sword in your hands? Don't you know that this is an offence punishable by death?"

Despite all Lin Chong's protestations of innocence, the magistrate ruled that Lin Chong be given twenty strokes of the bamboo, have the mark of a criminal tattooed on his cheek, and be exiled to Cangzhou. Two guards were designated to escort Lin to the place of exile.

Outside the gate, Lin's father-in-law and many of his neighbours were waiting. All repaired to an inn and took seats. The beating had not been heavy, and Lin Chong was able to walk there.

Clasping hands respectfully, Lin Chong addressed his father-in-law. "Bad times have befallen me, exalted father-in-law. I have something to say. I'm being exiled to Cangzhou and there's no telling whether I'll live or die. My lady will be left at home. I'm worried about her. I'm afraid Young Master Gao will try to force his suit.

"She's still young. I shouldn't tie her down. This is my own idea. It's entirely voluntary. In the presence of our honourable neighbours I want to write out an annulment of our marriage, consenting to her making a new match and promising not to contest it. Only in this way will I feel at ease, assured that Young Master Gao won't be able to harm her."

The old man wouldn't hear of it. He told Lin that when he left for Cangzhou, he would let his daughter and her servant move in with him. He had a bit of money and could support them for four or five years.

Lin Chong insisted, however, and finally the old man said, "Write out the annulment, if that's how you feel. In any event, I won't let my daughter marry another."

Lin Chong then sent for a scribe and had him write out the annulment. When the document was completed, Lin signed his name and added his thumb print. Lin rose, and having thanked his father-in-law and his neighbours, placed his bundle on his back, and went off with the guards.

7

We'll speak now of the two guards. As they were packing their things at home on the eve of their departure for Cangzhou, a waiter from a nearby inn came in and told them that a gentleman wished to see them in the inn. They went with the waiter to the inn. There they found a man who greeted them courteously, and asked them to have a drink with him. This gentleman was none other than Captain Lu Qian, Lin's best friend, whom the reader will remember for his role in Young Master Gao's attempt to seduce Lin Chong's wife.

Lu Qian invited the two guards to sit down and have some wine. "As you know," he said, "Lin Chong has incurred the marshal's displeasure. The marshal has ordered me to present you with ten ounces of gold. He hopes you will finish Lin Chong off in some secluded spot along the road. If Kaifeng people cause any difficulty, the marshal will take care of it personally."

The guards finished their wine. Lu Qian paid the bill and handed over the gold. Then all three left the inn and went their respective ways.

8

Let us now leave the city and follow Lin Chong and his two escorts on their journey to Cangzhou.

It was the height of summer and the weather was scorching. Lin Chong suffered greatly. He walked painfully, with dragging steps. The guards kept cursing him and urging him on.

As the second day of the journey was drawing to a close, they put up at a village inn. After they had had dinner, for which Lin Chong paid, the guards boiled a large pot of water. When it was bubbling hot, they poured it into a basin.

"Wash your feet, Arms Instructor," they told Lin Chong. "You'll sleep better."

Lin Chong struggled to a sitting position, but because of the rack around his neck he couldn't lean forward. One of the guards offered to wash his feet for him.

" How could I impose upon you? " Lin hastily

replied.

" Men travelling together shouldn't be ceremonious over such trifles, "said the guard.

Not realizing this was a plot, Lin Chong stretched out his legs. The guard seized them and plunged them into the boiling water.

"Aiya! " Lin cried out, hurriedly pulling his feet out of the basin. They had become red and swollen.

"Plenty of prisoners have looked after guards, but how often do you see a guard waiting on a prisoner?" said the guard who had plunged Lin's legs into the basin of boiling water. "With the best of intentions I wash his feet, but he has the nerve to complain the water is too cold, the water is too hot.... If this isn't returning evil for good, I don't know what is! "

They slept till daybreak. Lin Chong was so dizzy that he was unable to eat anything and barely able to walk. His feet were covered with blisters.

The guards led Lin Chong from the inn. He could hardly drag his feet along. "Walk! Faster! "shouted the guards. " Keep moving or we'll help you with this staff! "

It soon became obvious that Lin Chong really couldn't go much farther. They saw ahead of them a wild, evil wood shrouded in mist. The two guards led Lin Chong straight into the wood.

"I'm tired, "said one of the guards. "Let's rest here. "

Lin Chong groaned. With his back against a tree

trunk he slid to the ground.

On the pretext that Lin Chong would otherwise run off, the guards bound him hand and foot and tied aim tightly to the tree. Then they sprang up and seizing their staves advanced on Lin Chong.

"Killing you isn't our idea," they said. "It's Marshal Gao's order. Don't blame us two. We're only carrying out orders. We have no choice."

When Lin Chong heard this, his tears fell like rain.

"Officers," he cried, "there's never been any enmity between us. Spare me, and I'll never forget you!"

"Empty talk," said the guards. "Nothing can save you!"

9

The guard raised his staff and swung it fiercely at Lin Chong. But quicker than words can tell, from behind the pine tree came a thunderous roar. An iron rod shot forward, intercepted the staff and sent it flying into the air. Out leaped a big fat monk.

"I've been listening quite a while," he yelled. He brandished his Buddhist staff at the two guards.

Lin Chong recognized Sagacious Lu. He hastily cried, "Brother! Stay your hand. I have something to say. It's not their doing. Marshal Gao, through Captain Lu Qian, gave them orders to destroy me. How

177

could they refuse? It would be wrong to kill them! "

Unsheathing his knife, Sagacious cut Lin's bonds and helped him to his feet.

"Brother, "he said, "I've been worried about you since the day we parted. After you were convicted, I heard that you were being exiled to Cangzhou, and I looked for you outside Kaifeng, but in vain. Then I learned that a waiter had gone to the two guards saying, 'A gentleman wishes to speak to you at the inn,' and I became suspicious. I was afraid these oafs would try to harm you along the road, so I followed. "

"When these knaves brought you to the inn, I put up there too. I heard them plotting in whispers. You set out before dawn. I hurried ahead to the forest and waited to kill the two wretches here. "

"Since you've saved me, brother, there's no need to kill them, "urged Lin Chong.

"Scurvy trash, "bellowed Sagacious. "If it weren't for my brother here, I'd pound you both into mince-meat! "He put his knife away and shouted, "Help my brother up, and be quick about it. Come with me! " Supporting Lin Chong and carrying his bundle, the two guards followed the monk out of the forest.

After walking three or four *li*, they saw a little inn on the edge of a village. All four went in and sat down. They ordered some meat, two jugs of wine and some griddle cakes. When they had finished with the meat and wine, they got their luggage in order, paid the bill and left the village.

"Where are you planning to go, brother?" asked Lin Chong.

"I still don't feel at ease about you, brother. I'm going to escort you all the way to Cangzhou."

10

Along the road Sagacious Lu frequently bought wine and meat for Lin Chong, and the guards were permitted to join them. When the party came to an inn, they would retire early and rise late. Of course, the guards had to light the fires and do the cooking.

The guards conferred in private. "When we get back, Marshal Gao will surely punish us."

"I've heard that a newly arrived monk has been put in charge of the Great Xiangguo Monastery's vegetable fields. He's called Sagacious Lu. This must be the man. Let's tell the truth when we get back. We'll return the ten ounces of gold to Captain Lu Qian. Let him settle accounts with the monk himself."

11

To make a long story short, they marched for seventeen or eighteen days, with the monk never relaxing his watch over the two guards.

When they were only about seventy *li* from Cangzhou, Sagacious Lu said to Lin Chong, "Brother, from here to Cangzhou is not far. I'll part with you here. Some day we'll meet again."

"Go back, brother. Let my father-in-law know I'm all right," said Lin Chong. "If I live, I'll repay you for your protection in full."

Sagacious walked off dragging his iron staff behind him with one arm, swinging the other.

"Let's go, good officers," said Lin Chong. The three continued walking until noon. Down the highway they observed an inn. They entered, and Lin invited the guards to sit down.

The innkeeper told Lin Chong that in their village there was a wealthy man called Chai Jin, known in their parts as Lord Chai. This man made a practice of welcoming all bold men. He had left instructions at the inn that any prisoner on route to exile should come to his manor, and he would help him financially.

Lin Chong had often heard men in the Eastern Capital speak of Lord Chai. He suggested to the guards that the three of them pay Chai a visit.

They made their way to Lord Chai's manor. When they reached the place, they were told that he had left that morning to go hunting. As they were returning along the same road on which they had come, they saw a column of horsemen dash out of a grove and come galloping in the direction of the manor. A young nobleman riding a snow-white steed veered out of the column and trotted up to Lin Chong.

"Who is this gentleman wearing the rack?" he asked.

Lin quickly bowed and replied, " Your humble servant is called Lin Chong, formerly an arms instructor in the Eastern Capital's Imperial Guards. Because I offended Marshal Gao, he invented an excuse to send me to Kaifeng and have me sentenced to exile in Cangzhou. We were told at the village inn that the gallant hero who lives here, Lord Chai, keeps open house for men of talent. But I was unable to find him."

Leaping from his saddle, the nobleman rushed forward, crying, "I am Chai Jin. A thousand apologies for not being at home to welcome you!" He fell to his knees and saluted Lin Chong.

Lin hastily returned the courtesy. Chai led Lin Chong to the manor.

"I've long known of your fame," said Chai Jin. "Who would have thought that today you would come to our humble place!"

12

Lin Chong stayed at Chai Jin's manor for several days. At Lord Chai's insistence he demonstrated his skill in the use of various weapons. He was feasted daily on excellent wines and delicious food.

The guards began to press Lin Chong to leave. Chai gave him a farewell banquet. He also wrote two letters for the arms instructor, one addressed to the warden of the garrison prison, the other to the head keeper, both of whom were on intimate terms with him. He presented Lin Chong with an ingot of twenty-five ounces of silver, and bestowed five ounces of silver on the two guards.

Early the next morning, Lin Chong and his guards departed for Cangzhou. They arrived there about noon. The guards went directly to the prison and presented the order of exile to an official, who immediately brought Lin Chong before the magistrate. The magistrate wrote out an order committing Lin to prison. The guards bade him farewell and left for the Eastern Capital.

<h2 style="text-align:center">13</h2>

The reader must not allow us to take him to the Cangzhou garrison prison.

The letters Chai Jin had written to the warden and the head keeper of the garrison prison as well as the presents Lin Chong gave to the prison officials assured him of good treatment. The head keeper said, "Arms Instructor Lin, I've heard of your good name before. You're truly a splendid fellow. Marshal Gao has framed you, no doubt about it. Although for the time being you have to suffer this inconvenience, I'm sure you'll eventually make your mark."

The warden appointed Lin Chong to take care of the garrison prison temple. All he had to do was to burn incense and sweep the floor once in the morning and once again in the evening. This was the lightest work in the prison. Lin Chong thanked them for their protection and gave them another few ounces of silver.

The following day, Lin had the rack removed from his neck. From then on, Lin Chong slept and had his meals at the temple. Before he knew it, forty or fifty days had gone by. The warden and the head keeper, having been bribed, were always very cordial. He was left to come and go as he pleased, with no restrictions.

14

One day around noon as Lin Chong was strolling outside the garrison gates, he heard someone behind him call, "Arms Instructor Lin, what are you doing here?"

Lin turned around and saw the inn waiter Li Xiao—er, with whom he had first become acquainted in the Eastern Capital. Lin Chong had often shown kindness to Li, and more than once gotten him out of scrapes. Li was deeply devoted to Lin. He told the arms instructor that two fellows with Eastern Capital accents had invited the warden and the head keeper to the inn for a chat. They had a furtive manner and he thought there was something fishy about them.

Lin Chong had Li describe them. From the description he recognized one of them as Captain Lu Qian. He broke into a towering rage. " The filthy thief!"he cried. "How dare he come here to harm me!

Lin Chong bought a sharp dagger. Carrying it on his person, he made a search of all the streets and lanes in the city, but found no trace of the two men from the Eastern Capital. He continued his search for days, but nothing untowards befell him.

One day the warden summoned Lin Chong into his hall and told him that in order to improve his lot he had decided to give him the job of collecting fees from the people delivering fodder to an army fodder depot outside the city's east gate. He was to go there with the head keeper and take over from the old army man who was in charge.

Lin Chong was suspicious. "Not only haven't they harmed me," he thought to himself, "but they have given me this good job instead. I don't know what to make of it."

He packed his belongings, put his dagger in his belt, took up a spear and set out with the head keeper. They soon reached the depot.

The head keeper told the old soldier that the warden had sent Lin Chong to replace him. The old soldier took Lin Chong around, counted the stacks of fodder, and then gave him the keys and left.

15

Lin Chong placed his bundle and bedding on the bed and sat down to replenish the fire in the earthen brazier. It was a bitterly cold winter day. Although he huddled over the fire, he still felt cold. "The old soldier said there was a little marketplace two *li* from here," he recalled. "Why don't I go there and have some wine?"

He took some money from his bundle, tied a flask to the end of his spear, shut the door of his shack behind him, and headed for the marketplace. Lighting upon a wine shop there, he went inside.

Having had a platter of sliced meat and some wine, he started back against the wind. It was snowing very hard. When he unlocked the door of the depot, he uttered a cry of dismay. The thatched shack had collapsed under the weight of the snow.

"What am I going to do?" he wondered. "I've no place to build a fire. How am I going to manage?"

Suddenly he remembered a temple he had seen on the way to the marketplace. He decided to spend the night there. Rolling up his bedding and shouldering his spear with the dangling flask, he locked the depot door and proceeded to the temple. He walked into the temple, but could find neither occupants nor custodian.

Lin mounted a dais with an idol of a mountain spirit on it, placed the spear and flask in a corner, untied his bedding, covered himself to the waist with the quilt and tried to go to sleep. Suddenly, he heard a loud crackling outside. He leaped to his feet and peered through a vent in the wall. The fodder depot was in flames and burning fiercely. Lin grabbed his spear and was about to open the door and dash to the fire when he heard men's voices. He leaned against the door and listened. There were the sounds of footsteps of three men approaching the temple.

"We're much indebted to the warden and to you, Head Keeper," one of the men said. "When I return to the capital and report to the marshal, he undoubtedly will make you both big officials."

"We've taken care of Lin Chong properly this time," said another.

"I climbed over the wall and set a score of haystacks afire. I'd like to see him get away!" said a third.

"Even if he escapes with his life, burning down a military fodder depot is a crime punishable by death."

"Let's go back to the city."

"Wait a little longer. If we bring a couple of his bones with us to the capital, the marshal and the young master will praise us for doing the job thoroughly."

Lin Chong recognized the three men by their voices. One was the head keeper, one was Captain Lu Qian, and the third was Fu An.

Clutching his spear, Lin Chong pushed the door open.

"Where do you think you're going, you sons—of—bitches!" he roared.

The three, who had just begun to leave, froze, too shocked to move. Lin plunged the spear into the head

keeper's back. He then raised his arm and speared Fu An through.

"Spare me!" cried Captain Lu Qian, weak with terror.

Lin turned. He saw Lu Qian preparing to flee. Before Lu had gone three paces, Lin Chong grabbed him by the front of his tunic and threw him flat on his back in the snow.

"Filthy bastard," he cried, "I have never wronged you. How could you have injured me so?"

"This wasn't my idea," Lu pleaded. "The marshal ordered me to do it! I didn't dare refuse!"

Lin Chong ripped open Lu's clothes and stabbed his knife into Lu's heart. Blood spurted everywhere.

He went back inside the temple and finished off the wine in the flask. Then tossing the flask and the bedding aside, took up his spear, left the temple and started east.

16

He had gone only four or five *li* when he saw people from a neighbouring village rushing along with water buckets and pikes to put out the blaze.

"Hurry and save the place," Lin Chong called out to them. "I'm going to report the fire to the authorities!"

Spear in hand, he walked on rapidly. The snow fell more heavily. For several hours Lin Chong walked

187

eastward. He shivered in the merciless cold. In a grove of trees he saw a small house with a thatched roof. Firelight gleamed through cracks in the walls.

Lin Chong approached the house and pushed open the door. Some servants sat huddled around an open hearth where a wood fire was burning. Lin greeted them courteously and asked for permission to dry his clothes by the fire.

"Go ahead, "said one of the servants. "We don't mind."

Lin warmed his damp clothes until they were somewhat drier. He noticed a large jug was gently steaming by the embers, sending forth the fragrance of wine.

He asked one of the servants for a little of the wine. The man said they didn't have enough for themselves and refused to give him any.

"Only one or two bowls to ward off the chill."

"I said no. Forget it."

Lin Chong grew angry, and began to belabour them with his spear. Everyone jumped up in alarm. Lin drove them out with blows of the spear shaft.

"They're all gone. Now I can enjoy this wine!"

He scooped up the wine with a ladle, drinking until only half of the brew remained. Then he walked unsteadily through the door.

He staggered along for nearly a *li*. A gust of wind knocked him down beside a ravine. In vain he tried to struggle to his feet. He lay in the snow, stupefied.

The servants came rushing back, leading over twenty others armed with spears and clubs. They found Lin collapsed in the snow, his spear lying to one side. They seized and bound him. At dawn they brought Lin Chong to a large manor, where they swarmed around him and flailed him with sticks. He couldn't escape. At this moment, a man with an air of authority about him emerged from a building and walked over. He recognized Lin Chong and ordered the servants to desist and untie Lin's bonds.

"What are you doing here, Arms Instructor?" the man asked. Standing before Lin Chong was none other than Chai Jin.

The two went inside and sat down. Lin Chong recounted his adventures in detail, starting with the burning of the fodder depot.

"What bad luck you've had, brother," said Chai Jin. "But you needn't worry. this place is my eastern manor. Stay awhile, and then we'll decide what to do."

17

Meanwhile in Cangzhou the warden of the garrison prison laid an accusation against Lin Chong charging him with the murder of the head keeper, Captain Lu Qian and Fu An, and the burning down of the army fodder depot.

The magistrate immediately issued an order for

Lin Chong's arrest, and sent police to post pictures of him in every village and town, in every inn and shop, along with notices offering a large monetary reward for his apprehension.

Lin Chong, in Chai Jin's eastern manor, was on pins and needles from the time he heard about it. "You'd better not keep me here, Excellency," he said to Chai Jin. "If they find me in the manor, you'll be implicated. I'll find another refuge. If I live I'll repay you with my complete devotion."

"Since you insist on leaving, brother, I have a place to suggest. It's called Liangshan Marsh, in Jizhou, Shandong Province. The area is about eight hundred *li* in circumference. Three bold men have set up a stronghold there — Wang Lun, Du Qian and Song Wan. They've formed a band of seven or eight hundred to rob and pillage. Many who have committed capital crimes have found shelter among them. I'm on very good terms with the three leaders. Suppose I write a letter of introduction recommending you. How would that be?"

"Fine, if that's what you think best. I'm very grateful."

18

Cangzhou was plastered with notices for Lin Chong's arrest, and two army officers were checking travellers at the city gate. To get Lin Chong out of the city, Chai Jin gathered a party of twenty or thirty horsemen rigged out with bows and arrows, falcons, and hunting dogs, and they all gaily set forth with Lin Chong riding in their midst. The army officers at the city gate knew Chai Jin well and let the party through. After riding about fifteen *li*, Chai Jin told Lin Chong to dismount, remove his hunter's garb and put on his own clothes. Lin tied his sword to his waist, took his halberd in hand, bid Chai Jin farewell and marched off down the road.

He walked for over ten days. Towards evening on the eleventh day he saw in the distance a wine shop beside a lake. Lin hurried towards it and entered. He selected a place at one of the tables and ordered some wine and meat. As he was eating, he noticed a tall, stalwart man wearing a sable-lined jacket and deerskin boots, who walked to the door and looked at the snow.

Lin Chong summoned the waiter and asked him, "How far is it from here to Liangshan Marsh?"

" Only a few *li*. But you must go by water. There's no way to get there by land. You have to find a boat."

"Find one for me, then. I'll pay you well."

As Lin Chong was talking with the waiter, the man in the sable jacket walked up and grabbed him around the waist, exclaiming, "You've got your nerve! In Cangzhou you committed a capital crime, and here you are! A large monetary reward is offered for your

191

capture. What do you say to that?"

"Who do you take me for?"

"Aren't you Lin Chong?"

"My name is Zhang."

The man laughed. "Come, we'll talk in private."

He led Lin Chong to a room in the rear and told the waiter to light a lamp.

19

"I heard you asking for a boat to take you to Liangshan Marsh, brother. That's an outlaws' mountain stronghold. Why do you want to go there?"

"To be frank, the police are hot on my heels, and I have no place to hide. I've come to join the band on the mountain."

"In that case you need an introduction."

"I have one from a friend in Cangzhou. His name is Chai Jin," explained Lin. "But you must be one of them, and I didn't realize that all along. Please tell me your name." Lin bowed courteously.

The man returned the bow. "I'm the lookout for Chieftain Wang. I'm called Zhu Gui. Under the guise of running this wine shop I observe the movements of merchants and travellers. Since Lord Chai has written an introduction, Chieftain Wang is sure to welcome a man of your splendid reputation."

"How can I find a boat to ferry me across the lake?" Lin Chong asked.

"There are boats here, brother," said Zhu Gui. "Don't worry about that. First get some rest. Then please rise at daybreak and come here. I'll go with you."

Both men retired to their respective rooms. Zhu Gui woke Lin Chong at dawn before the sky was light.

Zhu Gui opened the window of his room. He fitted a whistling arrow to a bow and let it fly towards a creek in thicket of reeds on the other side of a cove.

"Why have you done that?" asked Lin Chong.

"That was a signal arrow to the mountain stronghold. A boat will come soon."

20

Not long after the whistling arrow left Zhu Gui's bow a scull appeared from the reeds opposite, rowed by four men. Lin Chong collected his luggage and weapons, and Zhu Gui conducted him to the craft. The boatmen propelled the vessel across the lake. Lin Chong and Zhu Gui disembarked, one of the boatmen going with them to carry Lin's things.

Zhu and Lin began climbing. Halfway up the mountain was a pavilion. A turn beyond that and they saw a large fortified pass. After brigands went on ahead to announce them, Lin and Zhu entered the pass. They crossed two narrow defiles before coming to the gate of the stronghold itself.

Zhu Gui led Lin Chong to Righteous Fraternity Hall. A bold fellow sat in an armchair in the middle. This was Chieftain Wang Lun. The man sitting to his left was Du Qian, and on his right sat Song Wan. The two men came forward and hailed the chieftains respectfully.

"This is Lin Chong, an arms instructor in the capital's Imperial Guards," said Zhu Gui. "Because Marshal Gao decided to ruin him, he was marked as a criminal and exiled to Cangzhou. There, the army fodder depot he had been put in charge of was burned down and he killed three men in a fight. He took refuge with Lord Chai, who has written a letter of introduction for him so that he may join our company."

Lin Chong presented the letter, which Wang Lun opened and read.

"Lord Chai is well, I hope?"

"He hunts and relaxes on the outskirts of the city every day."

Wang Lun fell silent. "I'm a scholar who failed in the civil examinations," he thought. "In a rage I came here with Du Qian and turned bandit. Later Song Wan joined us, and we formed this big company. I'm not particularly capable, and Du Qian and Song Wan have only ordinary skills in arms. This fellow was an arms instructor in the Imperial Guards. He must be an excellent military man. If we accept him and he sees what duds we are, he'll probably want to take over, and we won't be able to stop him. I'd better make some excuse and send him back down the mountain. That'll avoid trouble."

He ordered a feast laid in honour of Lin Chong. When they had all finished one of the men, on Wang Lun's instructions, brought in a platter bearing fifty ounces of silver and two bolts of fine silk, and placed them before Lin Chong. Wang Lun rose.

"Lord Chai has sent a letter recommending that you, Arms Instructor, join our humble band. But unfortunately we have little grain, our buildings are in poor condition, and our forces are small. It wouldn't be right if we impeded your career. We offer these paltry gifts in the hope you won't scorn them. Forgive us and seek a place in some big stronghold."

Lin Chong refused the gifts, saying that though he had no talents he hoped to be accepted. Nothing would make him happier than to place himself under their command.

Zhu Gui put in a word for Lin Chong. Du Qian and Song Wan agreed. They said that for Lord Chai's sake they should let Lin Chong join the band as one of their stronghold's leaders. If they didn't, Lord Chai would be offended and the whole fraternity of gallant men would despise them for lack of chivalry.

In the end, Wang Lun had to agree, but he demanded that Lin Chong present a membership certificate. It was explained to him that this meant that he had to go down the mountain, kill a man and bring his head to the stronghold to prove himself.

"I'll give you three days," said Wang Lun. "If you bring the membership certificate in that time, we'll accept you. If you don't, you'll have to excuse us."

21

Lin Chong rose early the next morning. After breakfast he tied on his sword, picked up his halberd and went down the mountain. All day he waited in a secluded place beside a path, but by dusk not a single traveller had come his way. He gloomily returned to the stronghold.

The following day he got up as the sky was turning light, took his weapons and proceeded down the trail. This time he tried a path on the other side of the mountain. But by dusk no one had appeared. Again he went back to the stronghold.

"Your membership certificate?" asked Wang Lun.

Lin Chong could only sigh. The bandit chieftain laughed. "If you don't get one tomorrow, there's no need for us to meet again. Just stroll down the mountain and find another place to stay."

On the third day, luck was with Lin Chong. At noon a big fellow came round the bend of the trail. Lin Chong strode forward to meet him.

The two men attacked each other with murderous

fury. They fought for thirty rounds, with neither gaining. Just as the struggle was approaching its climax, high on the mountain a voice rang out. "Stop fighting, brave fellows! "

Lin Chong and his opponent stayed their hands. Down the mountain came Wang Lun, accompanied by Du Qian and Song Wan.

" Beautiful technique, both of you, " Wang Lun commended.

" This is our brother, Lin Chong. And you, sir, would you tell me your name?"

" I'm called Yang Zhi. When I was younger, I passed the military examination, and was appointed an aide in the palace. I'm on my way to the Eastern Capital now."

"So that's who you are! We'd be very pleased if you would come to our stronghold for a few cups of wine. What do you say?"

At Wang Lun's insistence, Yang Zhi agreed to rest a while in the stronghold.

22

To dispense with idle chatter, what took place after Lin Chong got his membership certificate is recounted in detail elsewhere, and will be touched upon in our story of Chao Gai in volume three of this book.

BOOK TWO
CHAPTER SIX — MISTRESS GU

1

Among the chieftains of Liangshan Marsh were a number of valorous women. One that deserves particular mention is Mistress Gu.

Mistress Gu was known as the Tigress because when she fought, not even twenty or thirty men could touch her. Even her husband, Sun Xin, couldn't vanquish her, skilled as he was with weapons.

She and her husband lived outside the east gate of the city of Dengzhou, where they ran an inn. They also had a slaughter—house and a place to gamble.

2

A narrative of Mistress Gu's exploits had best begin with the story of Mistress Gu's two cousins, Xie Zhen and Xie Bao. One day a relative on her husband's side, Yue Ho, delivered a message from Xie brothers saying that they had been arrested on a trumped—up charge and thrown into prison . They asked to be rescued.

"When they killed a tiger a rich landlord, Squire Mao, stole it from them. Then he had them seized as thieves and taken before the magistrate. He bribed everyone, high and low," explained Yue Ho. "Sooner or later, Bao Ji the warden is going to have them murdered. They said no one but you could save them. That may be, but only if you act fast."

Mistress Gu uttered a cry of lamentation. She shouted to her assistants to fetch her husband. Several of them ran out, and soon returned with Sun Xin. His wife told him the story.

"You'd better go back, cousin," Sun said to Yue Ho. They're already in prison. We'll need you to look after them. As soon as my wife and I think of a plan for rescuing them, we'll join you directly."

Mistress Gu served Yue Ho wine and gave him a bag of silver. " Spread this around among the lower-ranking keepers," she said, "to make sure that they take good care of our cousins."

Yue Ho thanked her, took the silver, returned to the prison and put the money to use. Of that we'll say no more.

3

Mistress Gu conferred with Sun Xin. "Any ideas on how to save our cousins?" she asked.

"That jerk Squire Mao has money and power. He wants to prevent your cousins from ever coming out. He'll certainly see to it that they're killed. They have to be snatched out of that prison. There isn't any other solution."

"I'll go with you tonight,"said Mistress Gu.

"Don't be rash. We need a place to go after the jailbreak. We can't carry it off, anyhow, without the help of my brother and two other men I have in mind."

"Who are they?"

"An uncle and a nephew who are mad about gambling — Zou Yuan and Zou Run. At present they are robbers on Mountain in the Clouds. If I can get them, we can do it. I'll go immediately and invite them here for a conference. Mountain in the Clouds isn't far."

Mistress Gu instructed her assistants to slaughter a hog, and laid the table with wine and platters of fruit and delicacies.

4

By dusk Sun returned with the two bold fellows. Mistress Gu invited them into the inner room. She told the whole story and raised the question of raiding the prison.

"I have twenty men under my command I can trust,"said Zou Yuan.

"We won't be able to stay in these parts after we do the job,"said Zou Run. "There's a place I've been thinking of going to for a long time. I wonder whether you two would be willing to join us."

"We'll go anywhere you like, as long as you save

my cousins,"said Mistress Gu.

"Liangshan Marsh is thriving,and the leaders are very agreeable to accepting new members. There are several friends of mine under their command. They joined the band a long time ago. After we've rescued your cousins, we'll all go to Mount Liangshan and join up,too.What do you say?"

"Couldn't be better,"cried Mistress Gu.

5

"There's one thing, though,"Zou Run reminded them."When we've got our men, what if Dengzhou sends troops and cavalry after us?"

"My elder brother is a major in the garrison prison, and he's the best fighter they have,"said Sun Xin. "His reputation is known all over.I'll invite him here tomorrow and get his promise to help."

The next day Sun Xin's elder brother Sun Li came over. Mistress Gu came straight to the point: "Squire Mao is plotting against our cousins Xie Zhen and Xie Bao, and sooner or later is going to have them killed. We're going to raid the prison, rescue them, and then all join the band in Liangshan Marsh. I want to tell you of our plan. If you don't want to go with us, we'll go along. If we leave, nothing will happen to us. If we stay, we'll be prosecuted. What do you think of our idea?"

"I'm a military officer. How dare I do such a

thing?"

"Since you refuse, you and I must fight to the death, right now! "said Mistress Gu as she produced two sabres.

"Let me go home and pack some things first and see how the land lies. Then we'll go into action, "said Sun Li.

6

Bao Ji, the warden of the Dengzhou prison, had received money from Squire Mao and was waiting for a chance to murder Xie Zhen and Xie Bao.

As Yue Ho was standing in the passage of the prison gateway, he heard the entry bell ring.

"Who's there?"

"A woman with food, "Mistress Gu replied.

Yue Ho guessed it was she, opened the gate and let her in. Bao Ji spotted her.

"Who is that woman?" he yelled. "How dare she deliver food here?"

"She's the Xie brothers' sister. She's bringing them something to eat."

"Don't let her in. Give it to them yourself."

Yue Ho took the food, opened the cell door and handed the food to the brothers.

"How are things going?" they asked.

"Your cousin is already in. We're just waiting for the others to get set."

Yue Ho unlocked their fetters. Outside someone shouted, "Major Sun is pounding on the gate."

Mistress Gu moved swiftly towards the pavilion. Angrily, Bao Ji came down from the pavilion.

"Where are my brothers?" Mistress Gu shouted at Bao Ji. She pulled out two gleaming daggers. Bao Ji could see that he was in danger, and he started to hurry from the courtyard. He ran right into the Xie brothers, who had dashed out of their cell, their racks in their hands. Before Bao Ji could defend himself, Xie Zhen struck him heavily with the corner of his rack, crushing the warden's skull.

Mistress Gu had already stabbed four or five keepers. Yelling, she and the two brothers fought their way out. Sun Li and Sun Xin were at the gate. When they saw the four figures emerging, they went quickly towards the front of the prison office. At that point Zou Yuan and Zou Run came out. Shouting fiercely, the whole company marched off.

7

Crowded around Sun Li for protection, the party sped through the town gate and went directly to a spot they had agreed on. There, Sun Li's wife was helped onto a cart. Mistress Gu mounted a horse, and the procession continued.

After lagging behind to take their revenge on old Squire Mao, the Xie brothers caught up with them

203

thirty *li* further on. They took some horses from a manor along the way, marching swiftly through the night towards Liangshan Marsh. In a day or two they reached Shi Yong's inn. This was a lookout for the Liangshan Marsh stronghold. Shi Yong announced the arrival of the party to the stronghold.

When the new arrivals reached the edge of the lake, several chieftains were waiting there to greet them.

"We plan to join the stronghold, but we haven't shown the slightest merit," Sun Li said. "Suppose we offer a plan for cracking the Zhu Family Manor, which the Liangshan Marsh gallants have attacked twice, both times in vain. How will that be as an entrance gift?"

When the chieftains heard this, they were delighted.

8

Now the Zhu Family Manor was hostile to the outlaws of Liangshan Marsh. Lately the Zhu family had started provocations against the Liangshan Marsh brigands, whose leaders resolved to go down and punish them. It was decided that once they defeated the manor, they would seize its grain for the use of the fortress.

The Zhu Family Manor was ruled by Lord Zhu, who commanded a force of nearly twenty thousand.

Lord Zhu could count on help from the villages to the east and west. Lord Zhu had three sons, all of them terrific fighters.

Sun Li, Sun Xin and Mistress Gu knew that the Zhu Family Manor was a hard nut to crack, and could be taken by guile only, not by force. They discussed their scheme in detail.

When everything was ready, Sun Li changed his banner to read " Sun Li, Major of the Dengzhou Garrison" and rode to the gate of the Zhu Family Manor with his company of men and horses. The soldiers on the walls reported to their leaders.

On hearing of Sun Li's arrival, the Zhu family's arms instructor, Luan Tingyu, remarked, "He's like a brother to me. When we were children we learned to sport with weapons from the same teacher. I wonder what he's doing here."

Luan opened the manor gate, lowered the drawbridge and rode out to welcome Sun Li. They exchanged greetings.

" I thought you were with the Dengzhou garrison, "said Luan. "What are you doing in these parts?"

"I've been transferred here to defend the cities and towns against the bandits of Liangshan Marsh. We were passing by and I came to see how you are."

"How fortunate we are that you have come to protect us! We have had one clash after another with those bandits the last few days "

Luan was delighted. He presented Sun Li to Lord Zhu and his three sons.

Once Sun Li and his company managed to get into the manor, they immediately began to put their scheme into action.

Zhu and his sons were clever. But Sun Li had come with women and children, luggage and carts. What's more, he was an old friend of Luan Tingyu. Why should they suspect him? They ordered that cows and horses be slaughtered and a feast be laid, at which the guests were wined and dined.

At the feast Sun Li had Yue Ho sing a few ballads to the delight of the assembled diners. In the evening the gathering broke up, and all retired for the night.

9

Around noon of the fourth day, a manor soldier reported, "The Liangshan Marsh bandits are coming at us again."

The three sons of the Zhu family donned their armour and went out the manor gate. Lord Zhu took his seat in the tower stop the gate. To his left was Luan Tingyu, to his right was Major Sun Li.

The two sides were locked in slashing combat, and Sun Li could restrain himself no longer. "Give me my armour, helmet and ridged rod," he called to his brother Sun Xin. He put on his equipment and led out his own horse. After heaving the saddle on its back, he hung the ridged steel rod from his wrist, grasped his lance and mounted. To the accompaniment of crashing gongs, Sun Li rode onto the field.

We'll not describe this clash in detail. Suffice it to say that the three sons threw the Liangshan Marsh forces into disarray. Sun Li captured one of the chieftains, and six others were seized by Lord Zhu's sons.

Lord Zhu thanked Sun Li and invited him to a feast in the rear hall. The prisoners were locked in cage carts.

On the following day, Sun Li and the others strolled around the manor. Zou Yuan and Zou Run had already hidden big axes close by and were standing near the door of the building which held the prisoners. The Xie brothers, also armed with concealed weapons, stayed close to the rear gate. Mistress Gu paced in front of the hall, ready to strike with her pair of daggers at the signal.

The manor drums thundered three times, the front and rear gates swung open, the drawbridges were lowered and the army surged forward to engage the Liangshan Marsh outlaws who were again coming at the Zhu family in force.

Sun Li and a dozen men promptly occupied the front bridge. Zou Yuan and Zou Run, swinging their axes, cut down the few dozen soldiers guarding the prisoners and broke open the cage carts. The released captives seized lances from the weapons racks. When

Mistress Gu heard their shouts, she charged into the inner chambers and slaughtered all the women with her daggers. Lord Zhu recognized his peril and ran off to jump into a well, but was hacked down by one of the prisoners with a blow of his sabre. Near the rear gate the Xie brothers set fire to the haystacks. Black smoke funneled into the sky.

As a result of the capture of the Zhu Family Manor, the brigands obtained five hundred thousand loads of grain. The grain was loaded onto carts. Gold, silver and other valuables were given as rewards to the leaders and men of the Liangshan Marsh forces. All the cattle, sheep, donkeys, horses and the like were driven off for use in the mountain fortress.

The chieftains, big and small, assembled their fighters. Several new leaders were added: Sun Li, Sun Xin, the Xie brothers, Zou Yuan, Zou Run, Yue Ho and Mistress Gu.

10

Having dealt with the Zhu Family Manor, the supreme leaders of Liangshan Marsh determined the assignments of the various chieftains. "Sun Xin and Mistress Gu were innkeepers originally. Let them go on running an inn, selling wine and meat, and receiving bold fellows from all over. . . ." And so Mistress Gu and Sun Xin went off to assume their duties as lookouts on the outer perimeter of the stronghold.

Some time later, a great government army mustered by Marshal Gao and led by three famed commanders — Huyan Zhuo, Han Tao and Peng Qi — assaulted the Liangshan Marsh area. Shortly after the cessation of hostilities the following day, Mistress Gu arrived at the fortress and reported, " The imperial infantry swarmed all over us. They levelled our inns and houses to the ground. If our boats hadn't rescued us, we would all have been captured. "

The leaders consoled her. An inn was again erected to serve as a lookout for the brigands, and as before Mistress Gu and Sun Xin were put in charge.

When the necessity arose, Mistress Gu and her husband took part in battles against government troops and local despots. In records of the wars waged by the Liangshan Marsh brigands we find frequent mention of Mistress Gu and her exploits.

11

The reader may not have heard the story of how Mistress Gu helped to take the Northern Capital in order to save two chieftains who had been seized and cast in prison there.

When news of their capture reached Liangshan, the necessary troops were mustered and ordered to march immediately. The men were divided into four contingents. The third of these was led by Mistress Gu.

When the attempt to take the Northern Capital failed, the Liangshan Marsh forces resorted to guile. Taking advantage of the Lantern Festival celebration, a number of the chieftains stole into the capital in disguise. Mistress Gu and five others were made up as country couples coming to see the lantern display in the city.

Mingling with the crowds, they entered the city through the east gate in the evening. Two of the chieftains came forward fighting. Mistress Gu and her husband Sun Xin pulled out concealed weapons and aided them. At the same time their accomplices Zou Yuan and Zou Run began setting fire to the eaves of houses with torches on long bamboo poles. The concerted boom of numerous explosions in the city temple shook the earth. All over the city, people scurried about in terror. In a dozen places flames brightened the sky. Confusion reigned.

The two chieftains confined in prison were released.

12

A story that is widely known and often told is about how Mistress Gu attempted to rescue Chieftain Shi Jin in the town of Dongping.

This town had money and grain. Although the outlaws of Liangshan Marsh had never disturbed the townsfolk, when the brigands asked them to lend them some grain, they flatly refused.

Chieftain Shi Jin volunteered to go into the town to scout around before the town was seized. While there he was captured by the police and brought to the district court. He was given a severe beating to make him talk. Then a heavy rack was placed around his neck and he was put in the cell for the condemned.

When no news from Shi Jin reached Liangshan Marsh, the leaders summoned Mistress Gu and asked her to go into Dongping. She was instructed to disguise herself as a poor beggar. If Shi Jin was in prison, she was to try and get inside and tell Shi Jin secretly, "We're breaking into town the last day of the month around dusk. During the confusion, find a way of freeing yourself." Mistress Gu was also told to start a fire on the night of the last day of the month as a signal. That's when the raid would be launched.

Mistress Gu, her hair dishevelled, her clothes in tatters, entered the town. Her queries revealed that Shi Jin was indeed in prison.

The next day she walked back and forth in front of the prison holding a jug of rice in her hands. Finally, an elderly policeman came out. Mistress Gu dropped to her knees and bowed low, weeping bitterly.

"What are you crying about, woman?"

"My former master Shi Jin is in there. Nobody's sending him anything to eat, so I want to bring him this mouthful of food I've begged. Have pity. Take me in."

211

"He's a bandit from Liangshan Marsh, and he's committed a capital offence. No one would dare take you in there."

"Have pity on an old woman who only wants to deliver a mouthful of food in return for kindnesses in the past." Again Mistress Gu wept.

The old policeman thought to himself, "If she were a man, I wouldn't do it. But what harm is there in letting in a woman?" He led Mistress Gu into the prison, right to Shi Jin's cell.

Mistress Gu, pretending to weep and sob as she fed him from the jug, managed to whisper, "We're breaking into this town the last night of the month. Fight to free yourself."

It happened that the third lunar month had thirty days that year, instead of the usual twenty-nine. But when Shi Jin asked one of the jailers, "What's the date?" the man remembered wrongly and said, "The last day of the month." Shi Jin could hardly wait.

Near evening, he got one of the keepers, who was half-drunk, to take him to the latrine.

"What's that behind you?" Shi Jin suddenly exclaimed.

As the man turned, Shi Jin wrenched open his rack and struck him on the forehead with it, knocking him to the ground. With a brick Shi Jin smashed the wooden fetters on his feet. He charged into the central pavilion where there were several policemen sodden with drink. He killed a few, and the others fled.

Shi Jin opened the prison gate in anticipation of rescue from the outside. He released all the inmates, about fifty or sixty men. They came out of their cells cheering.

When the situation was reported to the governor, he was frightened out of his wits. He sent for the district commander and ordered that Shi Jin be surrounded at once.

The commander mustered all the keepers and guards, who were armed with spears and staves and dispatched to the prison gate. While Shi Jin didn't dare come out, neither did they have the courage to go in.

Mistress Gu could only bemoan the abortive venture.

13

And then there is the story of how Mistress Gu and her husband Sun Xin set fire to the government shipyards. The Liangshan Marsh leaders learned that Marshal Gao had set up a vast shipyard where hundreds of artisans were building large craft. The craft were obviously meant to be used for a large—scale assault on the Liangshan Marsh fortress.

Mistress Gu dressed up like a food server and had no difficulty in getting into the shipyard. Wearing soiled clothes and carrying a jug of cooked rice, she entered the yard with the other women noisily delivering food.

Towards midnight Sun Xin set fire to the left side of the yard, while Mistress Gu started a blaze on the right. The thatch quickly burst into flames. Yelling in alarm, the artisans knocked down the palisade and fled into the night.

Marshal Gao was aroused from his sleep by a man who rushed in crying, "The shipyard is on fire!" Gao got up quickly and ordered the army to the rescue.

The Mount Liangshan cavalry, who had been hiding in ambush, then dashed out. "Mount Liangshan bandits are here!" shouted Mistress Gu.

On seeing the government troops approach, however, the Mount Liangshan cavalry rode off. The government soldiers did not pursue them, but reassembled and went back to fight the fire.

Sun Xin and Mistress Gu were delighted. They were met by their cohorts who had come down the mountain to escort them to the stronghold.

14

When the Liangshan Marsh forces returned from the southern expedition, each of the chieftains was given an official post. Mistress Gu was appointed magistrate of Dongyuan County, but she preferred to return to the countryside. Soon she and her husband Sun Xin resumed their former jobs in Dengzhou.

BOOK THREE

CHAPTER SEVEN — CHAO GAI

1

The reader will no doubt recall mention of Chao Gai in our chapters on Lin Chong and Wu Song.

Outside the East Gate of the county seat of Yuncheng lay two villages separated by a large stream. One was called East Bank, the other West Bank. The ward chief of East Bank Village was called Chao Gai. Born of a well—to—do family, Chao Gai had always fought injustice and helped the needy. He liked nothing better than befriending gallant men, and putting them up in his manor, whenever they came to him. Extremely fond of exercising his skills with weapons, Chao was very strong.

One day the village constable called on Chao Gai and reported that they had nabbed a fellow sleeping in the temple. Chao Gai went to the gatehouse where the prisoner had been locked up to take a look at him.

"Where are you from, young fellow?"

"Your servant is a stranger from a distant district. I came to offer my services to a man, but they've arrested me as a thief."

"Who were you looking for in this village?"

"A gallant man called Ward Chief Chao."

"What did you want to see him about?"

"Chao is famed everywhere as a champion of righteousness. There's a rare chance for riches I'd like to tell him about."

"Seek no further. I am Ward Chief Chao Gai. If you want me to save you, pretend to recognize me as your mother's brother. In a little while when I come here with the constable, call me 'uncle'. Just say that you were only four or five years old when you left here. That's why you didn't recognize me when you came again looking for me."

2

The young fellow did as he had been told by Chao Gai. When Chao and the constable entered the gate house he shouted, "Uncle, save me!"

Chao Gai pretended to look him over. Then he cried, "Why, isn't that rascal Wang the Third?"

"Yes, it's me, uncle. Save me!"

Everyone was astonished. "How does he know you, Ward Chief?" asked the constable.

"He's my sister's son, Wang the Third. I haven't seen him for ten years. I've heard many people say the scoundrel is no good."

"Little Third," he shouted to the young man. "Why didn't you come directly to me? Why did you go into the village and steal?"

"But uncle, I didn't steal anything," the young

fellow protested.

"If you're not a thief, why have they brought you here?" Chao Gai demanded. Snatching a staff from the constable, he thwacked the young man about the head.

"Don't beat him," the constable urged. "Calm yourself, Ward Chief. Your nephew isn't a thief. I got suspicious, finding a big fellow like him asleep in the temple. I would never have arrested him had I known he was your nephew."

The constable untied the young man and turned him over to Chao Gai, who took him to the rear building and gave him some clothes and a hat.

The young man told Chao Gai about himself. His name was Liu Tang. Ever since childhood, he had drifted about. He had been to many places and made friends with many gallant men. He had often heard them speak of Chao Gai. He had made this trip specially to inform Chao Gai of a rare chance to lay hold of some riches.

"It's said that Governor Liang of Daming, the Northern Capital, has bought jewels and art objects worth a hundred thousand strings of cash to send to his father—in—law Cai, the premier in the Eastern Capital, as birthday gifts," he told Chao Gai. "The route by which they'll be sent has already been chosen. In my humble opinion, these things were purchased with unclean money, and there'll be nothing wrong in taking them. We've only to work out a plan for seizing them along the way. I've often heard that you're a real man, brother, and that you have a remarkable skill with weapons. What do you think of the idea?"

"Excellent! We must plan carefully. But you've just come. Why not rest a while in the guesthouse? Let me give the matter some thought. We'll talk about it later."

3

As soon as Liu Tang had gone, Chao Gai sent a messenger to invite Wu Yong, known as the Pedant, to the manor. The messenger was to tell Wu Yong that there was a matter on which Chao Gai needed his advice.

When Wu Yong appeared, Chao Gai led him and Liu Tang to an inner room in the rear building.

"Ward Chief, who is this person?" Wu Yong asked.

"A bold fellow in the fraternity of gallant men, Liu Tang. He came specially to let me know of a rare chance for riches. He has told me that Governor Liang of Daming has bought jewels and art objects worth a fortune to send to his father-in-law, the premier in the Eastern Capital, as birthday gifts. They'll soon be passing this way. Since they were purchased with unclean money, he thinks there's nothing wrong with seizing them."

Wu Yong smiled. "I thought there was something odd about the sudden appearance of brother Liu, and

218

was able to guess seven or eight-tenths of what was up. His proposal is excellent, but there's only one thing. With too many people involved, we can't succeed. With too few, we're bound to fail. But can just the three of us accomplish our aim? What we need is seven or eight gallant men."

"If you know of some courageous men you can trust, brother," said Chao Gai, "invite them to join us and see this thing through."

"I have three men in mind," said Wu Yong. "Gallant. Unusually skilled with weapons. We must get them if our venture is to succeed.

"What are their names, and where do they live."

"They are brothers, and they live in a village near Liangshan Marsh. They're fishermen, but they've also done a bit of smuggling in the marsh. Their family name is Ruan. Although they haven't had any education, they're very loyal to their friends, and are good bold fellows. If we can get these three to join in, our big project is a sure thing."

"I've heard of the three Ruan brothers, but we've never met. Why not send someone to invite them for a talk?"

"They'd never come. I'd better go myself and persuade them to join us."

4

Wu Yong left the same night, and after travelling

all night arrived in the Ruan brothers' village the next morning.

When they saw Wu Yong they hailed him respectfully. "Teacher, what good wind blows you here?"

"There's a small matter I've come specially to see you about."

They went down to the shore, got into their boats and sculled out onto the lake. They headed for the market centre, moored their craft and entered an inn overlooking the water. The four sat down at a table and ordered a bucket of wine.

"What brings you here, teacher?" one of the brothers finally asked after they had downed a few bowls of wine.

"These last few years I've been teaching in a village school near Ward Chief Chao Gai's manor. I hear he's expecting a very valuable shipment. I've come specially to ask whether you'd be willing to join me in snatching it on its way."

"No," said one of the brothers. "Since he's a noble and generous person, we couldn't do him any harm."

"I didn't realize you brothers were so highly principled. Your spirit is noble! I'll tell you the real story, if you're willing to help. I'm now living in Chao's manor. Your fame has reached him, and he's sent me here to talk with you."

"We three are completely honest. If the ward

220

chief has sent you on some important private business, and we can be of use, we pledge our help with our lives!"

"I assure you I don't want to induce you to do anything bad," said Wu Yong. "This is something big! Liang, the Governor of Daming, has spent a hundred thousand on birthday gifts for Cai, the Premier in the Eastern Capital. I've been asked to invite you to a conference. We'll plan how we few gallants can waylay the convoy in some mountain hollow and take their misbegotten treasure. Then we can enjoy ourselves for the rest of our lives. Does the idea appeal to you?"

"Marvellous!" exclaimed the brothers. "When do we start?"

"We'll leave for Ward Chief Chao Gai's manor tomorrow morning."

5

Early the next morning, the men set out for Chao Gai's manor. They walked all day, and finally came in sight of the manor. The ward chief and Liu Tang were waiting outside the gate. When Wu Yong led the three brothers forward, Chao and Liu greeted them warmly.

The six men entered the manor, went to a rear hall, and took their seats as host and guests. Wu Yong reported. Chao Gai was extremely pleased. A feast was laid to welcome the Ruan brothers. All ate, drank and chatted half the night. At dawn the next day they rose and went to the rear hall. Together they made this solemn vow: "Governor Liang in the Northern Capital harms the people. With the money he has extorted from them he has bought valuable gifts to send to Cai, the premier in the Eastern Capital, on his birthday. This is evilly obtained wealth. If any of us six has any selfish intent, let Heaven and Earth obliterate him! May the gods be our witness!"

6

At this moment, a servant entered and told Chao Gai that a Taoist priest was at the gate wanting to see the ward chief. Chao Gai told him to give the priest some grain and send him on his way. The servant departed. A few minutes later he returned. "I've offered him rice, but he refuses to leave. He says he has come here not for any handouts, but to see you."

The servant hadn't been gone very long when an uproar was heard outside the manor gate. Another servant rushed in and reported, "That priest is in a rage. He's knocked down ten of our fellows!"

Startled, Chao Gai hastily rose to his feet. "Excuse me a moment, brothers. I'd better see to this." He left the hall and went out to the gate.

There, a handsome, powerful priest was fighting off his attackers.

"Cool down, reverend." Chao called out. "You

came asking for Ward Chief Chao Gai, apparently wanting a contribution. They gave you rice. Why get into such a temper?"

The priest laughed. "I'm not interested in grain or money. A hundred thousand means nothing to me. I'm seeking the ward chief because I have something to tell him. These churls wouldn't listen to reason, and began swearing at me. That's why I knocked them about."

"I'm Ward Chief Chao Gai. What did you want to tell me, reverend? Won't you come into the manor and have some tea?"

The two entered the manor. After sipping tea for a while the priest said, "This isn't a good place to talk. Is there somewhere else we could go?"

The ward chief took him to the rear hall. "May I ask your name, sir, and where you're from?" queried Chao Gai.

"My family name is Gongsun, my given name Sheng. I was born in Jizhou prefecture. I've long known of the eminent Ward Chief Chao of Yuncheng County. But I've never had the good fortune of meeting you. In honour of making your acquaintance, I should like to present you with a hundred thousand worth of gold and jewels. I wonder if the you would accept?"

Chao Gai laughed. "You mean the shipment of birthday gifts from the Northern Capital?"

The priest was astonished. "How did you know?"

"I just guessed. I gather we're talking about the same thing?"

"A real treasure! This is too good an opportunity to miss. How does the idea strike you?"

7

The ward chief took the priest into a small room where he presented Wu Yong, Liu Tang and the Ruan brothers to him. "I've long known the fame of Gongsun Sheng among gallant men," said Wu Yong. "I didn't expect to have the pleasure of meeting you today." They drank together to celebrate the meeting.

"Our encounter here is a good omen. We seven can take the precious convoy easily. I suggest that Brother Liu Tang find out which route the convoy will take. It's too late today, but would you please set out early tomorrow?"

"No need for that," said Gongsun. "I already know. It's coming by way of the big road over Yellow Earth Ridge."

"Ten *li* east of there is the village of Anlo," said Chao Gai. "In Anlo lives an idler named Bai Sheng. He once sought me out, and I helped him by giving him a little money."

"We can use the man," said Wu Yong.

"Shall we employ soft or hard tactics?" queried Chao Gai.

Wu Yong laughed. "I've already thought of a

method. We'll meet force with force and guile with guile. I have a plan, but I don't know whether you'll approve."He outlined his proposal.

Chao Gai was delighted. "Marvellous! An excellent plan!"

"Let's not talk about it any more now,"said Wu Yong. "'The walls have ears and people pass outside windows,' as the old saying goes. We must keep this strictly among ourselves."

"Please go back, you three,"Chao Gai said to the Ruan brothers, " and return again when the time comes. Master Wu Yong, go on with your teaching as usual. Gongsun and Liu Tang can live here for the time being."

They drank until dark, and then retired for the night in the various guestrooms.

8

But enough of idle talk. While Yang Zhi, the chief steward, the two captains and the soldiers were proceeding labouriously with the birthday gifts in the direction of the Eastern Capital, Chao Gai, Wu Yong and the other bold fellows were preparing to carry out their plan to seize the birthday gifts when the convoy reached Yellow Earth Ridge. The plan had been rehearsed in every detail. Everyone knew his place and duty exactly. They had been informed beforehand by Bai Sheng of the approach of the convoy and had

hidden in a willow grove beyond the ridge. Chao Gai,
Wu Yong, Gongsun Sheng, Liu Tang and the three
Ruan Brothers were disguised as date merchants. Bai
Sheng was a wine vendor.

9

By a ruse they drugged the fifteen members of the
convoy and grabbed the birthday gifts. Before Yang
Zhi, the steward and the two captains came to, Chao
Gai and his companions had made off with the precious load.

On returning to his home village, Bai Sheng was
caught by the police. On being questioned, he named
Chao Gai as the leader of the seven who had stolen
the eleven loads of gold and jewels.

It so happened that news of this reached the ears
of Song Jiang, Chao Gai's close friend, clerk of the
county magistrate's court in Yuncheng. He was shocked. He knew that the crime Chao Gai had committed
was punishable by death.

He decided to warn Chao Gai of the danger threat-
ening him. He rode to his manor and found him
drinking with Wu Yong, Gongsun Sheng and Liu
Tang in the rear garden. Song Jiang hailed the ward
chief respectfully.

"Why have you come so unexpectedly sir?"

"You know my devotion, brother. I'd lay down
my life for you. They've broken the Yellow Earth

Ridge case! Bai Sheng has been taken to the prison in Jizhou. He's confessed and named you seven as accomplices. Escape quickly! Don't delay! The magistrate will send men this very night. You mustn't delay. If anything goes wrong, I won't be able to help you."

"Brother," said the startled Chao Gai, "I'll never be able to thank you enough."

Song Jiang mounted his horse and flew back to the county seat.

"What shall we do now?" Chao Gai asked his three companions.

"There's nothing to discuss," said Wu Yong. "'Of all the thirty-six possible solutions, the best one is — leave."

"But where should we go?"

"I'd say we should join the three Ruan brothers in their village. It's only a few steps away from Liangshan Marsh. The stronghold on the mountain top is thriving. When the officials and police go looking for robbers, they don't dare even glance in its direction. If the search gets too hot, we can always join the band."

"A very good idea."

They all agreed, and got started without delay. Wu Yong and Liu Tang packed up the purloined birthday gifts of gold an jewels into half a dozen loads, and directed his servants to set out shouldering the loads. The ward chief and the Taoist priest closed down the manor.

227

Meanwhile the magistrate of Yuncheng, having received instructions from the prefecture, summoned his sheriff and two constables and instructed them to proceed to Chao Gai's manor with a band of archers in order to arrest him for his part in the theft of the birthday gifts.

They left the town that very night. When they were in sight of the manor they stopped and conferred about how best to effect the arrest.

One of the constables proposed that they divide their forces into two groups. One of the groups would go quietly to the rear gate, the other would strike from the front gate.

Actually, both constables intended to let Chao Gai escape through the rear. They put on a show, creating a lot of noise and running about with the aim of speeding the ward chief's getaway.

Chao Gai ordered his servants to set fire to the manor. He and Gongsun Sheng, at the head of a dozen or so servants, dashed through the rear gate brandishing their halberds. Pretending to dodge an attack, the constables left a hole in the besiegers' line. The ward chief sent Gongsun Sheng and the servants plunging through, and then followed, protecting their rear. Chao Gai finally vanished into the night.

The pursuers soon straggled back. After hunting

all night they hadn't nabbed a single robber. All they could do was seize a few of the ward chief's neighbours and take them back to Yuncheng County.

11

The magistrate had the neighbours questioned, but they could give him no information.

"If you want to get at the truth," said one of the neighbours, "why not question his servants?"

The magistrate immediately dispatched men to Chao Gai's manor to apprehend the servants. After several hours they returned with two servants. When questioned the servants at first denied everything. But when they were beaten beyond endurance, they confessed.

"There were six of them who conferred with the ward chief," they said. "The only one we knew was a teacher in our township named Wu Yong. Another man is called Gongsun Sheng. He's a Taoist priest. Another is a big dark fellow named Liu. There were also three others we didn't know. Wu brought them. We heard him say, 'They're three brothers, fishermen, named Ruan.' That is the whole story."

The confession was recorded, and the magistrate wrote a detailed report to the prefect, who summoned Bai Sheng. Bai, seeing that denial was useless, named the three Ruan brothers and told him where they lived. The prefect was very pleased. "Now we're getting somewhere! Once we've taken the three Ruan brothers the case is half solved," said he.

12

We will now pick Chao Gai's story up at a later stage when he, with Lin Chong's help, overthrew the chieftains of Liangshan Marsh and assumed high command of the fortress.

Soon after Chao Gai took over the Liangshan Marsh stronghold, one success came after another. At a celebratory banquet, Chao Gai addressed the brigands.

"When we first came here seeking refuge, we hoped only to become junior officers under Wang Lun. Then Arms Instructor Lin Chong graciously relinquished the leadership to me. Now we have had two unexpected happy events in a row. First, we defeated the government troops, captured many men, horses and boats, and took District Garrison Commander Huang An, who led them. Second, we seized a great deal of gold, silver and other valuables. We owe all this to your talents, brothers."

From then on, Liangshan Marsh prospered. More and more men joined the stronghold. Bold fellows came like the wind from all over. New dwellings had to be built, and additional forts constructed on every side.

13

In Zengtou Village, southwest of the prefectural seat of Lingzhou, there lived over three thousand families. One was known as the Zeng Family Establishment. It was headed by Zeng the Elder. He had five sons, called the Five Tigers of the Zeng Family. The village was defended by six or seven thousand men and stockaded camps. They had built more than fifty cagecarts, boasting there was no room on earth for both the Liangshan Marsh chieftains and themselves.

They had composed a rhyme which was taught to all the children in the village. The rhyme went in part:

> . . . Liangshan Marsh we'll cleanly flush,
>
> Chao Gai to the capital we'll rush . . . .

Chao Gai was enraged. "How dare these animals be so unmannerly!" he fumed. "I'm going down there personally. If I don't capture those rogues, I won't return!"

"You're the leader of our fortress, brother," said the other chieftains. "You mustn't take action rashly. Let us go."

"You've gone many times. You must be weary from combat. This time I'm going."

The furious Chao Gai selected five thousand men and twenty chieftains, and set forth. He divided his forces into three columns and went down the mountain, ready to march on Zengtou Village.

Chao and his troops ferried across the river and soon neared Zengtou. Confronting them was a stockaded camp. The following morning Chao went with the chieftains for a closer look. Clearly, the village was strongly fortified.

Suddenly seven or eight hundred men emerged from a grove of willows. At their head was Kui, the fourth son in the Zeng family.

"You bandits from Liangshan Marsh are all rebels," he shouted. "I've been meaning to turn you over to the authorities and claim the reward, and now Heaven has sent you right into my arms! Get off your horses and be bound. What are you waiting for?"

Chao Gai was extremely angry. As he turned his head he saw Lin Chong riding forth to do battle with Kui.

The two horses met, and the warriors fought more than twenty rounds, with neither vanquishing the other. Kui realized he was no match for Lin Chong. He wheeled his mount and rode back to the willow grove. Chao Gai led his forces back to their camp. There they discussed strategy for attacking the village.

The battle continued for three days. The Liangshan Marsh forces suffered heavy losses. Of the twenty-five hundred men who had gone with Chao Gai only twelve or thirteen hundred were left.

Chao Gai and the chieftains hurriedly led their men in withdrawal. They had just traversed two turns in the road when they ran into a troop of enemy cavalry, who showered them with arrows. One arrow struck Chao Gai in the face, and he fell from his horse.

The chieftains came to see Chao Gai. The arrow was stuck in his cheek. They pulled it out. Blood flowed, and he fainted. Chao Gai had been struck by a poisoned arrow. The poison was working, and he was unable to speak. Lin Chong ordered that he be placed on a cart, and that the three Ruan brothers escort him back to the mountain fortress. The fifteen chieftains remaining in the camp conferred. Suddenly, a picket guarding the road rushed in. "Five enemy columns are heading this way."

Lin Chong immediately mounted his horse. The shouting foe were rapidly advancing. The chieftains did not resist. At Lin's order, they broke camp and withdrew. The Zeng family forces pursued them fiercely. The two sides fought a running battle for sixty *li* before the brigands could break free.

They hurriedly resumed the march in the direction of Liangshan Marsh. Halfway there they were met by a messenger bearing a command: they were to bring their troops back to the stronghold. There, new plans would be formulated.

The chieftains complied. On their arrival they went to see Chao Gai. He was no longer able to eat or drink, and his whole body was swollen. The chieftains all kept vigil outside his tent.

At dawn Chao Gai spoke to the chieftains. "Let whoever captures the bowman who slew me become the ruler of Liangshan Marsh."

Chao Gai closed his eyes and died.

BOOK THREE

CHAPTER EIGHT — WU YONG

1

The reader will undoubtedly recall mention of Wu Yong, the village school teacher they called 'Teacher' or 'Wizard', in our previous chapters.

This Wu Yong was instrumental in persuading the Ruan brothers to join in the venture of snatching the birthday gifts sent by Governor Liang of the Northern Capital to his father—in—law, Premier Cai in the Eastern Capital. It was he as well who had thought of a ruse for seizing the gifts.

When Chao Gai, Wu Yong and the others had escaped from the police with the help of Song Jiang, they decided to go up to the Liangshan Marsh stronghold. They first went to the inn run by Zhu Gui, which was a lookout for the brigands. When they told their story to Zhu Gui, he was delighted and immediately welcomed them.

Fitting a whistling arrow to his bow, he shot it into a cluster of reeds opposite the inn. Soon a small boat came out, rowed by one of the brigands. Zhu Gui wrote a letter of introduction for the fugitives, and gave it to the bandit, instructing him to deliver the letter to the stronghold.

The next morning Zhu Gui ordered a large boat, and invited the bold fellows on board. The boat set forth for the mountain fortress. They could hear drums beating and gongs clanging along the shore.

When the party disembarked, several scores of bandits came down the mountain and led them to the fortress gate. The leaders were waiting there to welcome them.

"I'm Wang Lun. The fame of Chao Gai, the Heavenly King has long thundered in my ears. It's a pleasure to welcome you to our humble stronghold," said the leader as he came out to great the party.

All went up the mountain and entered Fraternity Hall. Wang Lun insisted that the guests sit on the raised platform. Oxen were slaughtered, as well as pigs and sheep, and everyone feasted, to the accompaniment of drums and horns. As they drank, Chao Gai told the leaders the entire story. They continued their revels until evening. When the brigand chiefs escorted the visitors to the hostel.

Chao Gai was very pleased. "We've committed such serious crimes. Where else could we find refuge? If it weren't for the kindness of Chieftain Wang Lun we'd be in a real dilemma."

Wu Yong laughed coldly. Why was he sceptical?

2

The reason for Wu Yong's scepticism was that he

had been watching Wang Lun when Chao Gai was telling their story, and by the changes in the chieftain's facial expressions and manner during the narrative he could tell what was in his heart.

The next morning Lin Chong came to pay a call on Chao Gai and his friends. He complained bitterly of the treatment he had received at Wang Lun's hands since arriving at the fortress. During the conversation, Wu Yong threw out hints to Lin Chong that he sympathized with him, and would support him if things came to a showdown.

Just at this moment a bandit arrived from the stronghold to say that the chieftains invited them all to dinner.

"What shall we do, Teacher?" Chao Gai was uneasy.

"Don't worry, brother. The stronghold is going to have a change of masters. Lin Chong seems determined to have it out with Wang Lun."

Subsequent events, which are described in our stories about Lin Chong and Chao Gai, proved that Wu Yong's judgment was correct.

3

After Lin Chong had disposed of Wang Lun, Chao Gai proposed that Lin Chong be the leader of Mount Liangshan. But Lin would not accept the post. "I turned against Wang Lun because his heart was narrow, because he was jealous of the talents of Chao Gai and other heroes, " he explained. "Brother Chao is a gallant, generous man. He is intelligent and brave. He's famed and admired everywhere. I propose that he become the leader of the stronghold. What do you say?"

"Very appropriate, "cried the men.

Lin Chong pushed Chao Gai into the leader's chair. He called to the bandits to come to the pavilion and pay homage. A feast was prepared inside the fortress.

After dinner all the brigands proceeded to Fraternity Hall. Chao Gai was seated in the chair of honour, in the middle. Wu Yong took the second seat, as military adviser in charge of the military forces. Gongsun Sheng took the third chair, and Lin Chong the fourth. Liu Tang, Ruan the Second, Ruan the Fifth and Ruan the Seventh took the fifth, sixth, seventh and eighth places respectively. Other brigands took the remaining three seats. From then on, the positions of the eleven Liangshan heroes were fixed.

4

One day a bandit hurried up the mountain and announced, "Government troops from Jizhou, about two thousand of them, are sailing this way in five or six hundred boats, large and small! "

"They'll soon be here, " Chao Gai said to Wu

Yong in alarm. "How shall we deal with them?"

Wu Yong laughed. "There's nothing to worry about. I have a plan." Quietly he told the three Ruan brothers what to do, and then gave instructions to the other chieftains.

The troops from Jizhou were assembled in locally commandeered boats, and were divided into two squadrons. They proceeded separately across the lake, flags waving and soldiers yelling.

Three craft came towards the troops, each rowed by four men. One man was standing on the prow, a barbed spear in his hand.

One of the soldiers recognized them. "Those are the Ruan brothers," he told the commander.

"After them!" ordered the commander. "We'll catch all three!"

The soldiers sent a shower of arrows after the three craft. The Ruan brothers warded off the arrows with fox pelts, which they had whipped out of the cabins. The government vessels followed in hot pursuit. They had only gone two or three *li* when a small boat sped up from the rear.

"Stop chasing them," a man on the little craft cried. "The bandits have killed all our troops in the other squadrons and thrown them into the water. Now they've captured our boats!"

The commander groaned. He waved a white flag, signalling his other craft to abandon the chase and return. Just as they swung about, three vessels, followed by another dozen, were seen heading in their direction from behind, each with four or five men on board. Before the government commander could spread his flotilla in battle formation, cannon thundered from the reeds, which suddenly came alive with red flags.

A voice sang out from the rapidly approaching boats. "The commander can go — if he leaves his head behind! "

The commander ordered his men to row with all their might and get beyond the reeds. From both sides of the lake forty or fifty small vessels shot out and deluged the government soldiers with arrows. The commander tried desperately to get through this forest of feathered shafts. He had only three or four small boats left.

He leaped over into a fast little skiff. He could see his men were jumping into the water. Some were being hauled away on their boats. The vast majority had been slaughtered. Just as the commander was setting his skiff in action, a bandit who had been standing on the prow of a craft near the reeds reached out and caught it with a grappling hook. He bounded on board and grasped the commander around the waist.

" Struggle is useless, " shouted the bandit. He dragged the commander to the bank, and took him to the stronghold.

Great quantities of gold, silver and silk had been plundered. They were distributed among the rank and file as rewards. More than six hundred horses had been seized. Victories were won on the eastern lake and western lake.

The chieftains were very pleased. A feast was laid on at which fine home—made wine was served, as well as vegetables and fruit. Congratulations were exchanged all around.

This was the first of the many brilliant victories won by the Liangshan Marsh gallants after Wu Yong became the stronghold's Military Adviser.

5

Wu Yong was no known as 'Wizard' without reason.

One day, Song Jiang asked him if there were any people of note in the Northern Capital. Wu Yong recalled that there was a rich man called Lu Junyi, whose nickname was 'Jade Unicorn'. He was highly skilled in the martial arts. With cudgel and staff he had no equal.

"If we could get him to join our stronghold, we'd have no need to fear any government troops or police sent to catch us," said Song Jiang.

"You want him up here, brother? That's a simple matter." Without any further ado, Wu Yong laid out a plan for getting Lu Junyi to join the Liangshan Marsh outlaws.

The next day Wu Yong set out for the capital,

taking Li Kui along. When they came to the city gate, Wu Yong told the soldiers on guard that he was a wandering caster of horoscopes, and Li Kui his acolyte. They got in and strolled towards the centre of the city. Wu Yong rang a bell and chanted: "Fortune, destiny, fate. I predict life, foretell death. I know who shall rise high, and who shall fall low."

As they were passing Lu Junyi's warehouse, Lu, who was sitting in his office, asked one of his stewards what all the racket was about. The man told Lu that a Taoist fortune-teller from out of town was walking the streets offering his services.

"Invite him in," said Lu.

The steward went out and hailed him. "Reverend, the magnate asks you in."

"Who is he?"

"The Magnate Lu Junyi."

Wu Yong told Li Kui to come along, and entered the office. He approached Lu and bowed.

Lu bowed in return. "Where are you from, reverend? What is your name?"

"My name is Zhang Yung. I'm from Shandong originally. I can cast horoscopes. I predict births and deaths, high position or poverty. For an ounce of silver I can tell your fortune."

"When were you born?" asked Wu Yong.

"I'm thirty-two." Lu stated the year, month, day and hour of his birth.

Wu Yong took out an iron abacus, calculated a

moment, and then slammed it down. "Extraordinary!" he exclaimed.

Startled, Lu demanded, "What lies ahead for me?"

"I'll tell you frankly, if you don't take it amiss."

"Speak freely, reverend."

"Within the next hundred days, bloody tragedy will strike. Your wealth will be lost, and you will die by the sword."

Lu Junyi laughed. "You're wrong, reverend. I conduct my affairs with decorum. I do nothing unreasonable, I take no tainted money. How could I have incurred such a bloody fate?"

Wu Yong's face hardened. He rose, and walked towards the door. "People always prefer to hear what pleases them. Forget it. I'll leave you now."

"Don't be angry, reverend. I was only joking. I'd like to hear your instructions."

"Your fortune has always been good, Magnate. But within a hundred days, your head shall be separated from your body. This has been destined. There is no escape."

"Isn't there a way to avoid it?"

"Only if you go to a place one thousand *li* southeast of here," said Wu Yong. "Although you may suffer some shocks and frights, you will not be injured."

"If you can arrange that, I'll reward you."

6

Wu Yong thanked Lu Junyi, collected his abacus and went on his way. Their main job done, he and Li Kui left the city.

"Now we have to hurry back to the stronghold and prepare our welcome for Lu Junyi. Sooner or later, he'll come," said Wu confidently.

Wu Yong really had done his job well. Before long, Lu Junyi handed his affairs over to his most trusted adviser Yang Qing and bade farewell to his wife. Taking his chief steward Li Gu, a number of other servants and carts loaded with merchandise, he left the city.

On their way, an innkeeper warned Lu that he was nearing parts infested by bandits under Song Jiang. Lu only laughed scornfully and told his men to go forward. "I've always wanted to show my prowess with arms, but I've never met a worthy foe. Today, I have my chance, here and now," he cried.

As their convoy was passing a big forest, a shrill whistle rent the air. Lu ordered that the carts be pulled to one side, and kept under guard. The terrified drivers and porters crawled beneath the carts.

"When I knock the robbers down, you tie them up," Lu shouted.

Before the words were out of his mouth, four or five hundred outlaws emerged from the forest. From behind them came the sound of crashing gongs. Another four or five hundred brigands cut off Lu's retreat. A man leaped out of the forest. Lu recognize him: it was the fortune-teller. His acolyte, Li Kui, was behind him. Lu suddenly understood. Enraged, he twirled his halberd and charged. Li Kui met him with axes swinging. Before they had fought three rounds, Li Kui jumped from the combat circle, turned, and headed for the forest. Lu pursued, halberd leveled. By the time Lu reached the forest, his adversary was gone.

At this moment someone on the mountain slope called out, " You don't understand, Magnate. Our Military Adviser has made this plan. How can you escape?"

"Who are you, you bastard?" he yelled.

The man laughed. "I am Liu Tang."

"You thieving jerk, don't try to get away, " the magnate fumed. He dashed at Liu Tang, halberd in hand.

Before they had fought three rounds, Liu Tang fell back a few paces. Lu then found himself face to face with another brigand. As they were belabouring each other, gongs crashed on the mountain top. The brigand swiftly withdrew. Lu did not pursue him, returning instead to the edge of the forest to look for his carts and drivers. But the ten drivers and all the animals had vanished. He groaned.

Lu clambered to a high vantage point and looked around. Far in the distance, at the foot of a mountain slope, he saw a group of brigands driving the carts and animals in front of them. His chief steward and the other servants, tied together in a line, followed. They were being led to a grove of pines. Infuriated, Lu recklessly pursued the brigands.

Suddenly the sound of flutes wafted down from the mountain top. There, beneath a gold—spangled red silk umbrella, was Song Jiang, with Wu Yong to his left and Gongsun Sheng to his right. They were accompanied by a column of sixty or seventy men. All courteously hailed Lu Junyi.

"Magnate, we trust you've been well!"

Lu grew very angry, and cursed them by name. Wu Yong tried to soothe him.

"Calm yourself, brother. Song Jiang has long known of your virtue, and holds you in the greatest esteem He sent me to call at your gates and lure you up the mountain so that we might perform gallant deeds together. Please don't take it amiss."

7

To make a long story short, Lu Junyi frantically sought to escape, but in vain. He finally landed in the reeds, where he was picked up by a fisherman who was sculling a small boat. The fisherman was none other than Ruan the Second. Together with his two brothers, he seized Lu Junyi and hauled him ashore.

When they reached the bank, an attendant gave him an embroide red silk tunic and gown to wear. Eight brigands brought a sedan chair, assisted him into it, and set forth. Off in the distance a mounted troop was approaching to the accompaniment of drums and music. At its head were Song Jiang, Wu Yong and Gongsun Sheng.

Lu Junyi hastily got down from his sedan chair. Song Jiang knelt. The other chieftains did the same. Lu also dropped to his knees.

"Please sit in your sedan chair, Magnate," Song Jiang laughed.

To the sound of music, the procession climbed to Loyalty Hall. There, the hosts dismounted and led Lu into the hall. "Your fame, Magnate, has long thundered in my ears," said Song Jiang. "Being able to meet you today is one of the greatest good fortunes of my life. My brothers behaved rudely a while ago. We beg your forgiveness."

Wu Yong stepped forward. "The other day," he said, "on orders from brother Song Jiang, I called at your gates disguised as a fortune teller. My aim was to lure you up the mountain so that you might join us."

A large feast was laid on the next day in honour of the Magnate. When several rounds had been drunk, Song Jiang rose, goblet in hand. "Although our stronghold is small, and not a worthy place to water your horse, we hope you will consider our sincere fidelity. I gladly relinquish my position to you, Magnate. Please do not refuse."

But Lu Junyi refused categorically to become an outlaw. "I prefer death to accepting your proposal," he said.

The following day, Song Jiang gave the head steward Li Gu permission to return to the Northern Capital first with the carts, leaving Lu behind to rest for a few days. Wu Yong went on ahead to the shore of the lake to see Li Gu off. "Your master has already talked it over with us and agreed to stay, "he told the steward. "Today he's taken the second chieftain's chair. At first we were going to kill you all, but then we thought it would give our stronghold a bad name. So we're letting you go. Travel day and night and hurry home. But don't nourish any hopes that your master will return."

Li Gu bowed low. Wu Yong ordered that boats take the men and animals across the lake. They were shortly speeding along the road to the Northern Capital.

8

After Wu Yong went back to the banquet in Loyalty Hall, he besieged Lu with clever and persuasive arguments. The banquet did not end till late at night. Another feast was laid on the following day.

The day after, Song Jiang offered a feast, the next day it was Wu Yong, and the day after that it was Gongsun Sheng. There were over thirty chieftains, and each day one of them gave Lu a banquet. Time slipped away. More than a month passed by. Again

Lu proposed to leave.

"If you really must go, we'll have a few farewell drinks in Loyalty Hall." The following day, Song Jiang again laid on a feast. The other chieftains protested to Lu Junyi. "I risked my life in the Northern Capital to invite you here", Li Kui shouted, "and now you won't allow me to feast you. I'm going to hang on to your tail until you agree!"

Wu Yong laughed. "Who ever heard of such an invitation! Magnate, forgive him. But, in view of their sincerity, you really ought to stay a little longer"

Lu could not withstand the importunities of so many. He agreed to remain another short while. This stretched into an additional forty days. Autumn Festival time was rapidly approaching.

Lu longed to go home, and he spoke to Song Jiang about it. "That's easy enough," said Song. "Tomorrow, I'll see you to the shore."

Lu Junyi was delighted. The next day, his clothing and weapons were restored to him, and a column of chieftains escorted him down the mountain. They bade him farewell and returned to the stronghold.

9

The reader knows that Lu's chief steward Li Gu had gone on ahead to the Northern Capital. What the reader doesn't yet know is that Li Gu, in league with Lu Junyi's wife, had lodged a complaint against him with the governor, accusing Lu of having turned outlaw. On his return home Lu was seized, and after interrogation was taken to prison, and sentenced to exile on Shamen Island.

When Song Jiang heard of this, he dispatched two of his chieftains, Yang Xiong and Shi Xiu, to find out about Lu's fate, and report as soon as they got back from the Northern Capital. When Song Jiang learned that Lu Junyi had been captured and Shi Xiu subsequently arrested as well, he was shocked.

"You meant well at the time,"he told Wu Yong, "inviting the Magnate up the mountain to join our band. But because of this, today he's in trouble, and brother Shi Xiu as well. What can we do to rescue them?"

"Don't worry, brother. I'm not talented, but I have a plan. We can use the opportunity to relieve the Northern Capital of its money and grain for our own use! Tomorrow is an auspicious day. Divide our chieftains into two groups. Leave half here to guard the fortress. Give me the other half to attack the city."
Song Jiang mustered the necessary forces to march the following day.

"These two axes of mine haven't had any action for a long time,"said Li Kui. "I'm glad to hear that we're going to fight and pillage again. Let me have five hundred men and I'll take the Northern Capital, hack Governor Liang into mincemeat, and rescue Lu the Magnate and brother Shi Xiu! I'll do a thorough job of it!"

"Since you insist, you can go as a vanguard. Take five hundred bold fellows and set up an advance position. You can start tomorrow!"

The men had not seen battle for a long time, and they longed for action. They marched in contingents of a thousand men each.

Song Jiang was the commander-in-chief, Wu Yong his military adviser.

10

Meanwhile, a horseman sped to the commander of the government forces defending the city and announced that Song Jiang was approaching with an army of countless thousands. At dawn the next day, the defenders broke camp, moved forward, and deployed fifteen thousand infantry and cavalry in battle positions. The two government generals rode forward to meet Li Kui's vanguard. As one of the generals watched the Liangshan Marsh men galloping towards them, he remarked to the other scornfully, "Every day we hear about the bold fellows from Liangshan Marsh. Why, they're just a pack of dirty bandits, not worth mentioning. Why don't you nab the louts?"

Before the words were out of his mouth, a senior officer galloped forward with a hundred horsemen. Unable to withstand the charge, Li Kui and his men fled in all directions. The government troops chased them for a while. At this time, gongs and drums suddenly resounded behind a hill, and two cavalry units rode forth. Startled by the appearance of these reinforcements, the government generals abandoned their pursuit and hastily withdrew.

Again and again the government troops assaulted the Liangshan Marsh outlaws, but each time they would hear the thunder of drums and the crash of gongs, and a new contingent would appear and charge at them. The government armies suffered huge losses.

The two generals hurried to the city and reported to Governor Liang. That same night another government army was rushed to the battle area. The soldiers on both sides yelled. Song Jiang pointed with his whip and all three armies surged forward. Corpses soon covered the plain, blood flowed in rivers. It was a crushing defeat for the government troops. They lost a third of their men.

When Song Jiang made camp, Wu Yong said, "Beaten troops are always frightened. We ought to go after them before they recover their nerve. It's too good a chance to miss."

Song Jiang ordered his victorious forces to divide into four columns that evening and march through the night to attack the city.

As Song Jiang was making his plans to capture the city, a senior officer reported to the government generals that a row of fires had appeared on nearby hilltops. The generals mounted their horses and went with a troop of soldiers to take a look. Fires gleamed on the hills to the east and west. Suddenly, they heard thunderous shouts from behind. Racing in pursuit were Liangshan Marsh chieftains with their men.

The government troops were thrown into confusion. They broke camp and fled. But ahead of them drums pounded. A troop of cavalry was blocking their way. By dawn, the government troops had withdrawn to the outskirts of the city.

When Governor Liang heard the news, his soul was shaken from his body. He called a conference to discuss ways and means of saving the city. It was decided to write a letter to the premier, asking that crack troops be sent to the rescue, and all neighbouring areas notified to send relief troops quickly.

11

In the meantime, Song Jiang and his commanders attacked the Northern Capital every day, but were unable to break into the city.

One day Wu Yong came to see Song Jiang. "We've surrounded the Northern Capital for quite a while. Why hasn't an army been sent to its rescue? And no one comes out to do battle. We know that Governor Liang has dispatched emissaries to the Eastern Capital to report the emergency. Surely Premier Cai, his father−in−law, would send an army under an able general to his rescue. Could it be that instead of relieving this place, they're attacking our Mount Liangshan stronghold? That must be it. We should call in our forces, but not withdraw completely. We mustn't be hasty. Tonight, we'll have the infantry withdraw first. But we'll leave two cavalry units in ambush, on the two sides of the valley between here and our stronghold. When they learn in the city that we've pulled out, they'll surely chase us. This is the plan we must follow." Song Jiang approved the plan and gave orders accordingly.

The news of the withdrawal of Song Jiang's troops was reported to Governor Liang. The governor summoned his generals. "Evidently the premier has sent an army to capture their fortress," said one of the generals, "and the knaves are afraid of losing their lair, so they're rushing to get back. This is our chance to slaughter them and nab Song Jiang."

At this moment, a messenger arrived with a directive from the Eastern Capital ordering the governor's troops to join in exterminating the handits. "Pursue them if they retreat," the directive said. Governor Liang promptly ordered his generals to lead two contingents and harry Song Jiang's forces from the east and the west.

At the head of the withdrawing units, Song Jiang observed the soldiers pouring out of the city to give chase. He and his men moved quickly, as if their lives depended on it. Then cannon boomed behind the government troops.

The generals, startled by the blast, reined in their horses and looked. To their rear they saw a bristling array of banners and heard the wild thunder of battle drums. Then a thousand men under two Liangshan Marsh chieftains surged towards them from left and right in a murderous charge.

It was too late to take defensive action. The government commanders knew they had been tricked, and led a full speed retreat. They ran right into a troop of cavalry, which slaughtered them savagely.

The commanders fled back into the city and bolted the gates. Song Jiang's troops resumed their orderly withdrawal.

12

Next spring Song Jiang and Wu Yong conferred again on how to crack the Northern Capital, rescue Lu Junyi and Shi Xiu, and punish Li Gu and Lu's adulterous wife.

Wu Yong frequently sent scouts into the city to nose around. He found out that Governor Liang was afraid that the Mount Liangshan bandits were going to attack, and had got the jitters. Wu Yong also had proclamations put up in all the market places in and around the city, assuring the populace that they would not be harmed, and that when the Liangshan Marsh troops entered the city, they would seek out specific enemies. Premier Cai kept writing to Governor Liang, urging him to spare the lives of Lu Junyi and Shi Xiu.

"It's now the Lunar New Year and the Lantern Festival is rapidly approaching," Wu Yong said to Song Jiang. "I'd like to take this opportunity to slip some men into the city first, and then attack. By coordinating action inside and outside, we can break through the defenses."

Song Jiang was impatient to attack, but he agreed to this plan. The next day Wu Yong told two of his chieftains to assume the garb of rice merchants, push barrows into the city and find quarters. The moment they saw the signal — a fire atop a big building called Jade Cloud Mansion — they were to seize the city's East Gate.

Two other chieftains were instructed to disguise themselves as beggars. They were to sleep under the eaves of some buildings in the busiest section of the city. When they saw the signal, they were to hurry and lend a hand.

Two more chieftains were directed to dress up as travellers, and to put up at an inn outside the East Gate. On seeing the signal, they were to kill the soldiers guarding the gate, take it over, and keep it as a ready exit.

Wu Yong told Wu Song and Sagacious Lu to move into a temple outside the city in the guise of itinerant monks. At the signal they were to go to the South Gate and block the government troops attempting to charge out.

Other chieftains were given assignments as well, and they all set out on their various missions.

13

"Every year," said Governor Liang, "we put on a big display of lanterns to celebrate the first full moon, and make merry with the populace. But the Liangshan Marsh bandits have raided us twice recently. I' m afraid a lantern festival might attract trouble. I'm considering calling it off. What do you think?"

"I think the robbers have stealthily withdrawn," said one of the generals. "You needn't let them concern you, Your Excellency. If we don't have a lantern display this year and those rogues find out about it, they're sure to sneer at us. Follow the example of the Eastern Capital and celebrate the Lantern Festival for five full days, with revels all through the night. You too must join in, Your Excellency, and celebrate with the people. I'll lead a cavalry unit to the outskirts of the city to ensure that the populace is not disturbed."

Governor Liang was pleased with the suggestion. After he and his officials had discussed and agreed upon it, he had public proclamations issued accordingly. Every household in every street and lane had lanterns ready. An artificial hill was erected in front of the Jade Cloud Mansion. From morning till night the mansion resounded with music and song.

Scouts reported all this to Mount Liangshan. Wu Yong was delighted. He informed Song Jiang. Song wanted to lead the attack on the Northern Capital personally, buy Wu Yong disapproved.

"Let me go in your place," Wu Yong proposed. He mustered eight contingents, all cavalry. When the command was given, the eight set forth.

Now the chieftain whose mission it was to light a fire on the top of the Jade Cloud Mansion as a signal clambered over the city wall at night. Unable to find accommodation at an inn, he wandered the streets all day and at night rested in a temple. On the thirteenth he went to the centre of the city and watched the citizens hanging their lanterns. As he stood there watching, he saw the other chieftains who had infiltrated the city strolling by, mixing with the crowds.

14

Meanwhile, clamour arose in front of the Jade Cloud Mansion. Someone exclaimed, "The men of Liangshan Marsh are at the West Gate!"

At that moment, enormous flames shot into the sky from the roof of the mansion. That was the signal. Governor Liang hastily mounted and started to ride to the scene. But two big fellows pushed over their wheel barrows, blocking the road, and then proceeded to pour oil on them and set them afire.

Liang headed for the East Gate. Two other big

fellows strode murderously forward, twirling halberds. The guards at the gate fled, and the Liangshan Marsh men captured the gate.

With his retinue Liang flew to the South Gate. There he heard voices crying out that a big fat monk with a Buddhist staff and a pilgrim with a pair of sharp knives were yelling and slaughtering their way into the city.

Liang turned his steed and went back to his residence. He saw two Liangshan Marsh outlaws felling men left and right with their steel pitchforks. He hurriedly rode to the West Gate. But all over the city people were scurrying about in terror. Screams and wails resounded in every household. In a dozen places flames brightened the sky. Confusion reigned.

Liang raced to the top of the city wall above the South Gate and peered out. A huge array of men and horses was approaching. The contingent was nearly at the gate. He went again to the East Gate. There he saw an army advancing rapidly in the city.

Throwing all caution to the winds, Liang dashed through the South Gate. Murderous cries arose on both sides. He finally managed to break through, protected by his officers and men. Meanwhile, Liangshan Marsh outlaws had slaughtered the governor's family, old and young, good and bad.

Some chieftains had planted themselves in front of the prison to prevent anyone from entering. When they saw the signal fire, they smashed in the door,

unlocked the fetters and released the two prisoners.
All quickly emerged through the prison gate, and hastened to Lu Junyi's home. The Magnate led the
chieftains in search of his wife and his steward Li Gu.

When Li Gu heard that an army of bold fellows
from Liangshan Marsh had entered the city and saw
the fires raging on all sides, he was frightened out of
his wits. He consulted Lu's wife. They packed some
valuables and stole out through the rear gate. They
headed for the river, hoping to find a place to hide.
But Yan Qing and a chieftain from Liangshan Marsh
nabbed them there, dragged them down to a boat, and
headed towards the East Gate.

When Lu Junyi found his wife and steward gone,
he ordered his servants to pack his gold, silver and
other precious things, load them on carts and take
them to the mountain fortress for distribution.

The sky was already light. Wu Yong had the
trumpets blow the call for their forces to assemble. Li
Gu and Lu's wife were brought forward. Lu ordered
that they be kept under guard until their disposition
could be decided upon.

15

"We're short of money and grain," said Song
Jiang to the assembled chieftains, "but to the east of
here are two towns that have both. One is Dongping,
the other Dongchang. Although we've never disturbed

their people, when we asked them to lend us some grain, they flatly refused. We must capture these towns. I'll lead an army against Dongping, and let Lu Junyi command an army against Dongchang."

All the chieftains agreed. The arrangements were made, and the following day the two armies, each numbering ten thousand infantry and cavalry, set forth against the two towns.

Song Jiang sent chieftain Shi Jin into Dongping to scout around. But Shi Jin was seized by the police as soon as he entered Dongping. Song dispatched Mistress Gu to Dongping to find out what had happened to Shi Jin and to let him know that a plan had been made for him to escape at the end of the month. Wu Yong suggested to Song Jiang a way of getting her into Dongping. "First, you must attack the county seat of Wenshang. The people there are sure to flee to Dongping. As soon as they do, Mistress Gu can mingle with the refugees and slip into the town of Dongping with them."

Song Jiang mustered five hundred men and sent them against Wenshang. Sure enough, the residents scurried to Dongping to escape the battle. Mistress Gu mingled with the crowds and entered the town of Dongping.

We know already from the story about Mistress Gu that her plans miscarried through no fault of her own.

At Wu Yong's urging, the outlaws attacked

Dongping. On four sides outside the town cannon boomed. The gates swung wide. Song Jiang's forces surged into the town. First, they freed the chieftains that had been seized by the government troops. Then they broke open the granaries, sent part of the grain and money to the mountain stronghold and distributed the rest among the populace.

Song Jiang and the chieftains gathered in the prefectural office. Zhang Qin, the government commander, who had wounded many of their brothers in the battle for the town, was brought forward. The chieftains wanted to kill him. But Song Jiang ordered that he be untied, and came down the steps to greet him.

"We offended your mighty prestige by mistake," he apologized. "Please don't hold it against us." He invited Zhang Qin into the hall.

Before the words were out of Song's mouth, Sagacious Lu rushed up with raised staff to smite Zhang Qin. Song Jiang stopped him. "If you brothers insist on vengeance, Heaven will not protect you, and you'll die beneath the sword!" he cried.

The chieftains had no reply. The troops were mustered in preparation for a return to the mountain. The return journey was uneventful, and they soon reached the fortress.

16

A feast of celebration was held. Each took his

place according to rank. When everyone had eaten and drunk, Song Jiang addressed the gathering.

"Brothers," he said, "let each of you carry out your duties of leadership, and hearken without fail to orders. Whoever disobeys shall be punished according to military law."

He then read the chain of command. The two highest leaders were himself and Lu Junyi, the two chiefs of staff were Wu Yong and Gongsun Sheng. He also designated the commanders in charge of money and grain control, the main cavalry, the light cavalry, the infantry, water defenses, and so on.

Each chieftain received his seals, and the feasting ended. All were very drunk. The chieftains left to take up their posts.

Song Jiang, very drunk, wrote a poem which showed his eager pursuit of amnesty.

17

While this was taking place, in the Eastern Capital the emperor was conducting a session of the Council for Reports to the Throne. The emperor had approved a suggestion made by one of his ministers that a royal amnesty be issued and a high minister go to Liangshan Marsh to offer the amnesty to the Liangshan Marsh outlaws on the condition that they fight against the Liao Tartars who had occupied nine border prefectures, and swept down to pillage

Shandong, Shanxi, Henan and Hebei. The emperor designated Marshal Chen as emissary, and instructed him to proceed to the stronghold at once.

When Marshal Chen and his retinue reached their destination, they were greeted by Song Jiang and other chieftains. One of the chieftains read out the amnesty in a loud voice. The amnesty was couched in an insolent tone and aroused the ire of Song Jiang and his men.

Suddenly, Li Kui leaped down from a beam overhead. He snatched the amnesty and tore it into shreds. He then grabbed Marshal Chen and began pummelling him with his fists. The others pulled him away from the emissary and hustled him out of the hall.

18

Song Jiang summoned the chieftains to a feast. "Although the court decree wasn't very intelligent, you shouldn't have behaved so impetuously," he said.

"Don't delude yourself, brother," said Wu Yong. " There will be an amnesty some day. But why reproach the brothers for getting so angry? The court's attitude was too contemptuous. Forget about all that for now. Order full equipment for the cavalry, weapons for the infantry, and a refurbishment of our naval vessels. Sooner or later the government is going to send a big punitive army against us. We've got to slaughter their soldiers and down their horses in one or two battles, so that they're bereft of their armour and fear us in their dreams. That will be the time to talk about amnesty again."

"Absolutely right," said the chieftains. The feasting ended, and they retired to their respective quarters.

19

Meanwhile, Marshal Chen returned to the Eastern Capital to report to the throne. The emperor was very angry. He turned to the premier. "Those bandits have been wreaking havoc for a long time. Who can we send to annihilate them?"

"We cannot succeed without a large force. In my humble estimation, the Chancellor of Military Affairs should lead the expedition."

Wu Yong's judgment proved correct. Government troops numbering in the thousands, both infantry and cavalry, and countless war ships were put under the command of the Chancellor of Military Affairs, Tong Guan. Within ten days they were ready, and set forth Liangshan Marsh.

Wu Yong had it all planned out. When Tong Guan's troops approached, gonegs sounded behind the hills, and around the bend in the road came five hundred outlaw infantry led by Li Kui and other chieftains.

No sooner had Tong Guan's soldiers chased off in pursuit of the outlaws than cannon boomed on the rear of the mountain, and out flew a body of brigand cavalry. Another cavalry unit came sweeping around the west side of the mountain. Hurriedly the government generals repaired to the centre of the army and established defensive formations.

Riders bearing blue, red, white and black banners, twirling their weapons astride their steeds, advanced from different directions and halted at the edge of the battlefield.

The outlaw forces were laid out in a huge octagon, cavalry grouped with cavalry, infantry with infantry, all bristling with weapons – a formidable array! Infantry and cavalry together, the outlaw forces totalled two thousand. But their manner of deployment was not to be underestimated.

From his command platform Tong Guan looked over their octagon, the brigands' bold cavalry and their heroic infantry. His soul flew from him in fright, and his heart dropped.

"I couldn't understand why government troops were defeated each time they sought to capture these bandits," he cried, "Who knew they were so formidable!" He watched for a long time, and heard the steady beat of the gongs and war drums of Song Jiang's army.

20

Three units of Song Jiang's vanguard raced across the field. They ploughed into Tong Guan's army with swords and axes, and inflicted a crushing defeat. Badly mauled, the government troops scattered, abandoning arms and equipment, yelling in fright. More than ten thousand soldiers were cut down.

Wu Yong had the trumpeters blow assembly. "Stop the pursuit and slaughter," he ordered. "We only want to give them a sample!" The outlaws returned to their stronghold, where they reported their exploits, and claimed rewards.

Tong Guan was very disturbed over the losses his army had sustained, and summoned his generals for a conference. "Don't worry," his generals reassured him. "We've had a temporary set-back because our soldiers were unfamiliar with the terrain. We'll reorganize and rest for three days to let our men regain their morale and give our horses a breather. Then we'll stretch our entire army into a long line, all on foot, and advance. It'll be like a mountain snake. This next battle we're sure to win."

"An excellent plan," said Tong Guan. "Just what I was thinking myself." He issued appropriate orders. On the third day the government troops set forth.

There is hardly any need to say that this time again Tong Guan and his generals suffered a crushing defeat. Tong Guan, protected by his officers and men, fled to the Eastern Capital.

Song Jiang conferred in Loyalty Hall with Wu Yong and the other chieftains. "Once Tong Guan reaches the capital and reports to the emperor, he's sure to raise another expedition," Wu Yong predicted. "We must make suitable preparations." "I agree entirely," said Song Jiang. "We must send a man to learn what's going on. But which of our brothers should it be?" A chieftain named Dai Zong volunteered to go to the Eastern Capital to find out all about the military preparations being made. Liu Tang offered to go with him. That day the two men packed some belongings and went down the mountain.

21

In the capital, the premier designated Marshal Gao Qiu to lead another expedition against the Liangshan Marsh outlaws.

"Liangshan Marsh is eight hundred *li* in circumference," said Gao. "Without fighting ships it's impossible to advance. I request permission, therefore, to cut timber in the neighbourhood of the marsh and have carpenters build boats. Otherwise grant me funds to buy civilian boats and convert them to military use."

"I authorize you to do whatever is necessary and possible."

Meanwhile Dai Zong and Liu Tang spent a few

days in the Eastern Capital collecting information. Then they hastened through the night to the mountain fortress. When Song Jiang heard that Marshal Gao was personally going to lead an expedition against him, that he had mustered a hundred and thirty thousand troops from all over, and that ten commandants would be serving as generals, he was shocked and frightened. He went into conference with Wu Yong.

"Have no fear, brother," said Wu Yong. "I've heard of those ten commandants. They appeared very heroic when there was no one around to match them. But today, against our band of fine brothers, they're has-beens. You have nothing to worry about. Before the ten columns arrive, I'll give them a scare!"

"How will you do that?"

"They're to meet in Jizhou. I'll send two quick killers to wait on the outskirts. When the troops draw near, they will slaughter a few."

The two chieftains selected for the mission were given a thousand men earch. They were ordered to patrol the outskirts of Jizhou, and intercept and kill approaching government troops. The naval commanders were directed to seize enemy boats.

Although more than twenty days had passed, Gao was still in the capital. The emperor sent a message urging him to march. At last the army departed. One after another the ten columns neared Jizhou.

The advance unit arrived at a place called

Phoenix Tail Slope. They were just skirting a grove at the foot of the slope when a troop of cavalry trotted out from behind the base of the hill and blocked the road. The government troops gave battle, trying to break through. They smashed open the road block and fought their way free.

As the column passed the grove, another cavalry troop sudenly appeared before them. The commandant fled. The two Liangshan Marsh chieftains gave chase. They had nearly caught up when another government column cut in ahead at an angle. The Liangshan Marsh chieftains withdrew.

The ten government columns camped on the outskirts of Jizhou. The columns felled timber in the nearby hills and confiscated doors and windows from the villagers to build shelters and make beds for themselves. They caused severe losses to the local people.

Gao remained in his headquarters in the city, grabbing more recruits for his expedition. Anyone who had no silver for bribes was put in the foremost assault ranks. But if a man was able to spread a bit of money around he stayed at the centre of the forces and received frequent commendations for valour.

The naval forces arrived a day or two later. The marshal summoned the ten commandants for a strategy conference. The commandants had a proposal. "Let the infantry and cavalry go ahead and lure out the bandits. Then send in the naval forces to destroy their lair. They won't be able to fight on two fronts and we'll capture them all. " Gao agreed. He ordered his troops to set out. Each unit had its orders.

The two Liangshan Marsh scouts, Dai Zong and Liu Tang returned to the fortress and reported on their strategy. Song Jiang and his chieftains led the outlaw army down the mountain.

22

When the government infantry and cavalry failed to make headway, the naval forces went into action. But when they wound deep into the marsh, a cannon sounded from the mountain slope and from every side small boats converged. The soldiers on the government craft, who were rather frightened to start with, completely panicked when they saw the small craft swarming out from the depths of the reeds and cutting them off from each other. Most of them abandoned ship and fled.

The generals hastily turned their vessels around. But the shallow channel they had navigated earlier had been jammed by the outlaws with logs and brushwood that snagged their oars and blocked their passage.

Marshal Gao saw that his entire flotilla was in disarray and that his men were fleeing towards the mountains. His boats had been rounded up and captured. He ordered his troops back to Jizhou. His military prestige damaged, his energies depleted, Gao could only encamp in the city and wait for reinforcements.

The reinforcements did not arrive, and Marshal Gao fretted impatiently. Then one day the gatekeeper entered and announced the arrival of the reinforcements. "What about boats?" Gao asked.

"We confiscated over fifteen hundred large and small boats along the way. They're all waiting below the lock."

Gao was very pleased. He ordered that the craft be congregated in a wide bay and grouped in threes. Each group was to be decked with planks and chained together, so as to carry the maximum load of infantry. The cavalry would escort them along the banks.

By the time the dispersement of troops had been settled, the Mount Liangshan chieftains knew all about it. Wu Yong instructed Liu Tang to strengthen defenses along the waterways. He told the naval chieftains to prepare small boats, nail iron plates to their prows, and fill their holds with brushwood sprinkled with sulphur and saltpetre. These would wait in the inlets.

He also ordered that signal cannon be placed on all the surrounding heights. Gongs and drums and fireworks were to be readied along the river to create the impression that well—manned military encampments were at hand.

Wu Yong's plan for the men of Liangshan

Marsh was completed.

In Jizhou, Marshal Gao hastened the departure of his contingents. Gao donned his armour, the drums thundered thrice and the boats in the bay set sail, while on land the cavalry swung into a trot. The craft sped forward like arrows and the horses seemed to fly, as the government troops pushed into Liangshan Marsh. They gradually drew closer to the shore. The assault squad landed first. Six or seven hundred soldiers started clambering up the bank. A cannon boomed within the willows. On each side, war drums beat. A contingent of outlaws burst into view on the left. On the other side another contingent suddenly appeared. The two units, each composed of five hundred outlaws, swarmed towards the bank. By the time the government commander yelled out the order for his troops to return to the boats he had already lost more than half his men.

A string of cannon shots sounded on a hilltop and the reeds began to rustle. From the criss—crossing inlets in the reeds and water lilies a number of small craft sped out and dispersed amid the government flotilla. A drum sounded, and on each little boat torches were lit. This was in accordance with Wu Yong's plan, whereby the naval chieftains had loaded the craft with dry reeds and brushwood sprinkled with oil, sulphur and saltpetre. In an instant, great flames were leaping skyward, and the small boats closed in on the larger vessels. Soon, from one end to the other, the entire government flotilla was ablaze.

24

Corpses littered the waterways of Liangshan Marsh, their blood crimsoning the waves. Those soldiers who could swim escaped with their lives. Those who couldn't drowned. Prisoners were escorted under guard to the fortress.

Meanwhile Marshal Gao, leading his army of reinforcements to the water's edge, heard the continuous boom of cannon and the steady beat of drums. He saw soldiers emerging from the water and crawling up the banks and running. An officer told him that all the boats had been burned.

Gao's heart chilled with alarm. Drums suddenly thundered on the hills ahead. A troop of horsemen burst forth and blocked their path. When Gao and his contingent rounded the foot of a hill, they were attacked from behind by another troop and sufered some casualties. They travelled another six or seven *li*, and another outlaw troop caught up with them and inflicted further losses. After another eight or nine *li* still another troop harassed them from the rear, imposing still more casualties. These were tactics devised by the brilliant strategist and tactician Wu Yong — not preventing retreat but persistently raiding from behind.

Panic—stricken, Gao flew back to Jizhou. The battered government troops wanted only to flee and were incapable of protecting their rear. When they reached Jizhou they saw flames rising from the fort on the outskirts and heard shouts of alarm. The Liangshan Marsh men had set the city ablaze with a few torches. A count of Gao's troops showed that he had lost more than half his men.

25

Song Jiang and his chieftains were conferring when a messenger arrived from Jizhou. "The imperial court has sent an emissary with a decree granting amnesty and conferring official posts. I've been dispatched by Marshal Gao to invite all of you chieftains to the walls of Jizhou for a ceremonial reading of the decree."

When Song Jiang heard these joyous tidings, a smile broke out over all his face. He ordered his chieftains to prepare for the reading of the imperial document.

"Don't be so hasty, brother." urged Lu Junyi. "Marshal Gao is probably up to something. You can't rush into this!"

"We've beaten that rogue Gao so badly, his gall is chilled and his heart is shattered." said Wu Yong. "No matter how elaborate a scheme he may have, it won't work. Besides, we're all gallant warriors. There's no need to worry."

Wu Yong arranged for a thousand infantry to lie in ambush on the east road to Jizhou, and another thousand cavalry to lie in ambush on the west road. If they heard a series of cannon shots they were to charge to Song Jiang's rescue at the North Gate. After all the arrangements had been made, the chieftains descended the slope.

Meanwhile, in Jizhou flags were displayed on the city walls, except above the North Gate, where an imperial yellow banner was unfurled bearing the words "The Emperor's Edict". Gao, the emissary and high officials then mounted the wall and awaited the arrival of the Liangshan Marsh chieftains.

A chieftain with an advance cavalry unit of five hundred made a circuit of the city, and headed north. This was reported to Marshal Gao, who then went to the ramparts of the outer wall himself.

Song Jiang's army could be seen approaching far to the north. On horseback, the foremost of the chieftains — Song Jiang, Lu Junyi, Wu Yong, Gongsun Sheng — bowed from their saddles and hailed Marshal Gao.

On Gao's instructions, an officer shouted from the top of the wall, "The imperial court has deigned to pardon your crimes and has sent a special decree. Why do you come in armour?"

Song Jiang sent one of the chieftains to the foot

of the wall with his reply. "We have not yet heard the gracious statement and don't know what it contains. We therefore dare not come unprotected. If Marshal Gao will summon all the residents of the city and let them hear the decree together with us, we will remove our armour."

Gao issued the appropriate order, and before long all the citizens of Jizhou were assembled. Only then did Song Jiang and his chieftains advance and dismount.

From atop the wall, the emissary read:

> Edict: . . . We hear that for a long time a band has congregated on Mount Liangshan, unresponsive to kindly exhortations to restore goodness to their hearts. We dispatch our emissary with this decree: obliterate Song Jiang ... Lu Junyi and the other chieftains' crimes, we grant them amnesty. Let the leaders report to the capital to give thanks. Let their followers return home...

When the words "obliterate Song Jiang" were read out, Wu Yong said to one of the chieftains, "Did you hear that?"

The chieftain shouted, "Since you won't amnesty our Big Brother, why should we surrender?" He notched an arrow to his bow, pulled it to the full, and yelled to the emissary, "Take a look at my magic arrow!" The feathered shaft struck the emissary be-

277

tween his eyes.

All four gates of the city opened. spewing out government troops. Cannon thundered, and Li Kui came charging from the east with brigand infantry, while from the west a cavalry troop charged in an attack. Song Jiang and his unit then turned around and charged, so that the local contingents were being attacked from three sides. Thrown into great confusion. they were slaughtered by the score as they fled. Song Jiang and his men did not pursue them, but returned to the Liangshan Marsh stronghold.

26

After the murderous battle at the walls of Jizhou, Song Jiang was anxious. "Twice they have come with amresties, and both times we injured the emissary. That makes our crimes more serious than ever. What are we going to do? The court will surely dispatch an army to punish us."

He sent a scout down to find out what was happening and report back as soon as possible. In a few days the man returned with the details. Song Jiang learned that Gao had raised a navy, and that a fleet of hundreds of vessels, large and small, was being built. Also that the Eastern Capital had dispatched reinforcements under capable generals. "How can we stop their ships when they come flying across the water?"

Wu Yong laughed. "What is there to be afraid of?

It will take them several months to build their vessels.
We've forty or fifty days yet. Send a couple of
brothers down to get into their shipyard and stir them
up a bit!"

We know already from the story of Mistress Gu
how she and her husband Sun Xin stole into the
shipyard and started a blaze there, setting all the
vessels under construction afire. Yelling in alarm, the
artisans and labourers knocked down the palisade and
fled into the night.

27

To cut a long story short, Marshal Gao mobilized
thousands of people and built a great fleet and
attacked Mount Liangshan. In three battles the
outlaws wiped out more than half his forces. The
marshal himself was seized and taken to the
stronghold. Song Jiang not only did not kill him, but
treated him royally and sent him back to the capital.
All the prisoners were also let go. While he was on
Mount Liangshan, the marshal made a solemn oath to
petition the emperor for an amnesty for all the
outlaws. Song Jiang dispatched two of his cheiftains
with him. But the marshal had them confined in his
residency and wouldn't let them out.

Upon Wu Yong's suggestion, two more chieftains
were sent to the capital to inquire what was going on
and to find someone who could convey their wishes to

the emperor. They were told to try to get in touch with Marshal Su, an extremely virtuous and generous man, to ask him to intervene for them with the emperor.

The following day, when the emperor held court and received the homage of his officials, Marshal Su came forward and knelt before the throne. "Although I have no talent, I would be glad to go to Mount Liangshan and order Song Jiang and his men to return to the capital."

The emperor was very pleased. "I'll write the document myself," he exclaimed. After penning the amnesty, he impressed the imperial seal on it. The marshal took his leave of the emperor and left.

When Gao heard what had happened he was terrified. He was afraid to appear before the emperor.

Mounting his horse, Marshal Su left the city. Officials saw him and his entourage out of the capital. The party proceeded rapidly towards Jizhou. As soon as Marshal Su and his entourage reached Jizhou, word was sent to Mount Liangshan. The following day, all the chieftains, big and small, welcomed the emissary with great fanfare to the fortress, and escorted him to Loyalty Hall.

One of the chieftains read the imperial decree:

    " . . . Song Jiang, Lu Junyi and their men are loyal and righteous, and do not engage in violent persecution. Although they have committed crimes, it was not without reason. In view of their sincerity, I sympathize with them. I have directed Marshal Su to deliver my amnesty to Song Jiang and the other offenders presently residing in Liangshan Marsh.... From the date of this decree let them cast doubt aside, return quickly and submit. Imperial tasks will be given them! "

Song Jiang directed that wine be poured, and invited Marshal Su to be seated in the centre of the hall. The chieftains paid their respects.

After several days, though Song Jiang and his chieftains were reluctant to let him go, Marshal Su said he had to leave for the capital. "You don't understand," he explained. "It's been some time since I delivered the amnesty. If you heroes return promptly, all will be well. If you don't, false and jealous ministers will very likely gossip."

The next day, to the beating of drums and trilling of fifes, the chieftains accompanied the marshal down the mountain.

28

Song Jiang ordered that a ten-day close-out be held and all the property of the stronghold be disposed of. The neighbouring populace was invited to come and attend. From the storerooms gold and silver, silks and satins were apportioned among the chieftains and officers and men. When everything had been distributed, everyone packed up and left for the capital.

29

We'll not recount in detail how Song Jiang and his men were treated in the capital. Suffice it to say that the emperor was pleased with them. But his ministers were jealous of their talents and concocted plots against them.

That year, the king of the Liao Tartars dispatched his armies over the mountains. In four columns, they swept down and overran Shandong, Shanxi, Henan and Hebei.

Four crooked ministers hatched a scheme. They arranged for one of them to propose to the emperor that Song Jiang and his chieftains be ordered to smash the invaders. They concealed the true force of the Liao Tartars and the danger situations of the country. They hoped thereby to exterminate the whole hundred and eight of Liangshan heroes.

They hadn't expected that another important minister would interfere. This was none other than Marshal Su. He overheard them making the proposal to the emperor, and appealed directly to the emperor: " The Liao Tartars have occupied nine prefectures with a hundred thousand troops, and every county is petitioning for relief. We have sent some units, but the enemy is too powerful. Our forces can't cope with them. In my humble opinion, if we dispatched Song jiang and his fine generals and all the troops under their command to the border, they could defeat the Liao bandits. I beg Your Majesty to consider my proposal."

The emperor personally drew up an edict naming Song Jiang as the Vanguard General against the Liao Tartars, and stating that his chieftains would be awarded official rank according to how well they distinguished themselves.

Marshal Su brought the edict to Song Jiang's camp and told him the emperor's intention.

The next day the emperor received Song Jiang and his chieftains in the Hall of Martial Heroes. "Go forth and crush the Liao Tartars,"the emperor urged. " Let us hear news of victory soon. We shall make much important use of you. As for your generals, they shall be awarded rank according to their merit. Let there be no delay!"

Song Jiang returned to his camp and ordered his commanders to prepare to march. Every day the army covered sixty *li* before making camp. The march was uneventful, and after a time they neared the borders of the Liao territory.

" The Liaos have been invading us in four columns,"Song Jiang said to Wu Yong. "Should we divide up and go after them, or attack their cities and towns?"

"It's a vast territory and thinly populated. If we split up we won't be able to coordinate. Better take a few cities first, and then we'll see. If we hit them hard they'll naturally call back their soldiers."

"An excellent plan," said Song Jiang. He summoned one of the chieftains who knew the north well. "Which is the nearest prefecture?"

"Tanzhou is right ahead. It's a vital entry to Liao territory. A deep river called the Lushui winds around the prefectural city and connects with the River Weihe. You'll need warships to attack Tanzhou. Once our flotilla arrives we can assault from land and water togethe, and take the city."

Song Jiang dispatched a chiftain to urge his naval chieftains to hasten their armada and assemble in the Lushui.

30

We will not tire our reader with a detailed narration of the wars of the Mount Liangshan gallants against the Liao Tartars. We will just mention that in every operation and every battle Wu Yong displayed fully his talents as a strategist and tactician.

Using force and guile, Song Jiang's forces captured four major Liao cities and killed a number of skilled Tartar generals. Liao was beset by troubles. When the Liangshan Marsh forces neared Youzhou, the gateway to the Tartar capital, two chieftains volunteered to lead the advance units through the mountains to Youzhou.

From a bluff Song Jiang observed the powerful Liao army. Then in his tent he conferred with Lu Junyi, Wu Yong and Gongsun Sheng. "Although we defeated them in battle and killed two of their vanguard generals," said Song Jiang, "the army I saw from the bluff is huge and strong. They're coming in endless lines. Only a tremendous force can deal with them. But we're comparatively few. What can we do?"

"Skilled generals among the ancients were able to defeat larger foes and do it beautifully," said Wu Yong. "There have been many such cases. What are you worried about? Order our soldiers to go into battle with arrows notched to their bows, swords out of their scabbards. Set deer antler stakes in deeply, alertly defend our camps. Construct good trenches and fortifications, have our weapons all laid out, our ladders and cannons in working order, and everything in proper readiness. Though they come with a million soldiers, they won't dare attack!"

"Well put, Military Adviser," said Song Jiang. He transmitted his instructions and directed the chieftains to await his orders.

Ten *li* from Youzhou is a flat plain called Fangshan. It is fringed by mountains and streams. Here, the army deployed into a Nine-Unit Octagon battle position.

Before long, the Tartars came into sight, in three

columns. All three spread out in battle positions when they saw Song Jiang's army.

What was the outcome of the battle? The outcome was that the great Liao forces fled in utter defeat, more than three thousand cavalry mounts were captured, and fallen banners and weapons filled the plain. The Tartar army suffered the loss of three generals: one was killed, one captured alive, and a third fled, no one knew whither.

31

Song Jiang's victories induced the Liao King to consider saying for peace. An emissary was sent to Song Jiang's camp to negotiate. The Tartars had hoped to be able to bribe Song Jiang. The emissary brought with him a number of valuable gifts. But Song Jiang, having heard him out, said sternly, "Do you think Song Jiang is the sort who can be bribed? Don't ever try that again!"

The Liao King sent a high official to the Eastern Capital to request an audience. The emperor formally approved the surrender in writing and pardoned the crimes of the Tartars.

The war was ended and Song Jiang withdrew his troops. When Song Jiang and his chieftains returned to the capital the emperor gave a banquet in their honour. Song Jiang was given the honorary title of Defender of Righteousness, and Wu Yong and other

chieftains became full commanders. Monetary rewards
were issued to all.

32

Some time later, when Yan Qing and Li Kui were
strolling along the streets one day, they overheard
someone saying that a bandit in the south named
Fang La had rebelled and that the emperor had ordered that an expedition be dispatched across the
Yangtze to clean the rebels out. Excited, they rushed
back to camp, where they reported the news to Wu
Yong. The military adviser was very pleased. He told
Song Jiang about it.

"Being idle here is not right," said Song Jiang.
"We should ask Marshal Su to petition the emperor to
let us join the expedition." He discussed the matter
with his chieftains. They all liked the idea.

When Song Jiang called on Marshal Su and made
his request, the marshal replied, "This is of great
importance to our country and our people. Why
should I petition the emperor? Go back. The emperor
is sure to give your request serious attention."

Marshal Su was right. The emperor accepted
Song Jiang's proposal gladly. Song Jiang was
proclaimed Commander-in-Chief of the Southern Pacification, and Lu Junyi named second in command.

Song Jiang fixed a date for his march. The army
was divided into five columns. Their destination was

Yangzhou, where they were to meet the naval forces. The march was without incident, and they soon reached Huai'an County and made camp.

33

A few words about Fang La and his depredations in the south are necessary here. Fang La had been a woodcutter in the hills of Shezhou Prefecture. It is said that one day, while washing his hands in a stream, he observed his reflection in the water. He seemed to be wearing a crown and a dragon robe. Fang La therefore announced he was destined to be a king, and started his rebellion.

He set up palaces in various places, designated civil and military ranks, created ministries, and appointed premiers and generals. Fang La controlled a toatal of eight prefectures, containing twenty—five counties. He proclaimed himself king, and appointed provincial, prefectural and departmental officials.

Fang La ravaged the south. The people of the cities and towns controlled by Fang La were groaning under the oppression of his ministers and troops.

34

There is hardly any need to recount in detail Song Jiang's punitive expedition against Fang La. Suffice it to say that as a result of the expedition all the major cities in the south formerly controlled by Fang La were recovered. Fang La himself was captured alive and sent to the Eastern Capital. Most of Fang La's sons and other relatives, as well as his high officials and ministers, were either killed or taken alive by Song Jiang's men. Military Adviser Wu Yong was instrumental in devising ways of crossing the Yangtze, in capturing Runzhou (present—day Zhenjiang) , Hangzhou and other important cities and points in the south.

The Mount Liangshan forces lost a great number of their chieftains. When Song Jiang returned victoriously to the capital, a count of the chieftains revealed that only 27 were still alive out of the original one hundred and eight.

35

When the punitive expedition against Fang La was concluded, Wu Yong was appointed commander of the Wusheng Military District. Not long after he assumed his office, Wu Yong learned of the demise of Song Jiang.

BOOK THREE

CHAPTER NINE — SONG JIANG

1

We now come to the last story — the story of the central figure among the chieftains of the Liangshan Marsh stronghold, Song Jiang.

Song Jiang was a clerk in the Yuncheng county magistrate's court. He wrote legibly and well, and was familiar with administrative procedures.

Because he was filial to his parents, generous to his friends, and a chivalrous to all, he was famed throughout the provinces of Shandong and Hebei. He made friends only in the gallant fraternity, but he helped anyone, high or low, who sought his aid, providing his guest with food and lodging in the family manor. He never refused a request for money. He always made things easy for people, solving their difficulties, settling differences, helping in cases of hardship, and saving lives.

He was known to all as Timely Rain, for like the rain from the heavens he brought succour to every living thing.

Song Jiang was especially fond of sporting with weapons, and was adept at many forms of fighting.

2

One day as Song Jiang was leaving the magistracy, he was accosted by Police Inspector Ho Tao of Jizhou Prefecture. Ho Tao greeted Song Jiang courteously, and asked him to step into a tea house where they could have a private talk.

When the waiter had brought the tea, Inspector Ho explained that his business concerned several important people in the prefecture. He further told Song Jiang that the matter involved the theft of birthday gifts that were being sent by Governor Liang of the Northern Capital to Premier Cai in the Eastern Capital. They had caught one of the robbers, and he had confessed that there were seven men involved in the robbery, all from Yuncheng county. "We hope you'll give us every assistance."

Inspector Ho said that the police didn't know the names of six of the robbers, but the leader of the band was Ward Chief Chao Gai.

Song Jiang was shocked. Chao was one of his dearest friends. This crime was a capital offense. "I must save him," he thought. "If they capture him, he's sure to die!"

Concealing his anxiety, Song Jiang declared, "The dirty scoundrel! Everyone in the county hastes him. So now he's come to this. We'll make him pay!"

"Please help me apprehend him."

" I'm only a clerk. I couldn't assume

responsibility for an important matter like this. What if word leaked out!"

Inspector Ho wanted to see the magistrate immediately, but Song Jiang told him that the magistrate had been busy all morning and was taking a rest. He would call the inspector as soon as court was resumed. Saying that he had to go home to attend to a few things, he went off.

On arriving home Song Jiang saddled his horse and led it out the rear gate. There he mounted the horse, and in less than half an hour arrived at Chao Gai's manor.

He told Chao Gai that the magistrate would without doubt send men that very night and he must leave immediately. Otherwise, Song Jiang wouldn't be able to save him.

They exchanged a few brief courtesies and Song Jiang flew back to the county town on horseback.

3

When Song Jiang returned to the county town, he found the inspector standing outside the door of the tea house, looking for him.

"Sorry to have kept you waiting so long."

"May I trouble you to take me in?"

Song Jiang led him into the magistracy.

"Documents from Jizhou Prefecture," Song Jiang told the magistrate, "brought by Inspector Ho because of the urgency of the case."

The magistrate read the documents. He was shaken. "We must send men to catch the criminals!"

"If they go during the day, word is liable to leak out. Night would be the best time. Once we take Chao Gai, we'll be able to bag the others."

There is no need to relate in detail how Inspector Ho raided Chao Gai's manor and how, warned by Song Jiang, Chao Gai and his accomplices escaped to Liangshan Marsh.

4

Some months passed. One day when Song Jiang went into a tea shop across the street from the magistracy, a big fellow dripping with sweet and breathing hard as he walked passed the tea shop. He was clearly hesitant about something. He looked familiar to Song Jiang, and Song got up and followed him. The man had gone about thirty paces when he turned around and stared at Song Jiang.

"Now where have I seen that fellow before?" Song Jiang mused.

The man went into a barber shop. "Can you tell me the name of that official outside?" he inquired.

"That's Clerk Song Jiang."

The man approached Song Jiang and hailed him respectfully. The two entered an inn and sat down in a secluded room.

May I ask your name, sir?" Song Jiang asked.

"Benefactor," the man replied, "how could you have forgotten your younger brother?"

"Who are you? You really look familiar, but I don't remember."

"My name is Liu Tang. I had the honour of meeting you in Ward Chief Chao Gai's manor, when you came to warn him. You saved our lives."

Song Jiang was startled. "Brother," he cried, "you're very rash. It's lucky no policeman has seen you, or you might be in serious danger!"

"Even if it meant my life, I had to thank you!"

"How are Ward Chief Chao Gai and the others? Who sent you here?"

"Brother Chao is very grateful to you for saving his life. He feels he must express his thanks. He's now the highest leader of our stronghold on Mount Liangshan. There's no way we can repay you for your great benevolence, but I have been sent with a letter and a hundred ounces of gold as a token of our gratitude."

Liu Tang opened his pack, produced a letter and gave it to Song Jiang. Liu also took a bundle of gold from the pack and placed it on the table. Song chose only a single gold bar, wrapped it in the letter and put both in a pouch which he again concealed underneath his gown.

Song Jiang asked a waiter to bring wine, fruit, a platter of beef, and some vegetable dishes, and to pour the wine for his guest.

"Listen to me, brother. You seven have just gone to the mountain stronghold. It's a time when you can use money. I have a family income I get along on. Keep the rest of this gold for me in the fortress. I'll come for it when I need it. I won't ask you to stay the night, brother. If you were recognized, it would be no joke. Don't hang around here. Give my best regards to the leaders and say I hope they'll forgive me for not coming to congratulate them in person."

Song Jiang had the waiter bring a pen and some paper, wrote a letter to Chao Gai, and asked Liu Tang to place it in his pack. When Liu Tang saw that Song Jiang was determined not to accept the gold, he wrapped it up and put it away.

It was getting late. "Since you have a reply, brother," said Liu Tang, "I'll deliver it tonight." He bowed four times, shouldered his pack and left.

5

Song Jiang had for some time been living with a girl called Yan Poxi. That evening, after having seen Liu Tang off, he went to the house he kept for Poxi.

Poxi was a frivolous young girl. She had lately been having a love affair with one of Song Jiang's assistants, a young man named Zhang. When her mother called out, "Your beloved is here," she thought it was the young rake. She got up quickly and fixed her hair. She flew down the stairs and looked through the lattice wall. When she saw it was Song Jiang, she was bitterly disappointed and promptly turned to go ack up the stairs, where she threw herself on the bed.

Her mother was insistent that she receive Song Jiang however, and pulled the clerk to her room. The girl sat with her face turned, and her mother had to drink with Song Jiang herself. He reluctantly drank a cup of wine.

"Quit sulking. Have some wine," the old woman said to Poxi.

Getting no answer, she collected the cups and dishes and went downstairs to the kitchen, where she put everything away and retired.

Song Jiang, sitting on a stool, glanced at the girl and sighed. He took off his tunic and hung it on the clothes rack. His sash, with its attached dagger and pouch, he draped over the bed rail.

6

In the middle of the night Song Jiang, swallowing his rage, unbolted the door and went out, pulling the door closed behind him. He put his hand into his gown and felt for his pouch. It wasn't there. "I must have left it on that creature's bed rail last night," he thought. "The gold doesn't matter, but it's wrapped in Chao Gai's letter. If Poxi gets her hands on that letter, it will be very bad!"

Meanwhile, Poxi got up after hearing Song Jiang leave. In the light of the lamp by the bedside she saw the sash hanging on the rail. When she picked it up, the pouch felt unusually heavy. Poxi opened it and spilled its contents on the table. Out came a gold bar and a letter. She picked up the gold bar.

"A gift from heaven," she laughed. "My Zhang has been getting too thin. Now I can buy him some good things to eat."

Opening the letter, she saw Chao Gai's signature and what he had written.

"Aha!" she said. "Song Jiang is all that prevents me and Zhang from being man and wife. Today I've got him in the palm of my hand. So he's in cahoots with the bandits in Liangshan Marsh, and they've sent him gold. I'll fix him!" She wrapped the gold bar back up in the letter and put it in the pouch.

No sooner had she done this than Song Jiang returned. Bursting into the room, he went straight to the rail of the bed. His belongings were gone. Song was in a panic. He shook Poxi by the shoulder.

"For the sake of my kindness to you before, give me back my pouch."

The girl feigned sleep. Song Jiang shook her again.

"Who wakes me so rudely?"

"Quit acting. You know very well it's me. I want my pouch."

"I took it, and I'm not going to give it back. You

can have me arrested as a thief!"

"I didn't say you stole it."

Song Jiang's panic was growing.

"I'm not a thief, I'll have you know!"

"Dear sister, keep your voice down! If the neighbours hear, it won't be any joke!"

"If you're afraid people will hear, you shouldn't consort with bandits and robbers! I'm going to hold on to that letter!"

7

Song Jiang yanked off the quilt covering Poxi. The sash was there.

"So that's where it is!" Song Jiang gave another hard pull. The dagger fell out on the mattress. He instinctively pounced on it. The girl looked at the dagger in his hand and screamed.

"Murder! He wants to kill me!"

Before Poxi could scream again Song Jiang pushed her down with his left hand and with his right slit her throat. Fresh blood spurted out.

Song Jiang quickly opened the pouch, extracted Chao Gai's letter and burned it in the lamp flame. He fastened the sash around his waist and went downstairs. The old woman, lying in bed downstairs, had heard the quarreling, but hadn't paid any attention until Poxi screamed "He wants to kill me!" She jumped out of bed and hurried up the stairs. She

collided with Song Jiang, who was coming down.

"What are you two raising such a racket about?" she demanded.

"Your daughter was insufferable! I killed her!"

"How could you do such a thing? Now I've no one to support me in my old age."

"You needn't worry. I have a bit of property. I will see to it that you have plenty of food and clothing for the rest of your days."

"Oh, thank you, sir clerk."

They went downstaris. The old woman locked the house behind her. Then she and Song Jiang walked in the direction of the county office in search of a coffin. As they neared the magistracy the old woman suddenly clutched him.

"I've got a murderer here!" she yelled.

Song Jiang clapped a hand over her mouth.

"Shut up!"

Several policemen ran over. But when they saw that the old woman was clutching Song Jiang, none of them was willing to lay a hand on him.

At that moment a friend of Song Jiang's, the peddlar Tang, came by. He put down the tray he was carrying and rushed over.

"Old bawd," he shouted. "Why are you hanging on to our clerk?"

Tang was furious. He pried her hands loose and slapped her so hard she saw stars. She staggered dizzily and let go. Song Jiang walked directly into the market crowd.

8

There is no need to dwell on how Song Jiang, known as Timely Rain, escaped punishment for killing his concubine Yan Poxi.

To begin with, he found refuge in Lord Chai's manor. After staying here for some time he made his way to Clear Winds Mountain.

After travelling for some days, he saw a high mountain in the distance, thickly covered with tress. Before he realized it darkness began closing in, and he looked around in alarm. He continued along the road for some time, growing more and more worried. He could not see, and stumbled over a trip cord. Immediately, a bell tinkled among the trees. A dozen robbers who had been lying in ambush came out yelling. They seized and bound Song Jing, taking his dagger and bundle, and then escorted him up the mountain by torchlight. Before long, they reached the stronghold.

There, in the main hall, stood three armchairs draped with tiger skins. The robbers trussed Song Jiang up and tied him to a pillar.

Some time later four or five robbers emerged from the rear of the hall. "The big chieftain is here," they announced. Song Jiang stole a glance at the man who appeared. The chieftain seated himself in the middle armchair.

"Where did you get this fellow, boys?" he asked.

"We were lying in ambush behind the mountain when this lone traveller stumbled over the trip cord."

"Fine. Invite the other two chiefs to join me."

The robbers went and soon returned with the two chieftains. All three chieftains took their seats. "Let's get started, boys. Cut out his heart and liver and cook us three portions of sour and peppery broth."

A robber brought in a large bronze basin filled with water which he set down in front of Song Jiang. Another robber rolled up his sleeves and grashped shiny pointed knife.

The captive sighed. "What a pity that Song Jiang should die here!"

The big chieftain heard him. "Stop!" he shouted to the robbers. "Did that fellow say something about Song Jiang?"

"He said, 'What a pity that Song Jiang should die here!'"

The big chieftain rose from his chair. "Do you know Song Jiang?"

"I am Song Jiang."

"Not Song Jiang the Timely Rain from Shandong Province? The one who killed Mistress Yan and fled, Song Jiang of the gallant fraternity?"

"Yes. But how did you know?"

Astonished, the chieftain grabbed the knife from the robber, cut Song Jiang's bonds, and led him to the middle chair. He shouted to the other two chieftains and all three knelt and bowed. Song Jiang returned the courtesy.

"Not only do you let me live, but you treat me with such respect! What's the meaning of this?"

"Imagine not recognizing a good man! If I hadn't seen you, if I had asked a few less questions, I might have finished off a noble warrior! Fortunately you uttered your great name, or I'd never have known! In the ten years or so I've been in the greenwood I've often heard chivalrous men tell how just and generous you are, helping those with hardships and saving those in danger. Today heaven has let us meet. I'm happy with all my heart!"

"What virtue or ability have I to deserve such kindness?"

Song Jiang related how he had rescued Chao Gai, killed Mistress Yan, and lived with Lord Chai for a long time. Finally he explained why he was at that point seeking refuge at Fort Clear Winds. The three chieftains listened delightedly. They presented Song Jiang with clothes, ordered sheep and horses to be slaughtered and laid a feast that very night.

9

To cut a long story short, Song Jiang stayed on the mountain six or seven days. The mountain was not far from the twon of Qingzhou. Song was anxious to find Hua Rong, the military commandant of the town.

Bidding the chieftains farewell, he took the road to the town. He found Hua Rong's residence without trouble. All day Hua Rong and his family wined and dined Song Jiang. A few days later while Song was taking a walk around the town accompanied by Hua Rong's officers, the wife of the Civilian Commandant, Liu, caught sight of him. This woman had been abducted by the bandits of Clear Winds Mountain while Song Jiang was staying there. She told her husband that Song was one of the chieftains of the bandits on Clear Winds Mountain who had kidnapped her.

Startled, Liu ordered his guards to grab Song Jiang. He was tied up and taken into the hall. Hua Rong's men, who had been accompanying Song Jiang, ran back and reported to Hua.

On hearing that Song Jiang had been seized, Hua Rong was deeply shocked. He immediately penned a missive to Liu, asking him to release Song, who he said was his relation. But Liu, who was at odds with Hua, tore the missive to shreds, and ordered the messenger to be thrown out.

Hua Rong mounted his steed, and with forty or fifty men armed with spears and staves set out for Liu's compound.

Song Jiang was rescued and taken back to Hua Rong's enclosure.

But Song knew well that Liu would do his best to get him back into his own hands. He decided to take refuge on Clear Winds Mountain that very night. He advised Hua Rong to deny knowledge of the matter the following day.

Towards dusk, two soldiers saw Song Jiang off just beyond the gates of the fort, and from there Song Jiang made his way through the night alone.

But Liu was a very crafty man. He guessed that Hua Rong would let Song Jiang leave for Clear Winds Mountain that very night. he sent twenty or thirty soldiers down the road to lie in wait for Song Jiang. The soldiers soon returned with Song, his hands tied behind his back. Liu was delighted. He ordered that Song be locked in the rear yeard so that no one would know about his capture.

Liu wrote a formal accusation against Song Jiang which he dispatched to Qingzhou Prefecture.

10

Meanwhile, Hua Rong assumed that Song Jiang was already on Clear Winds Mountain, and made no inquiries.

In Qingzhou the prefect was holding court. When the police officers handed him Commandant Liu's accusation, he was startled. "Hua Rong is the son of a military commandant who has made great contributions to the nation. How could he be conspiring with the brigands on Clear Winds Mountain?"

The prefect ordered Huang Xin, commander of

the prefectural army, to investigate the case. Huang Xin that very night proceeded to Liu's enclosure. Without bothering to examine Song Jiang, Huang Xin ordered that a cage cart be made and Song Jiang put in it. A red band was tied around Song Jiang's head and a paper pennant inserted in it reading, "Zhang San of Yuncheng, Chieftain of the Clear Winds Mountain Bandits".

Upon Huang Xin's suggestion, a feast was laid in the main hall of the fort, and forty or fifty men concealed all around. Hua Rong was invited to attend. "When you see me fling down my cup," Huang Xin told the prefect, "that will be the signal to grab him! I'll take them both with me back to the prefecture."

The plan was carried out. Hua Rong was taken during the feast, and he and Song Jiang were sent to the prefecture in cage carts, in spite of all their protests.

Before the procession had gone forty *li*, they saw ahead a large forest. As they neared it, a guard pointed and exclaimed, "Men are watching us from among those trees!"

The procession halted. Suddenly twenty or thirty gongs began crashing in unison. The soldiers, panic-stricken, turned to flee.

At this moment, nearly five hundred bandits, all fierce-visaged stalwarts, surrounded the company on all sides. They stood, halberds in hand, blocking the

305

road. In the middle stood the three chieftains of Clear Winds Mountain.

Huang Xin had no time to consider the unit under his command. On flying steed he raced back alone. A swarm of bandits seized Liu. Hua Rong who had already pried his cage open, jumped out and snapped his bonds. He broke open the other cart and rescued Song Jiang. They were escorted to the Clear Winds Mountain by the bandits.

11

Not long after Song Jiang was rescured by Clear Winds Mountain band, he succeeded in persuading them go to Mount Liangshan.

One day, before they started for Mount Liangshan, Song Jiang got a letter for him from his younger brother, Song Qing.

Song Jiang tore open the envelope and read:

"Early in the first lunar month father died of illness. Please return immediately. Do not delay!"

Song Jiang cried out in anguish and beat his chest. "Unfilial son that I am! He is dead and I am not there to perform my duties as a son!" He beat his head against the wall and lamented. Nothing anyone could say consoled him. He wept till he was dazed.

"I'm not without feeling for our men," he said at last, "but my old father was the one I loved best. Now he's gone. I must return home tonight. Tell our broth-eis to go up the mountain themselves."

Without touching any food and wine, he walked directly out the door.

12

Song Jiang travelled all night and reached his own village late the following afternoon. He stopped to rest at a wine shop run by a man named Zhang, who was on good terms with Song Jiang's family. Zhang observed his sorrowful expression and tear-filled eyes.

"You've been away for half a year, but today, fortunately, you've come back. Why are you so dejected? You ought to be happy. A general amnesty has been declared. Your crime surely has been lessened."

"That may be true, uncle, but it's only of secondary importance. How can I help feeling distressed when my old father has passed away?"

"You're joking. He was here drinking a short time ago. He's just gone back. Why are you talking like that?"

"Don't make fun of me, uncle ." Song Jiang showed him the letter. "My brother Song Qing has written here very plainly that our father died early in the first lunar month. He urges me to come home and attend the funeral!"

"Nonsense. Nothing of the sort. He was drinking here at noon with Squire Wang of East Village. I wouldn't lie."

Song Jiang didn't know what to say. He thought for a long time. When it began getting dark, he said goodbye to Zhang and hurried home. He entered the manor gate. All was peaceful. The servants greeted him respectfully.

"Are my father and brother here?" he asked.

"The squire has been wearing out his eyes looking for your return," they said. "How fortunate that you've come back. He's just returned himself. He was drinking with Squire Wang at Zhang's wine shop in the village. He's having a nap inside."

Song Jiang was astonished. He hurried into the house. His younger brother Song Qing, dropped to his knees on seeing him, and bowed. He was not wearing mourning. Song Jiang was enraged.

"How dare you, you monster! Father is alive and well. How could you write such a lying letter?"

Before Song Qing could reply, Squire Song appeared and said, "Calm yourself, son. It's not your brother's fault. I was thinking of you every day, and told him to write saying I had died, knowing that would bring you home quickly. I heard there were many robbers on White Tiger Mountain. I was afraid you might be inveigled into joining them and become a disloyal, unfilial person. The idea was mine entirely. It had nothing to do with your brother. Don't blame him."

Torn between happiness and anger, Song Jiang

bowed to his father. "Have you heard anything lately about my case?" he asked. "An amnesty has been proclaimed. The charges against me are sure to be reduced."

"A general amnesty has been issued. Charges on all major criminal acts have been lessened by one degree. The edict is already in force. If you were brought before a judge now, at worst you would be exiled, but you no longer could be punished by death. So let them do what they will. We'll find some way to cope."

It was a happy family reunion. When everyone in the manor was asleep, suddenly a loud clamor arose at the front and rear gates. On all sides torches surrounded the manor, and voices shouted, "Don't let Song Jiang get away!"

13

Squire Song placed a ladder against the wall, climbed up to the top and looked out. Over a hundred men were outside with torches. At their head were two newly appointed Yuncheng County sheriffs — the brothers Zhao Neng and Zhao De.

"If you know what's good for you, Squire Song," they shouted, "you'll send your son Song Jiang out and let us deal with him. If he doesn't turn himself over to the authorities, we'll arrest the both of you!"

"Song Jiang hasn't come home," the old man said.

"Don't lie," Zhao Neng retorted. "He was seen drinking in the village at Zhang's place. And he was followed home from there. You can't deny it."

"Don't argue with him, father," Song Jiang urged. "I'll go out and give myself up. An amnesty has been announced. I'm sure to be given a reduced sentence. It's no use arguing with these wretches. The Zhao brothers are a pair of shysters. Pleading with them is a waste of time."

Song Jiang mounted the ladder and called out, "Quiet down, out there. Leniency for my crime has already been declared. It's no longer a capital offense. If you two sheriffs will come into our manor and have a few cups of wine with us, I'll go with you to the magistrate tomorrow."

Song Jiang came down from the ladder, opened the manor gate, and invited the two sheriffs into the guest hall. That night they were wined and dined. Bars of silver were presented to the two as "thanks for their kindness".

At dawn the next day Song Jiang proceeded with the two sheriffs to the county. When it was daylight, they brought Song Jiang before the magistrate, who had just opened court. The magistrate was delighted. He ordered the prisoner to submit his confession. Song Jiang took a pen and wrote, "The crime occurred because last autumn I purchased Yan Poxi as a concubine. She was no good, and I accidentally killed her in a quarrel when I was drunk. I ran away to avoid being punished. Today, captured and brought before the court, I set forth these details and state that I shall willingly accept whatever sentence the court decrees."

The magistrate read the confession and ordered Song Jiang to be remanded into custody.

14

Everyone in the county heard of Song Jiang's arrest, and there wasn't a person who didn't pity him. They pleaded with the magistrate to forgive him, telling him what a good man Song Jiang was ordinarily. The magistrate was more than inclined to go easy. He formally accepted the confession and directed that Song Jiang be confined to the prison, but added that he need not be fettered.

Squire Song bribed high and low. The magistrate drew up his findings and when the sixty-day detention period was over, sent the prisoner to the prefecture of Jizhou for sentencing.

The prefect reviewed the case. He ordered that Song Jiang be given twenty strokes and exiled to the prison in Jiangzhou. In the presence of the court a rack was placed around Song Jiang's neck for the journey and documents of transfer issued. Two guards were designated as escorts.

On receipt of the documonts, the guards set off with their prisoner. Song Jiang's father and his brother Song Qing were waiting outside the prefectural compound. They served the guards wine and gave them silver. Song Jiang bid farewell to the old man, and departed weeping.

15

Song Jiang proceeded along the road with the two guards. The three marched all day. At night, they put up at an inn, where they made a fire and cooked some rice. Song Jiang bought wine and meat, and treated the guards.

"I'll be frank," he said. "From here on we'll be skirting Mount Liangshan. On the summit are a number of bold men who know my name. They might come down to rescue me and give you a fright. I suggest we get up early tomorrow and follow small paths which detour around the mountain. Even if we have to travel a few extra *li* it'll be worth it."

"We'd never have known if you hadn't told us, sir clerk," the guards replied. "We're familiar with a few paths. We definitely won't run into them there." Plans were made accordingly that night.

The three rose at dawn the next morning. They soon left the inn, and walked along narrow trails for about thirty *li*. Suddenly a band of men appeared round the bend of the mountain ahead and advanced towards them.

Song Jiang groaned. Leading forty or fifty

brigands was none other than Liu Tang. They plainly intended to finish off the two escorts. The terrified guards fell to their knees in a heap.

"Brothers," Song Jiang called, "whom do you want to kill?"

"Those two thugs, of course. Who else?"

The guards moaned.

"Why do you want to kill them?"

"Our brothers on the mountain top sent a man to Yuncheng to enquire about your trial. We learned you were being exiled to Jiangzhou. To make sure we didn't miss you, chiefs, big and small, have been posted on every road and path. We're here to welcome you and invite you up the mountain. Naturally, we've got to kill these guards."

"This won't honour me. It will disgrace me. I'll become disloyal, unfilial. If you insist, I have no choice but to kill myself." Song Jiang raised his blade to his throat.

Liu Tang grabbed his arm. "Wait, brother. Let's talk this over." He wrenched the knife from Song Jiang's hand.

"Pity me, brothers," Song Jiang pleaded. "Let me go on to the Jiangzhou prison. When my term is up, I'll come back and we'll meet again."

"That's not in my power to decide," said Liu Tang. On the main road ahead our Military Adviser Wu Yong and Commandant Hua Rong are waiting to greet you. If you'll allow me, I'll ask them to come and confer."

"You can confer all you like. I've nothing more to say."

A bandit was sent to report. Not long after, Wu Yong and Hua Rong were seen galloping towards them, followed by a dozen men on horseback. The two dismounted and bowed.

"Why hasn't the rack been removed?" Hua Rong demanded.

"What a thing to say," Song Jiang remonstrated "It's affixed according to government law. Who would dare touch it?"

Wu Yong laughed. "No problem. We won't ask you to remain in our mountain stronghold then. But Chieftain Chao Gai hasn't seen you in so long. He's hoping to have a private talk. Stay with us for a while, and we'll send you on your way,"

"Only you, Teacher, understand." Song Jiang raised the two guards to their feet and said, "Don't worry. I'd rather die than let them harm you."

"We owe you our lives, sir clerk," they cried.

16

The column left the main road and came to a thicket of reeds along the bank. Boats were waiting. They crossed over to the road on the other side and got into sedan chairs. When they reached the mountain top, Chao Gai expressed his thanks to Song

Jiang.

"Ever since you saved us at Yuncheng and we came here, there hasn't been a day that we haven't remembered your great kindness. What's more, you brought us several heroes to grace our humble lair. We don't know how to express our gratitude."

"After leaving you, I killed a lecherous wench and wandered about for a year and a half. I intended to come back and see you, brother, but I received a letter from home saying that my father had died. Actually, my father was afraid that I'd join your band of gallant men, and used this method to get me to return. Although I had to face trial, I was protected by officials high and low, and I wasn't hurt much. They exiled me to Jiangzhou, a good place. Since you summoned me, I had to come. Now we have met. But there's a time limit on my journey and I don't dare overstay. I must bid you farewell."

Chao Gai ordered his chieftains to pay their respects to Song Jiang. Lieutenants poured wine. After a few rounds, Song Jiang rose to his feet.

"Your affection touches me, brothers. I'm a criminal, a prisoner. I dare not remain. I must leave you now."

His tears streaming like rain, Song Jiang threw himself on his knees. Chao Gai and Wu Yong raised him to his feet.

"Since you are determined to go to Jiangzhou brother," they said, "relax and spend the day with us

We'll see you down the mountain tomorrow morning."

After much persuasion, Song Jiang agreed to stay the day with them. They gave him a farewell banquet and gifts of silver and gold. But of this we'll say no more.

17

Song Jiang rose early the next morning and announced he was leaving.

"Hear me, brother," said Wu Yong. "The superintendent of the two prisons in Jiangzhou is a very good friend of mine. His name is Dai Zong, and he's called Superintendent Dai. Because he knows some Taoist magic and can walk eight hundred *li* in a day, everyone refers to him as 'Marvellous Traveller'. He's extremely chivalrous and generous. Last night I wrote a letter of introduction for you. You two can become acquainted."

A feast was laid to bid farewell to Song Jiang. With a man carrying his pack, they all escorted him down the mountain. Wu Yong and Hua Rong accompanied him across the lake and twenty *li* along the road. Then they two returned to the mountain stronghold.

18

Song Jiang and the guards pushed on towards

Jiangzhou. They marched more than half a month. When they had crossed Jieyang Ridge, they could see on the slope below an inn with a wine pennant hanging from a tree by the door.

"We're hungry and thirsty, and there's an inn that sells wine," said Song Jiang. "Let's have a few bowls before going on."

They entered the inn. The guards eased themselves of the luggage, and leaned their official staves against the wall.

An hour passed and no one appeared.

"Host, where are you?" Song Jiang called.

"Coming, coming," From an adjoining room a big fellow emerged. He greeted the three respectfully.

"How much wine will you have, sirs?"

Song Jiang ordered a measure of wine and some sliced beef.

"There are many evil men around these days," one of the guards remarked. "It's said they drug the travellers' wine and meat, steal their valuables and put their flesh into dumplings."

The host laughed. "Don't eat, then. My meat and wine are drugged."

Song Jiang and the guards were hungry and thirsty, and the meat and the wine were spread before them. They tucked in. The eyes of the guards began to bulge, and they drooled from the corners of their mouths. Staring at each other, they toppled over backwards.

Song Jiang jumped up. He went to raise them to their feet, but suddenly he too felt dizzy and his eyes swam. He fell heavily to the floor.

"How lucky," said the host. "I haven't had a speck of business in days, and now heaven sends me these three pieces of merchandise."

He dragged Song Jiang to the butchering hut and placed him on the skinning bench. Next, he hauled over the other two. Then he returned to the inn and took Song Jiang's pack and luggage into the rear room and opened them up. They were filled with silver and gold.

"In all the years I've been running this inn I've never seen a prisoner like him. It's like a gift from the sky."

He went outside to watch for the return of his helpers so that he could start butchering. He stood by the door for a while, but there was no sign of them. Further down the slope he saw three men climbing rapidly towards him. Recognizing one of them, he hurried forward.

"Where to, brother?" he hailed in greeting.

The big fellow replied, "We're looking for a man. He should be coming this way about now. I've been waiting for him every day at the foot of the mountain, but he hasn't shown up,

"Who is he?"

"The clerk of Yuncheng County, in Jizhou prefecture. Song Jiang."

"Not Song Jiang of Shandong Province, famed in the gallant fraternity as Timely Rain?"

"None other."

"Why would he be coming here?"

"I don't know. The other day I met a friend from Jizhou and he told me that Song Jiang had got into some kind of trouble in Jizhou and had been exiled to the prison in Jiangzhou. He's got to pass this way. There isn't any other road. What's business like these days?"

"Frankly, it's been practically dead the past few months. Today, thank Heaven, I've caught three pieces of merchandise, and they have got some stuff on them."

"Who are they?"

"Two are guards and the third is a prisoner."

"Is the prisoner a dark, short, chunky man?" asked the big fellow in alarm. "You haven't gone to work on him yet?"

"I dragged him into the shed only a short while ago. I can't start till my helpers get back."

"Let me take a look at him first."

The four men entered the butchering shed. The big fellow didn't know Song Jiang.

"Go get the guards' pack we can read the documents."

They went into the house, obtained the guards' bundle and opened it up.

"A lucky thing," the four exclaimed.

"Heaven sent me up this ridge today. If you'd set to work a little earlier you'd have taken my brother's life," the big fellow cried.

The host prepared a herbal mixture to revive Song Jiang. The four then carried him to the front part of the inn. He slowly came to and opened his eyes. The big fellow dropped to his knees.

"How did you know who I was?" asked Song Jiang.

"A friend of mine who has just been in Jizhou on business told me about you. I'd often thought of going to your county to pay my respects, but I have never been fortunate enough to have the chance. Today, Heaven happened to send me and these two brothers up the ridge. May I have the temerity to ask why the clerk of Yuncheng County is being sent to Jiangzhou prison?"

Song Jiang told what had happened from the time he killed Yan Poxi to when he was exiled to Jiangzhou.

"Why not stay here?" asked the host. "Why go to prison and suffer hardships?"

"The men on Mount Liangshan begged me to remain with them, but I refused because I was afraid of implicating my father," Song Jiang explained. "How can I stay with you?"

"Our brother is a man of principle. He won't do anything wrong. Now you'd better revive those guards."

After several days Song Jiang was determined to continue his journey. He again put on his rack, gathered his luggage and bid farewell to everyone. On leaving Jieyang Ridge, he and his guards proceeded towards Jiangzhou.

When the guards and Song Jiang at last reached Jiangzhou, they went to the office of the prefectural government. The escorts handed the documents to the prefect, delivered Song Jiang to the prison, obtained a receipt and returned home.

Song Jiang invited the head keeper to his cell and gave him ten ounces of silver. He sent the same amount to the warden. Nor did he forget to tip the others working in the prison and the soldiers on guard. As a result he was well liked.

Not long after, he was brought to the registration room and his rack was removed. According to law, as a newly exiled prisoner he should have been beaten a hundred strokes "to quell his arrogance", but the warden, who had been bribed, exempted him from the punishment. He was set to work as a copyist.

While he was moving to the Copying Section, the superintendent, Dai Zong came to see him. When the superintendent learned that the prisoner was Song Jiang from Yuncheng County, Shandong Province, he pulled him aside and said, "Brother, this is no place to talk. In the city we can speak freely. Please come with me."

Song Jiang handed the superintendent Wu

letter. They entered a wine shop and sat down.

"The head keeper spoke to me of you several times. I intended to call on you and pay my respects, but I didn't know where you lived. That's what delayed our meeting. Today we have met and all my wishes have come true."

Once both men had revealed their feelings and motives they were very pleased with each other. They summoned the waiter and ordered wine and tidbits. Over the wine, Song Jiang told of the bold heroes he had met on the road. Dai Zong spoke frankly of his relations with Wu Yong.

19

The next day, Song Jiang was sitting in an inn waiting for friends. He was alone and depressed. He told the waiter to bring him a jug of wine and some meat. He drank steadily.

The wine went to his head and he wept, very depressed. Suddenly, he decided to write a poem. The waiter brought a pen and ink "Why not write a poem on the wall?" he said to himself. "Some day, when I've earned my place in the world, I'll come here and read it again, and think of my present misery."

Stimulated by the wine, he ground a thick mixture of ink, soaked his pen in it, and wrote on the white wall:

Since childhood I have studied classics

and history,

And become shrewd and intelligent.

Today, a tiger enduring in the wilderness,

I crouch with tooth and claw, intent.

A criminal's tattoo upon my cheek,

An unwilling exile in far Jiangzhou.

I shall have my revenge some day,

And dye red with blood the Xunyang's flow.

Song Jiang laughed uproariously, delighted with his effort. He drank several more cups of wine. Again he took up his pen and added four more lines:

Heart in Shandong, body in Wu,

Drifting, I breathe sighs into the air.

If I achieve my lofty aim,

No rebel chief will with me compare.

At the bottom in large script he wrote: "By Song Jiang of Yuncheng", and tossed the pen on the table. He was very drunk. He paid his bill, staggered down the stairs and returned to the prison. He oppened his door and collapsed on the bed.

20

In the town of Wuweijun, across the Xunyang River from Jiangzhou, lived a former deputy prefect named Huang Wenbing. He'd read a bit of the classics, but was a narrow-hearted sycophant who envied men of nobility. Those superior in talent he injured, those inferior he mocked. His speciality was harming people throughout the township.

He knew that Prefect Cai of Jiangzhou was the son of the premier, and frequently crossed the river to call on him and ingratiate himself. He hoped that this would lead to an appointment making him an official again. It was Song Jiang's fate to arouse this man and be treated by him as an adversary.

That day Huang was sitting idle at home. He called two servants, bought some attractive gifts, crossed the river and went to call on the prefect. The prefect was in the midst of an official banquet. Huang headed back toward his boat and went into the Xunyang Pavilion, where Song Jiang had drunk wine the day before.

Huang glanced at the many poems upon the wall. He then read Song Jiang's verses. "This is rebellious," he exclaimed. He looed at the signature: "Song Jiang of Yuncheng". He read the poem through. "If that's not a proclamation of revolt I don't know what is!"

Huang read the signature again: "Song Jiang of Yuncheng".

"Where have I heard that name before?" he pondered. He summoned the waiter. "Who wrote this poem?"

"A man who was here last night. He drank a whole jug all by himself."

Huang asked for a pen and ink, copied the poem

on a sheet of paper, and placed it inside his robe. "Don't scrape it off," he cautioned the waiter.

21

The next day Huang again proceeded to the prefecture. An officer announced him. After some friendly chatter, Huang asked, "May I be so bold as to enquire whether there has been any word from your honorable father the premier lately?"

"I received a letter from him just a couple of days ago."

"What's the news from the capital?"

"He says the Royal Astrologer in a report to the emperor states that an evil star is shining on our land of Wu, and that there are probably troublemakers abroad who must be annihilated. What's more, says my father, children on the streets are chanting this rhyme: 'The destroyer of our country is home and free... Shandong will put us in a terrible fix....' He advises me to keep a careful watch on my prefecture."

Huang thought a moment. Then he smiled. "I'm not surprised, Excellency." He took from his robe the poem he had copied and handed it to the prefect. "Here's the reason."

The prefect read it. "A rebellious poem. Where did you get it?"

"From the wall in the Xunyang Pavilion."

"What sort of person is the author?"

" He's put his name down. Song Jiang of Yuncheng."

"He tells us in his poem: 'A criminal's tattoo on my cheek, An unwilling exile in far Jiangzhou.' He's an exile, a criminal in the city prison."

"What can a fellow like that do?"

"Don't underestimate him, Excellency. He fits in exactly with the children's rhyme your honorable father mentions in his letter. This is a warning from Heaven. How fortunate for the populace?"

"Is the fellow still here?"

"It's easy enough to find out. Check the prison register."

The prefect ordered an attendant to fetch the register of the city prison, and examined it personally. Sure enough, there was the entry: "Fifth month. Our newly exiled prisoner — Song Jiang of Yuncheng County."

"The man in the rhyme. This is very important," said Huang. "If we delay, news that we're on to him will leak out. Better seize him immediately and lock him up. Then we can discuss what to do next."

The prefect summoned the superintendent of the city's two prisons and ordered him to take some police, go to the prison and bring Song Jiang of Yuncheng to the prefecture. "He's written a rebellious poem in the Xunyang Pavilion. I don't want a moment's delay."

Shocked, Dai Zong groaned inwardly and left the

prefect's office. He mustered a number of prison guards and told them to assemble later at his quarters.

Using his magic method of travelling, Dai Zong sped to the prison's Copying Section and pushed open Song Jiang's door. His friend was there.

"Brother," exclaimed Dai Zong, "what sort of poem did you write on the wall of the Xunyang Pavilion?"

"Who knows! I was drunk."

"Just now the prefect summoned me and ordered me to arrest you for having written a rebellious poem in the Xunyang Pavilion. I was very shaken, but I told my men to wait at my quarters to give me time to let you know first. Brother, what are we going to do?"

Son Jiang scratched his head in perplexity. "I'm a goner," he moaned.

"There's a way, though it may not work," said Dai. "I can't delay any longer. I'll have to bring my polic and arrest you. Muss up your hair, spill your fifth on the floor, roll in it, and pretend to be mad. When I come with my men, speak wildly and act as if you were out of your mind. I'll go back to the prefect and report that you're insane."

"Thank you, brother. Save me, I beg you."

22

Dai Zong quickly bid Song Jiang farewell and returned to the city. At his quarters he assembled his

327

police and proceeded with them to the prison at a rapid pace. "Where's the exile Song Jiang?" he shouted with feigned ferocity. He led his men to Song Jiang's room in the Copying Section.

There they found the clerk, his hair in disarray, rolling in his own filth upon the floor.

"Seize the wretch," Dai roared.

Eyes glaring, Song Jiang fought in a frenzy, speaking wildly, as if he were out of his mind.

"He's crazy," said the policemen. "What's the use of arresting him?"

"You're right," said Dai Zong. "Let's go back and tell them. If we have to take him, we'll come again."

They returned to the prefecture. "Song Jiang has taken leave of his senses," they reported.

The prefect was about to enquire further when Huang emerged from behind a screen. "Don't believe them," he advised the prefect. "That poem he wrote was not the work of a madman. There's something fishy going on. Bring him in. If he can't walk, carry him."

After being beaten until he was more dead than alive, Song Jiang abandoned his ruse and confessed that he had written the poem when he was drunk.

23

Having obtained the confession, the prefect

directed that a rack for capital felons be placed around the prisoner's neck and that he be thrown into a cell for the condemned. Dai secretly ordered the guards to treat him well, and arranged for food to be sent in.

Huang persuaded the prefect to rush a man to the capital with a letter to the premier reporting how he was dealing with this matter of national importance. He urged him to suggest that if the premier wanted the man alive, the prefect would send him by prison cart. If he didn't, the prefect would execute him in Jiangzhou.

The prefect wrote the letter. He decided to let Dai Zong, who knew certain charms by which he could cover eight hundred *li* in one day, deliver the letter to the premier. The prefect also filled two hampers with gold and jewels, sealed them and told Dai Zong to present them as well to his father.

That day Dai Zong set out on his journey. He returned to his quarters and put the letter into his pouch along with some money for the road. The hampers he carried on a shoulder pole.

Once outside the city, he attached two charms to each of his legs, murmered some magic words, and set forth. He traveled all day, and put up at an inn in the evening.

He rose early the next morning, had some food and wine, and left the inn. Again he attached the four charms, shouldered the hampers, and travelled — so rapidly that the wind and rain whistled in his ears, and his feet didn't touch the ground.

By mid-morning he had covered nearly three hundred *li* without encountering a single clean inn. Hungry and thirsty, he noticed a tavern ahead beside a lake at the edge of a grove. Dai Zong was there in the twiddle of a thumb. He went in, chose a secluded table, rested his hampers, and removed his gown.

As he sat down, the waiter approached.

"How much wine, sir? Would you like some meat to go with it?"

"Go easy on the wine. And bring me some rice."

The waiter soon returned with the wine. Dai quickly finished several bowls. He was waiting for the rice when the earth and sky began to turn dizzily. His sight fading, Dai fell backwards off the bench.

From within the inn a man emerged. It was Zhu Gui, a member of the Mount Liangshan stronghold.

"Take his papers inside and see whether he's got anything on him," Zhu Gui ordered.

Two assistants searched Dai and found a paper packet. Zhu Gui removed the paper, revealing an envelope inscribed: "Peaceful Family Letter, with the Utmost Respect to His Father from His Son Prefect Cai." Zhu Gui tore open the envelope and read the missive from beginning to end. it read:

> "Today we have arrested a man who fits the prediction rhyme and who has written a rebellious poem — Song Jiang of

Shandong, and are holding him in
prison. . . . We await your orders for his
disposition."

Zhu Gui was shocked beyond speech. His assistants were lifting Dai Zong to carry him into the
butchering shed when Zhu Gui noticed a red and
green object attached to the sash lying on the bench.
He picked it up. It was an official's identification
plaque. Etched in silver were the words: "Dai Zong,
Superintendent of the Two Prisons, Jiangzhou."

"Wait," Zhu Gui said to his cohorts. "I've often
heard our military adviser talk of his friend Dai Zong,
the Marvellous Traveller from Jiangzhou. This must
be the man. But why is he bearing a letter that will
harm Song Jiang? Heaven has sent him into my hands.
Give him the antidote and bring him round. I want to
question him."

The attendants poured a mixture into some water,
raised Dai Zong up and fed it to him. He soon opened
his eyes and struggled to his feet. He saw Zhu Gui
with the letter in his hands.

"Who are you?" shouted Dai. "How dare you
drug me? And you've opened the letter to the premier.
Don't you know what a crime that is?"

Zhu Gui laughed. "So what? What's opening the
premier's letter to a man who's opposing the
emperor?"

Dai Zong was astonished. "Who are you, bold
fellow? What's your name?"

"I'm Zhu Gui, of the gallant band in Liangshan Marsh."

"Since you're one of the leaders, you must know Wu Yong."

"He's our military adviser. He controls all our military operations. How do you know him?"

"He's a very close friend."

"You're not Superintendent Dai, the Marvellous Traveller of Jiangzhou, he so often speaks about?"

"I am."

"When Song Jiang was on his way to exile in Jiangzhou, he stayed at our stronghold, and Wu Yong gave him a letter to you. Why are you helping to take his life?"

"Song Jiang is like a brother to me. He wrote a rebellious poem and I couldn't prevent his arrest. I'm on my way to the capital right now to find a way to save him. I'd never harm Song Jiang."

"If you don't believe me," retorted Zhu Gui, "take a look at this."

Dai Zong read the letter the prefect had written. He was shocked.

"In that case please come with me to the stronghold and talk it over with our leaders," said Zhu Gui. "We've got to rescue Song Jiang."

24

Zhu Gui went to the pavilion overlooking the

lake and shot a whistling arrow to the opposite cove. A bandit promptly rowed over in a boat. Zhu Gui helped Dai Zong put his hampers on board. They landed on the opposite shore and climbed to the fortress. When it was reported to Wu Yong that they were at the gate, he hurried down to greet them.

Dai related in detail the story of Song Jiang and his poem. Chao Gai was very alarmed. He proposed to the other leaders that they immediately muster men and horses, raid Jiangzhou and bring Song Jiang back to the fortress.

"That's not the way, brother, "Wu Yong said. "It would mean Song Jiang's life. What's needed here is guile, not force. I have a little plan by which we can rescure Song Jiang. It involves Superintendent Dai."

"Let's hear it, Military Adviser."

"Dai has to bring back a reply to the letter Prefect Cai is sending to the Eastern Capital. We'll write a false one and turn the tables on them. The reply Superintendent Dai will deliver will say: 'Take no action against the prisoner Song Jiang. Send him here under appropriate guard. After thorough investigation we shall execute him and put his head on display to discredit the prediction rhyme.' When Song Jiang is being escorted through this area, our men will snatch him. What do you think of the plan?"

"Suppose he doesn't pass this way. We'll miss our chance, "said Chao Gai.

"That's no problem. We'll dispatch scouts near

and far to inquire. Whichever path he travels, we'll be waiting for him."

It was thus decided. Wu Yong had two friends, one of them a skilled calligrapher, the other an excellent seal cutter. The next morning Dai Zong was given two hundred ounces of silver. Disguised as a deacon, he went down the mountain to invite the two men to the stronghold.

On their arrival at the stronghold, the two men were greeted by Chao Gai, Wu Yong and the other chieftains. They were given a feast of welcome and told what was expected of them. To reassure them, their families were brought to the stronghold to join them.

They set to work and soon finished the forged letter from the premier. A banquet was laid for Dai Zong, who was given detailed instructions. The superintendent bid all farewell and went down the mountain, where an outlaw ferried him across to Zhu Gui's inn.

After seeing Dai off, Wu Yong and the other chieftains returned to the stronghold and feasted. Suddenly, Wu Yong cried out in despair.

"What's wrong?" everyone asked.

"That letter I prepared is a death warrant for Dai Zong and Song Jiang!"

"What's the matter with it?"

"I thought only of one thing and forgot another. There's a terrible error in that reply!"

25

Wu Yong explained what was wrong with the letter.

"The seal reads: 'Cai Qing, Member of the Hanlin Academy'. But a father writing to his son would never use that formal title. I forgot about that. When Dai returns to Jiangzhou he'll surely be questioned. If the truth comes out, it will be terrible."

"Let's send a man after Dai, quickly, and bring him back."

"No one could catch him. We can't delay. Dai and Song Jiang must be saved."

"How can we save them?" asked Chao Gai.

Wu Yong spoke softly in Chao Gai's ear for several minutes, concluding with, "Issue the order quietly among our men. Tell them how to act. Instruct them to move promptly, without fail."

26

Dai returned to Jiangzhou and reported to the prefect. Prefect Cai was very pleased. He rewarded Dai with a flowery silver ingot and ordered that a cage cart be built.

A day or two later, all was in readiness to take the prisoner to the capital. Just at this moment the gate keeper announced that Huang Wenbing was calling. The prefect showed him the letter from the capital.

Huang, having read the letter, shook his head.

"That letter is a fake."

"You must be misteken. That's my father's own handwriting."

" Please don't think me meddlesome, but the letter is a forgery. If you don't believe me, Prefect, question the messenger closely. If he answers incorrectly, then the letter is false."

The prefect sent attendants to look for Dai Zong. When Dai came in, he was conducted to the prefectural office.

The prefect asked him in detail whom and what he had seen at the premier's residence. Dai of course couldn't answer many of the questions correctly.

The prefect was not hoodwinked. He summoned Huang. "Dai is obviously in league with the Liangshn Marsh bandits, "said Huang. "They're organized, and plotting a revolt."

The superintendent was beaten till his skin split and fresh blood flowed. He couldn't take it, and confessed that the letter was false.

27

Dai Zong and Song Jiang's confessions were taken and formal documents drawn up. Both were sentenced to be decapitated in the marketplace. Proclamations of the convictions were posted.

On the appointed day a crossroads in the marketplace was swept to serve as an execution ground. After breakfast soldiers and executioners were mustered — well over five hundred men — and assembled outside the prison gate. Everything was in readiness. The prisoners' arms were bound. Racks were locked around their necks. Song Jiang, followed by Dai Zong, was led out of the prison gate. The spectators heard the announcements of criminal convictions.

At this time, from the east side of the market a band of snake charmers pushed their way through the crowd of nearly two thousand jamming the execution ground. The soldiers tried to beat them back, but they wouldn't leave. In the midst of this disturbance, a group of medicine peddlars elbowed through the crowd of spectators on the west. The soldiers shouted at them, but they wouldn't go back.

Just then a convoy of porters carrying goods on shoulder poles arrived from the south.

"We're bringing things to your prefect." the porters shouted to the soldiers, who tried to block their way. "How dare you stop us!"

From the north a troupe of merchants approached, pushing two carts. They insisted on pushing through the execution grounds. The soldiers wouldn't let them go on. The merchants gathered together in a stubborn knot and refused to retreat.

Not long after, a group of officers on the execution grounds dispersed, and a man stepped forward and announced, "Time for the execution."

"Cut off their heads," ordered the prefect.

Quicker than it takes to say, rioting broke out.

28

It's hardly necessary to say that the snake charmers, the medicine peddlars, the porters and the merchants who had swarmed the execution grounds were none other than Liangshan Marsh outlaws, come to Jiangzhou to rescue Song Jiang and Dai Zong. In the ensuing melee, they killed countless solidiers and whisked off the two prisoners.

They walked six or seven *li* along the road outside the city. Song Jiang opened his eyes and saw Chao Gai and the others. "Brothers," he exclaimed, weeping, "this must be a dream."

"I see some boats along the opposite bank," said Ruan the Seventh. "My brothers and I will swim over and haul a few back. How will that be?"

After stripping and tying on daggers, the Ruan brothers dived into the river. Soon they were back again, each towing some boats after him.

Shortly after, a bandit came running up and reported, "A huge host of men and horses has been assembled in Jiangzhou City and is marching forth to catch us."

"If we fight, we fight to a finish," shouted Chao Gai. "Rally around me, bold fellows. "We'll return to Liangshan Marsh only after we've slaughtered every man in the Jiangzhou army!"

29

The rescue of Song Jiang and Dai Zong was celebrated with a feast.

During the drinking, Song Jiang rose and addressed the assembly. " Superintendent Dai and I would be dead now if you hadn't come to our rescue. Our gratitude is as deep as the sea. We don't know how to thank you. I hate only Huang Wenbing. He tried to ruin us. I must have vengeance. I beg you bold gallants to do me a great favor once again and attack Wuweijun, kill Huang Wenbing and slake Song Jiang's burning hatred. What do you say?"

" How shall we proceed? " mused Chao Gai. " Perhaps we should return to the mountain stronghold and muster a larger force. We'll get Wu Yong, Gongsun Sheng and Lin Chong to join us. "

"We'll send a man into Wuweijun first, to reconnoiter. We've got to know how to get in and out of there, and where exactly Huang Wenbing lives. Then we can make our move, "said Hua Rong.

To cut a long story short, Song Jiang took Wuweijun by using a clever ruse. Huang Wenbing was captured while crossing the river, and his whole family was slaughtered by bold fellows from Liangshan Marsh.

Huang was tied to a willow tree. Song Jiang asked the chieftains, all thirty of them, to sit around in a circle. He called for a pot of wine and cups for all

When the cups were filled, Song Jiang turned to his captive.

"Huang Wenbing, you bastard! I've never done anything against you. Why should you want to harm me? Four or five times you tried to get Prefect Cai to kill me and Dai Zong. How could you be so vicious? You scum, you do nothing but injure people. In Wuweijun you're known as Huang the Wasp. Well, today I'm going to remove your sting!"

"I acknowledge my crimes," said Huang. "I ask only fo a quick death."

"Which one of you brothers will do the deed for me?" Song Jiang asked.

Li Kui leaped forward. "I'll take care of the villain for you, brother."

He took a sharp knife, looked at Huang and laughed. "In the prefect's rear hall you lied and slandered, stirred him up, invented stories out of whole cloth and deceived him. So you want a quick death? I'm going to see that you die slowly."

It took Li Kui some time to slice Huang to ribbons.

Everyone congratulated Song Jiang.

30

After Song Jiang's trouble in Jiangzhou he went to join the brigands on Mount Liangshan, and later, after Chao Gai's death from a poisoned arrow in the

340

battle for Zengtou Village, he was made supreme leader of the Liangshan Marsh stronghold.

Some time later, he was happy to announce that there were then a total of one hundred and eight chieftains, and that on each occasion they had led troops down the mountain they had always returned intact.

"It was not due to the talent of any man," said Song Jiang to the assembled chieftains. "None of us can claim any credit."

That day Song Jiang ordered a grand feast laid. He addressed the gathering. "Brothers, let each of you carry out your duties of leadership, and hearken without fail to orders. To do otherwise would harm our chivalry. Whoever wilfully disobeys shall be punished according to military law. None shall be let off lightly."

He then read off the chain of command. The two highest leaders were himself and Lu Junyi, the two chiefts of staff were Wu Yong and Gongsun Sheng. He also assigned duties to all the other chieftains.

In chorus the chieftains swore their eternal unity.

31

From that day on, the gallant fellows often went down the mountain, alone or at the head of a body of men, and patrolled the roads. Ordinary travellers and merchants were not molested. But if the brigands encountered a high official, they lightened his coffers of their gold and silver. Loot was delivered to the mountain stronghold and put in the treasury for collective use.

Ranging within a radius of three hundred *li*, the outlaws openly plundered the wealth of prominent families which oppressed the people. Who dared oppose them? No one spoke out and they were never exposed.

The Ninth Day of the Ninth Lunar Month Festival was fast approaching. Song Jiang directed that a feast be laid. All those who were away from the fortress were summoned back.

There was a mountain of meat and a sea of wine that day. Before they knew it, it was dusk. Song Jiang, very drunk, called for paper and a pen. He was determined to write a poem. When he had finished, he sang it to musical accompaniment. It went like this:

> Welcoming the Double Ninth
> With newly fermented good wine,
> We gaze at the blue waters, red hills,
> Yellow reeds and dark bamboo.
> The grey in my hair is ever increasing,
> But a yellow chrysanthemum is tucked over one ear.
> Let us savor our friendship,
> More precious than gold or jade.
> We've controlled the savage foe and can defend our borders.
> Our orders are wise, our discipline is

tight.

We want only to repel the barbarian in
vaders,

Defend our people and our country

Constantly we burn with loyal ardor,
though wicked officials

Are blind to our exploits.

May the emperor soon hand down and
amnesty,

Then will our hearts be fully at ease.

"Day in and day out you talk about amnesty,"
Wu Song shouted. "You're cooling our enthusiasm!"

And Li Kui glared and exclaimed, "Amnesty,
amnesty, who needs a frigging amnesty!" He kicked
over the table, smashing everything on it.

"How dare that swarthy oaf behave so rudely,"
Song Jiang cried. "Guards, take him out and cut his
head off!"

The chieftains dropped to their knees. "He's
drunk. Forgive him, brother," they pleaded.

"Rise, brothers. Put him in jail, then."

The chieftains were relieved.

The incident shook Song Jiang into sobriety. He
was very depressed. Wu Yong spoke to him
soothingly.

"Everyone is enjoying this feast you ordered. Li
Kui's a crude fellow and goes a little wild when he's
drunk. Why take it to heart? Join the brothers in their
revelry."

343

"When I got drunk in Jiangzhou and wrote that rebellious poem, he fought for me, "Song Jiang said. "Today I wrote another and nearly had him killed. Luckily, you brothers spoke up. My emotional ties with Li Kui are the strongest. We're as close as flesh and bone. I can't help feeling depressed."

He turned to Wu Song. "Brother, you're an intelligent man. I advocate amnesty so that we can return to a respectable life and become government officials serving our country. Why should that cool your enthusiasm?"

"All the ministers, whether civil or military, are crooks, " said Sagacious Lu, "and they've got the emperor fooled. Those sons—of—bitches are as black as my cassock. An amnesty won't solve anything. Let's have a ceremonial parting, and tomorrow each can go his separate way and be done with it."

" Listen to me, brothers, " said Song Jiang. "Because the emperor is surrounded by corrupt ministers, he's temporarily confused. But the day will come when the clouds will part and the sun will emerge again. He'll know that we never harm the people and will pardon our crimes. We'll serve the country with one heart and strive to distinguish ourselves. What could be finer? That's why I hope we'll be amnestied soon. I want nothing else."

The chieftains thanked Song Jiang profusely. The banquet broke up and they returned to their respective posts.

32

From about this time onwards, events of great import for the destinies of Song Jiang, the gallants of the Liangshan Marsh stronghold, and their country took place in rapid succession.

We have mentioned a few of them in some detail in previous chapters, and will touch upon others now.

The first event that occurred after the rescue of Song Jiang and Dai Zong from Jiangzhou was Song Jiang attack against the Northern Capital, which ended in the deliverance of chieftains Lu Junyi and Shi Xiu, who had been seized by the police.

This was followed by Song Jiang's victories over some of the emperor's outstanding military leaders who attempted to take the Liangshan Marsh fortress.

Beset by external and internal difficulties — the raids of the Liao Tartars on the northern provinces, the Fang La rebellion in the south — the emperor was unable to deal with Song Jiang and his men and was compelled to grant an amnesty.

The Liangshan Marsh stronghold thereupon announced a ten—day close—out, during which the stronghold's property was dispensed among the neighbours free of charge. Song Jiang and all his men were invited to the capital to become respectable citizens.

Not long after their return to the capital, Song Jiang was ordered to smash the Liao Tartars. A royal edict was issued appointing Song Jiang the Vanguard General to smash them, and Lu Junyi the Vice—Vanguard General. They and their men were ordered to set out at once, go directly to the ememy's lair, save the people, and purge the border regions. By force and guile, Song Jiang won one victory after another, forcing the Tartars to capitulate.

No sooner had Song Jiang and his bold fellows returned to the capital than they heard that an expedition against Fang La was about to cross the Yangzi.

Song Jiang immediately went to the Military Affairs Council in Marshal Su's residency to propose leading an expedition.

There's no need to say that the emperor agreed readily to Song Jiang's proposal. He proclaimed Song Jiang Commander—in—Chief of the Southern Pacification, and Vanguard of the Expedition Against Fang La. He named Lu Junyi the second in command. A time limit was set for the departure of the expeditionary force.

We have recounted in detail elsewhere how Song Jiang's forces crossed the Yangzi, how they captured one after another of the major cities held by Fang La, and how Fang La himself was seized by Sagacious Lu as he fled to the mountains.

33

The capture of Fang La, the killing of his

relatives and ministers and the seizure of his territory meant the end of the Fang La rebellion. But Song Jiang's victories cost the life of many a chieftain. Of the original one hundred and eight chieftains, only twenty-seven returned to the capital.

34

In the meantime, the wicked ministers surrounding the emperor were plotting to get rid of Song Jiang, whom they considered their enemy. The high honours and substantial rewards given to Song Jiang and his chieftains profoundly disturbed Marshals Gao and Yang. They conferred about it.

"Song Jiang and Lu Junyi are our enemies," said Gao. "Now they've been made high officials and honoured by the imperial court. We ministers have become laughing stocks!"

"I have a plan," said Yang. "We'll get rid of Lu Junyi first. It will be like cutting off Song Jiang's right arm."

"Let's hear your plan."

"Let's send an emissary to Song Jiang with imperial wine in which we'll put a slow-working poison. In half a month he'll be beyond saving."

"An excellent idea," said Gao.

During the first ten days of summer, Song Jiang heard that an emissary had arrived from the capital with imperial wine. Accompanied by other officials, he went out of the city to welcome the emissary and escort him in. In the public hall the emissary read the emperor's greeting, presented the wine and urged Song Jiang to drink. When Song Jiang requested the emissary to join him, the man refused, saying he was a teetotaler. Song Jiang ceremoniously drank and the emissary returned to the capital.

Song Jiang's stomach began to pain him soon after, and he suspected something had been added to the wine. He made enquiries and learned that the emissary had in fact done some drinking while stopping at a hostel along the road. Song Jiang realized he had been tricked. He was positive the wine had been poisoned by the evil ministers. He sighed.

"What have I done to deserve this! It doesn't matter if I die, but Li Kui, who is today commandant of Runzhou, will certainly take to the hills again when he hears about this dirty trick the imperial court has played. There's only one thing I can do."

He dispatched a man that same night to Runzhou with a message for Li Kui to come and see him immediately.

When Li Kui came, Song Jiang gave him some poisoned wine.

"Brother, don't blame me!" said Song Jiang. "The emperor sent me some poisoned wine the other day, and I drank it. I'm going to die soon. I was afraid that after I died you would rebel and spoil our reputation for loyalty and righteousness. And so I asked you here and gave you the poisoned wine also. When you return to Runzhou you'll surely die."

Li Kui's body felt heavy. Weeping, he bid Song Jiang farewell. When he reached Runzhou, sure enough, the poison took effect.

As Li Kui lay dying, he instructed his attendants, "After I'm gone you must take my coffin to Liao Er Flats outside Chuzhou's South Gate and bury me beside Big Brother." Later, his orders were carried out.

Song Jiang felt bad when Li Kui sailed away that day. On his deathbed he said to his trusted followers, "You must fulfil my request. Bury me on high ground above Liao Er Flats. Promise that you will." So saying, he died.

His followers prepared to bury him in Chuzhou with due ceremony. The prefectural officials, informed of his request, agreed to honour it. Together with his intimates, functionaries young and old carried his coffin to a place above Liao Er Flats and buried him there. A few days later, the coffin of Li Kui was brought from Runzhou. He was interred next to Song Jiang.

35

A temple dedicated to Song Jiang's memory was built in Liangshan Marsh.

Song Jiang's spirit appeared frequently in Liangshan Marsh, and the people continually sacrificed to him. He appeared too in Liao Er Flats. There the people also built a large temple. People came from near and far to worship, and their prayers were always answered.

Those who defend their country and protect the people have incense burned in their memory for ten thousand years. Sacrifices are made to them generation after generation.

* THE END *